Ill V

By John Pendleton

Contents

Chapter one
Upping
sticks

BLACK night was friendly above the shores of Loch Breaganish. The skies were clear, the stars twinkled merrily and the moon shone brightly. Two or three house lights could be seen on the far banks of the loch, but nothing more.

No human sounds could be detected. Gentle waves lapped the edge of the loch, a waterfall made a plunging sound as it fell into a deep pool between the Black Burn and the loch and an occasional harsh cry from an oyster-catcher pierced the tranquillity.

After a few minutes, though, the sound of someone tramping along the shingle broke the stillness. The beam from a small torch came into view as it jerked up and down to the rhythm of the walker.

The moonlit shadow of another human form passed over the beach immediately behind the walker. There was a muffled groan. The torch fell to the ground. The next sound was of something being dragged roughly across the larger stones between the shingle beach and a grass bank leading to a sheep field.

They say that without a hearer there is no sound. There was at least one hearer present – an ever-attentive heron standing at the edge of the burn at the point where it met the loch, listening for food.

****

It was raining at Fort William. It always rains at Fort William.

The BMW crept gingerly along a busy estate road on the outskirts of town.

Its two occupants struggled to follow their directions which had been hastily scribbled on a cut-out piece of a Kellogg's Bran Flakes packet.

"Go right, now", ordered the brunette passenger to her husband, the driver.

"Are you sure?" he asked, disbelieving her.

"Yes. I'm sure," she screeched.

The right turn took them into a council estate. On first glance, the houses, dating from the Fifties, were spruce looking, well decorated in white and with well-kept gardens. Council houses are like this in the Highlands of Scotland.

As the car slowly negotiated the road humps the woman opened the window and craned her neck, looking for road names.

"It's next left – Cameron Road," she said.

"Are you quite sure?" asked the driver, far from convinced.

"Yes. Quite sure."

"It doesn't look like it was described in the brochure," said the driver. "Where's the Caledonian Canal? Where's the view of the Nevis Range?"

"Oh. I don't know. You booked the place. Here it is – Cameron Road, then right into Mackenzie Place."

The road became narrower and the council houses with their large gardens gave way to council flats with tiny patches of grass separating them.

"There's no B and B down here," said the driver. "It's just a council estate."

Then he looked to his right. And, there, nestling uncomfortably cheek by jowl with two rows of four-storey flats, was a single old cottage, with aging red brickwork and pink and yellow roses growing up the wall.

A sign outside declared "Mountain View – Bed & Breakfast – Vacancies". It also carried a reassuring three star recommendation from the tourist board.

"This is it," he said, as he parked the car with two wheels up on the pavement.

"Where *have* you brought us to?" said his wife.

The husband looked around, trying to find some saving graces in the property.

"It's got a lovely garden. Perhaps there are views out the back,"

"But I can't see the Caledonian Canal. And, according to the map, it's nowhere near here."

"Oh, well. We're here now."

They got out of the car, opened the neat white gate, and strolled apprehensively along a grey stone path towards the front door of the cottage.

The husband, Jack Easter, was 50, of medium height, with a trim figure for his age. He had thick, dark brown hair, which was swept back and hung over his shirt collar. There was just the hint of a bald patch at the top of his head.

With his blue denim shirt, brown corduroy trousers, suede shoes, and rather lugubrious demeanour, he could have been taken for a secondary school teacher or a university lecturer. But, if such had been his profession, his finely chiselled face and beautiful blue eyes would have made him a favourite among his female students.

His wife, Sophie, was a natural brunette, although the colour of her long, straight hair had been somewhat darkened and enriched at the hairdressing salon. She was aged 45, 5ft 9in tall, with a well-proportioned figure. She had perfectly formed ample breasts and shapely long legs. Her gentle, smiley, face had a soft, dreamy quality. She had aged well; some darkness around the eyes and a few insignificant laughter lines were her only concessions to middle age.

Jack rang the doorbell and waited patiently. There was no reply. He rang it again. No reply. And again. Still no reply, even though he could clearly hear it ringing.

"Don't worry," he said. "The lady said she was going out to do some shopping so she might not get back until latish afternoon."

"It's four o'clock," said his wife. "I would call that late afternoon. Wouldn't you?"

"Perhaps we should sit in the car for a while – and wait for her to turn up," he suggested.

They sat in the car for three-quarters of an hour. But no one arrived.

Jack decided to have one more try at the door, while Sophie looked around the neighbourhood for someone who might be able to help. There was still no sign of life at the cottage, but at that moment a car drew up outside the next-door council flat.

A large slovenly looking woman emerged from the driver's seat and three noisy children leapt from the passenger seats.

"Excuse me," said Sophie. "Do you live here?"

The woman gave a friendly nod.

"I wonder if you could help me? We have booked in for bed and breakfast at this house but nobody seems to be in. You don't know where they might be, do you?"

In a gentle Highlands accent the woman replied: "I don't know them very well. I haven't seen them for a day or two. They have a wee car but I don't see it in the driveway. I'm sorry but I haven't a clue where they might be."

Sophie thanked the woman for her time. She beckoned Jack towards the car and they sat inside, looking dejected.

"I think we might as well give up," he said. "If we drive back towards the town centre we are bound to find somewhere else to stay. There are hundreds of places around here."

Sophie agreed and Jack started the car and began to drive away slowly.

"Stop!" shouted Sophie, pointing to the cottage, "A curtain just moved in the window. Just there."

"Oh, yes," said Jack.

"I'll nip out and knock on the door again," said Sophie.

This time when she knocked she could hear someone fumbling with the lock and doorknob on the inside.

"Oh bugger! Balls! Shit!" said a woman's voice.

At last the door shuddered on its hinges and flew open. The woman inside, who was hanging on to the knob, fell backwards on to the floor on to her bottom. She scrambled back to her feet, hastily rearranging her clothing.

"Oh, I'm sorry dear," said the old woman, who was five foot nothing with a shock of blue hair, badly drawn eyebrows pointing skywards and black mascara running down her cheeks.

10

Sophie smiled beatifically and said: "Don't worry. Doors can stick terribly sometimes, particularly in damp weather like this."

"That's just it dear. We've had such a lot of rain recently. Quite unusual."

Sophie nodded assent. Actually she was thinking this was typical Highlands' disingenuousness. Everyone knew it hardly ever stopped raining in those parts.

"What can I do for you, dear?" asked the old woman, in a slurred sing-song voice. Sophie had already noticed her breath smelt strongly of alcohol.

"We're booked in for bed and breakfast – Mr and Mrs Easter."

"Oh. I'm so sorry, dear. I had forgotten you were coming. When did you book in?"

"About a week ago," said Sophie. "I believe my husband said he had spoken to Mrs Macpherson."

"Aye. That's me right enough. I'm terrible. I have the book here. Do come in."

She went into the hallway and took a book from a window ledge.

"Aye, yes. Here we are. Mr and Mrs Easter. One night. I just don't know where my brain is. Still, there's no harm done. We have a double bedroom here for you. It just needs heating up a little. Michael!"

In a few moments a small, grey-haired, old man appeared. He was swaying and hopping from one foot to

11

the other, clearly drunk, and had watery, bloodshot eyes.

"I'm here now," he said. "What can I be doing for you, Margaret?"

"Michael. This lady has come for the bed and breakfast. Can you turn the heating on in Number Four bedroom? And then help this lady with their luggage."

"I will, my love."

He proffered a clammy hand to Sophie, who shook it and gave him a friendly smile.

"We have been having a little party here today," said Michael. "We have some friends here from Uist."

"Oh. Very nice," said Sophie.

"Just come in the parlour and meet them," slurred Margaret. "They will be pleased to see you. Indeed they will."

She took Sophie by the hand and opened the door to a room leading off the hallway. The noise of traditional Scottish music and people conversing loudly was immediately apparent.

There were two old couples in the parlour, very merry and very welcoming, and with telltale red faces and glazed, watery eyes. Empty whisky bottles and beer cans were lined up on a table, along with the remains and all-pervading smell of fish and chips.

The old people took it in turns to shake Sophie's hand and tell her how unseasonably wet the weather was – and how lovely it had been up until that very day.

Sophie thanked them for their welcome and then made her excuses when she remembered she had left Jack waiting in the car.

She went back towards the front door, pursued by Margaret.

"Now, I'll get Michael to bring in your suitcases," she insisted.

"There's no need," said Sophie. "We only have a couple of quite small overnight bags."

"Ah, but you will be needing some help with those," Margaret persisted. "Michael! Where are you now? Come and help bring in the luggage."

Sophie went to the car where Jack greeted her with a quizzical expression.

"They are all drunk in there," said Sophie. "What shall we do?"

Jack was about to suggest driving away when Michael appeared at the car, grinning widely.

"Hello there," he said. "Very pleased to meet you. Can I carry your luggage for you?"

"No," replied Jack. "It will be quite all right."

"I have put on the wall heater in your bedroom. You should be very snug in there," said Michael. "It is a pity about the rain. It was so nice earlier. I just don't know where the rain has come from."

Jack shrugged his shoulders and stared at Sophie in a questioning way. What were they to do? he implied.

Sophie wrinkled her nose, suggesting that they seemed to have little choice but to stay.

13

Jacked pursed his lips and nodded in acquiescence.

They took their bags from the car, Michael insisting on carrying them, even though he was still swaying with the effects of drink. He managed to crash both bags against both gateposts and then repeated the procedure against the front door surrounds as he tried to squeeze through in one motion with a bag in each hand and his knee holding open the door.

He showed Sophie and Jack into their bedroom, which, to their pleasant surprise, was immaculate. It was tastefully decorated and smelt sweetly of pot pourri. The walls were adorned with paintings of castles and hunting scenes and every nook and cranny had some twee Scottish ornament or souvenir in it. There were birds and animals shaped out of native wood and a variety of tartan-patterned candlesticks. Fresh flowers cheered up an ancient mahogany dressing table.

The room had the feel of a well preserved Scottish cottage, but it had all the expected mod cons: en suite lavatory, bath and shower; smart tea and coffee making facilities, with complimentary shortbread and chocolate biscuits; a flat screen TV hanging from the wall and offering Sky and Freeview channels; and a pile of tourism brochures giving details about the surrounding area.

Things were looking up.

Margaret, evidently sobering up, bustled into the room.

"Fancy me forgetting you were coming. What must I have been thinking? Now you just come and go as you please. Here's the keys: this one for your room and this one for the front door. Come in at any time you please.

"Will you be wanting a cooked breakfast? We can give you a traditional Scottish breakfast or you can have some poached haddock if you would prefer that."

Jack and Sophie assured her that the traditional Scottish breakfast would be very much to their liking.

Margaret chattered away incessantly as she explained the various facilities which could be made available at the B and B.

"Just two things," said Jack, when at last he managed to get a word in. "Can you tell us how we get to the Caledonian Canal? We would very much like to see it before we go."

"Of course you would," replied Margaret. "It's just a stone's-throw away.

Pointing to the bedroom window, she continued: "If you turn left at the end of this road and then walk past a couple of shops you will see a pub called The Herring Boat. Go through the car park at the back of the pub and you will see a footpath with a sign pointing to the canal. It's about 15 minutes' walk from there."

Sophie looked at Jack with a resigned expression. The B and B's website entry clearly stated that the cottage was adjacent to the canal and the

Nevis mountain range – an exaggeration to say the least.

"And is there anywhere good for an evening meal within walking distance of here?" asked Jack.

"Aye, indeed," said Margaret. "The very pub I mentioned – The Herring Boat. They do lovely meals there. Very reasonably priced. We were all there for a meal ourselves last night. It was lovely, wasn't it, Michael?"

Her husband, who had just appeared at her shoulder, concurred: "Aye. They'll not be found wanting at The Herring Boat. They do good wholesome food and you will not be out of pocket."

"That all seems very good," said Jack. "We were thinking we might have to find somewhere else because we couldn't make you hear earlier."

"Oh. We were partying pretty strong," said Michael. "We would not be able to hear the door."

"And we having forgotten you were coming," added Margaret. "I am as daft as a brush sometimes."

"Will you join us for a whisky before you go out?" asked Michael.

Jack and Sophie declined and, after another 20 minutes or so of banter with their hosts, they at last managed to shut the bedroom door. Both slumped on the bed, exhausted.

They quickly fell asleep, fully clothed, on top of the bed.

After a day's drive from Warwickshire, the couple slept soundly for an hour. When they awoke they were feeling hungry.

"I need food," said Sophie.

"Me too," said Jack. "Shall we head for The Herring Bone?"

"Herring *Boat*, I think," said Sophie. "Yeah. Let's go."

The couple followed Margaret's instructions and soon approached what was easily identifiable as a pub. A group of five smokers were standing outside the doorway of a shabby white-painted building. A sign above the door read "Herr oat". This must be the place.

Jack tried to read a menu board at the side of the doorway but was unable to get a clear view of it because the smokers, totally unaware of his presence, were standing in the way.

"Oh, well. We may as well go in and have a look," said Jack.

They sidled past the smokers into a large bar with linoleum floors and plastic tables and chairs and a pool table which dominated the room.

At one table sat two men, the only people in the bar. One was a burly fellow in his sixties with heavily tattooed arms and a large beer gut. Sitting opposite was a smarter, but equally fat, man in a clean, white, knee-length coat. He looked very much like a down-at-heel hospital doctor.

The two men had bags of fish and chips paper spread across the table and were sharing the contents by dipping into the bags with greasy fingers.

Jack and Sophie noticed – to their amazement and not a little hilarity – that the fish and chips were also being shared by two big black cats which had positioned themselves on the table and were helping themselves with gusto.

Jack nudged Sophie and pointed to a door at the side of the bar. A notice hung on it which said: "D. Macmillan DDS, Dental Surgeon, Monday and Wednesday, 4pm-6pm."

All was explained. The fish and chip guzzler in the white coat was a dentist!

Hardly liking to interrupt the busy pair, who had not even noticed there were new customers in the bar, Jack asked tentatively: "We wondered if you were serving bar meals tonight?"

The tattooed man swung round and greeted the couple with a warm welcoming smile: "I'll go and ask the wife what's on the menu.

"I can recommend the carry-oots from the chippy across the road," he giggled wheezily.

The man got up from the table and disappeared through the door behind the bar.

The dentist, talking through a mouthful of chips, said, reassuringly: "You'll be all right here right enough. Jessie's a very good cook."

The tattooed man, who was the pub landlord, reappeared, looking apologetic. He said: "I'm afraid we have a limited menu tonight. We haven't had time to go out and do much shopping. We can do you braised beef or steak and ale pie."

Jack and Sophie looked at each other.

"What do you think?" asked Jack.

"I think braised beef sounds ok," said Sophie. "How much is it?"

"Let's say £7.50," said the landlord.

Jack nodded: "Two braised beefs, then, please."

"Would you like them with chips and salad or mashed potatoes and veg?"

They both chose mashed potatoes and vegetables and the landlord showed them to a table where they then sat waiting with some trepidation. They wondered if the cats, which had by now polished off the fish and chips, would choose to share their meal too.

Half an hour went by. The dentist had left the pub having downed a pint and the remaining customers were still outside smoking. Neither the landlord nor his wife was to be seen.

Jack and Sophie were contemplating making a hasty exit when suddenly a short, fat, rosy-faced woman approached, carrying two large rectangular plates. She was followed by her husband, the landlord, who had two terrines brimming with vegetables.

The plates each contained five layers of beef covered in an inviting looking mushroom sauce. There were Yorkshire puddings, new potatoes, tomatoes, broccoli, carrots, caramelised onions, a slice of black pudding and, oh joy, a mound of haggis with neeps.

"Wow!" exclaimed Sophie. "This looks absolutely great."

"It certainly does," agreed Jack, enthusiastically.

"We hope you enjoy your meal," said the landlord. "Please tell us if you need anything else."

"This should be fine," said Jack.

The couple tucked into their food with relish. When Jack had finished his, he said to Sophie: "Well, what did you think to that?"

Sophie replied: "Do you know, I think it was the best main course I've ever tasted."

Jack agreed.

They stayed at the pub to enjoy a dessert of clootie dumpling and then walked home happily arm in arm to the B and B. The Caledonian Canal would wait until the morning.

****

In the living room of a neat white cottage at Upper Beindow on the Isle of Skye an old woman of about 75 sat in a comfortable armchair, staring vacantly at her merry wood-burning fire.

Suddenly she was jolted into full consciousness and sat bolt upright. Her eyelids opened wide, painfully wide - so wide that they looked as if they could never meet again.

The homely fire disappeared from her gaze. In its place the woman saw a young man cutting peat in a field which she recognised as being alongside the main road between the villages of Beindow and Dunvegan. She knew so well the fluffy white bog cotton plants which skirted the field.

She also knew the man very well, a local man she had known all her life.

On a track alongside the peat field was a tractor and hitched behind that a long trailer with a wooden floor, the receptacle waiting for the cut peat.

The man - a tall, slim figure, bare-headed and wearing olive green overalls - shoved his spade into the earth. As he did so he heard a woman's cry.

"I'm here. Come and get me, lover!"

The man left his spade in the ground and looked over his shoulder. Running towards him through the grass from the direction of the adjacent sea loch was a slim, long-legged young woman, pale-faced with girlish freckles and long red, rather unkempt hair. The old woman recognised her too.

The young woman was wearing a billowing white blouse and skin-tight jeans, torn at the knees and at various other points along the legs. The man held out his arms, ready to embrace her, but she swerved past him and ran in the direction of the trailer.

She jumped into the trailer, sat down on the floor and took off her blouse, leaving herself naked from the waist up and exposing pert breasts with erect black nipples.

"Come inside," she laughed.

The man vaulted over the side of the trailer and stood in front of her, eyes wide open and smiling gently.

The woman laid back, unzipped her jeans and pulled them off together with her knickers. She was prone in front of the man, and stark naked.

"Come inside," she said again, smiling broadly.

The man eagerly removed all his clothing and lowered himself on top of her. He kissed her and caressed her breasts then slid backwards and kissed her pubic hair. A few seconds later he had entered her and they made passionate love, causing the whole trailer to rock fiercely and clatter. Her shrieks of joy rang out..... and made the old woman by the fireside start and sit up even taller in her chair.

Her living room fire came back into view for a few seconds and then another picture presented itself to the old woman.

She saw the same couple again, standing together in the same field. The woman was holding a baby and shouting, pleading, with the man. The man leapt on to his tractor and drove it away, leaving the distraught woman and the crying baby standing on the track.

These images disappeared and the old woman was left staring at the fire again, her eyelids burning and her eyes bloodshot and aching. A spark flew out of the fire and hit her face.

She brushed it away in panic and shouted out "No, no. Not again, please God, not again."

The woman looked red and flustered and she tore at her grey hair, disturbing its neat new perm. She rose from her seat and made towards the living room door, where a long grey mackintosh was hanging from a peg.

She hurriedly put on her coat and a headscarf which she took from the top drawer of a tallboy. Then, from the same drawer, she found a fold-up umbrella.

Thus prepared, she left her cottage and went scurrying along the lane, down a steep slope which led her to the main road. It was early summer, with plenty of daylight still to come at around eight o'clock in the evening when the woman undertook her journey.

But it was cold and windy and as she reached the main road a chilly rain started to come down in torrents. The old woman knew it was pointless putting up her umbrella as the wind was far too strong.

She walked another half mile and came to a smart, white-painted church. Next to it was a large house, also, predictably, white – the manse.

The woman went to the front door of the house, rang the doorbell, and waited, looking forlorn and bedraggled. Soon the middle-aged, grey-haired Church of Scotland minister opened the door:

"Miss MacInnes! What are you doing out on a dreadful night like this?

You will catch your death. Come inside. Please come inside."

That phrase "Come inside" struck a discordant note with Miss MacInnes. She thought of the peat trailer and the disgraceful goings-on she had witnessed.

"Oh, please don't say that, minister. Don't say that."

"What do you mean, don't say that? You must come in. You will be soaked."

"Oh, I will explain," she said, stepping into the wide hallway. "I'm so sorry, minister - so sorry to be troubling you at this time of night. But you see it's happened. It's happened again, the Lord help me."

The minister could see she was panicky and upset as he ushered her into his large study.

"Now calm down, Miss MacInnes. Give me your raincoat and I'll hang it on the boiler. I'll ask Jane to make a pot of tea. Come and sit down."

The minister, the Rev John Grimmond, pointed politely towards a wooden armchair and Miss MacInnes sat down. When he returned he spoke to her rather more abruptly than before:

"It's not your usual trouble, Miss MacInnes, is it?"

"Oh, minister. I'm so sorry. It is. I don't know what to do."

"What have you seen this time?"

The old woman related the scenes she had seen in front of her as she had sat quietly at home contemplating the fire.

The minister had pulled up a chair and listened patiently to her story.

"Now what do I do now?" she asked.

The minister spoke to her sternly.

"Now you know what I'm going to say to you, don't you?"

The woman nodded sadly.

"I think this second sight nonsense is the work of the Devil. I would urge you, as I have before, to put all of this out of your mind. Don't go upsetting people. Keep it all to yourself and no harm will be done."

The old woman welled up. She was unconvinced.

"But I feel I must warn those people about the death of the baby. The spark from the fire was a sure sign. I have ignored such warnings before on your insistence and you know what has happened."

The minister's visage softened. He was a man of stern, unbending, beliefs, but was kindly and understanding in his dealings with his flock.

"What happened before must have been a co-incidence. You have to understand that second sight, as you call it, is a superstition – and superstitions are devised by the Devil to divert us from our true path – the path of Jesus. Now let's pray together for a minute or two – pray that this curse of ridiculous visions is removed from you."

He took her hand and muttered some words of prayer in her ear.

"Thank you, minister," she said. "I am so sorry to have wasted your time. I wish I could have your faith. I am afflicted by a gift I have never asked for."

The minister sighed deeply.

"It isn't a gift. It's a delusion. You are afflicted by a delusion which is the Devil's work."

"I know you think I am a silly old woman – and probably I am. I will not take up any more of your time," she said.

"You will take your tea first, won't you?" said the minister.

"No. Thank you kindly, but I would rather get home. It's getting late for me to be out."

"Don't you go worrying yourself any more," said the minister. "Believe in the power of prayer. We will see you at church on Sunday?"

"Aye, indeed you will - as you always do," she replied.

The minister fetched her mackintosh, shook her hand and showed her to the door. It was still raining heavily and he insisted on giving her a lift home in his car.

****

The next morning Jack and Sophie went down to breakfast to be greeted by a loquacious B and B landlady. Margaret's breath smelt strongly of alcohol – not that stale morning-after-the -night -before smell with which drinkers so often regale the rest of us. This was the smell of whisky recently imbibed, very likely during the cooking of breakfast.

She provided a hearty Scottish breakfast, although the juice from the baked beans and the tinned tomatoes did mean that the fried eggs tended to swim from side to side of the plate, eluding capture by knife and fork until finally breaking up and adding to the attractive stew.

Nevertheless the meal gave adequate sustenance for the couple's journey ahead to the Isle of Skye.

Margaret chattered away incessantly about the lives and achievements of her numerous relatives, right up until Jack and Sophie left to get into their car. It was, needless to say, raining heavily, but that did not deter her from continuing the conversation while Jack hovered on the doorstep with the overnight bags, getting both himself and the luggage thoroughly soaked.

But the soaking they received before finally entering the car did nothing to dampen the couple's spirits. For they were anticipating the greatest adventure of their lives.

Jack had been a bit of a Jack-of-all-trades. On leaving university with an English degree he had become a journalist, working his way from being a junior reporter on a small weekly newspaper in the Birmingham area to becoming features editor of a big regional daily in the same city.

But journalism never really interested him. Creative writing was what made his adrenalin flow. The humdrum life of meeting deadlines and writing mundane advertising features for spoilt clients never had much appeal.

So, at the age of 30, having married Sophie two years previously, he decided to change direction. He had a string of jobs – taxi driver, gardener, caravan site manager and museum curator being just some of them. But always, at night and at weekends, he would dedicate much of his spare time to writing.

After sending several novels around scores of publishers he eventually struck gold – an acceptance. After that he had never looked back. His genre of murder mystery novels set in remote, often weird, places, with even weirder, psychologically flawed, characters, began to gain a following - so much so that he was now able to make a reasonable living just from writing.

Sophie was also a creator, whose career path had followed a similar haphazard pattern to her husband's. She had been a model, a pub manager, a fashion designer, a window dresser for a department store and, latterly, a set designer for the Royal Shakespeare Company at Stratford-upon-Avon. But her great and abiding love was for landscape painting.

Her landscapes were bold and colourful, not dissimilar to the North Yorkshire landscapes of David Hockney. But whereas Hockney focused on trees and the patchwork of rolling hills and fields, her best work was of mountains, lakes and fast flowing rivers.

The couple made their home at Stratford and were generally happy there. They produced two daughters, both bright girls who were now at university, one at Edinburgh and the other at Glasgow.

The location of their universities was significant.

For a number of years the family had spent most of their holidays together in the Scottish Highlands. The scenery and inaccessibility they found there inspired both Jack and Sophie in their work. For Sophie, the landscapes were to die for. For Jack, the remoteness of the region lent itself to the mystery of his novels and the quirky, often quaint, Highland characters he met demanded to be moulded for use in his plots. Their daughters just loved the freedom of the region.

When the girls, Portia and Cordelia, made Scotland their choice for higher education, their parents saw the ideal opportunity to up sticks and make a new home in the Highlands.

Jack's parents had both died in the previous three years and Sophie's had emigrated to Australia to live with Sophie's brother and his family. So there were now no close remaining family ties in England.

The couple had no hesitation in choosing for their new home the Isle of Skye, which had become their favourite holiday haunt.

There is something about the light and the colours of Skye which is different from that of any other part of Scotland. That is why so many artists and photographers have chosen it as their home and as the subject matter for their work.

The mountains are one aspect – the forbidding Black Cuillins and the mellower Red Cuillins, really a sort of brick pink. But it is the seascapes which give Skye its irresistible charm. The sea can display a wide spectrum of greys and blues, from slate grey when the weather is poor to azure when it is fine and a turquoise which would do justice to any South Sea island when the sun is out and the seabed is bleached white.

The sea is set against images of distant mountains, which are purple, mauve, blue and grey, illusively suffused by the mist. The scenery is gentle and restful.

When all mist clears, the view changes completely. The sun paints as pretty and as colourful a picture as you will see anywhere in the world.

It is the quick changes of scene which give Skye its excitement. It can go from rain-tossed gloom, through clement mist to radiant sunlight within five minutes.

Jack and Sophie had sold up at Stratford and bought a delightful two-bedroomed cottage at Breaganish, a tiny settlement on the banks of a loch by the same name in the north-west of the island.

They had made several trips to furnish and decorate the cottage. Now they were ready to move in. A quick look at the Caledonian Canal, followed by a three-hour journey from Fort William, would see them to their new home.

Chapter two
Meeting the
neighbours

AS JACK and Sophie crossed the Skye Bridge their spirits lifted. All was space and light, above rich blue water.

On their left was the small island, now locked under the bridge, where there is a disused lighthouse and a museum dedicated to author Gavin Maxwell. Famous for writing Ring of Bright Water about his close relationship with an endearing otter, Maxwell lived for a time in the lighthouse cottages.

What is not quite as well known is that Maxwell came to the area to catch and kill sharks. After The Second World War he bought the adjacent Isle of Soay, to establish a basking shark fishery. He was unsuccessful, but his plan demonstrated a less cuddly side to his nature than is usually appreciated.

Skye attracts romantics, adventurers and bohemians. The pop

singer Donovan set up a commune on the small island of Isay, off Skye, and Ian Anderson, of folk rock group Jethro Tull, owned Skye's Strathaird Estate and salmon fishery. Centuries earlier Dr Samuel Johnson and his biographer James Boswell famously visited the island and wrote about it in A Journey to the Western Islands. And, of course, Skye was host to that most romantic and hopeless of lost causes, Jacobitism, Flora MacDonald famously harbouring and rescuing Bonnie Prince Charlie.

Also to the left of the bridge is the village of Kyleakin – still looking spruce with its immaculate white-painted houses, but having a forlorn and forgotten feel to it. Before the Skye Bridge opened in 1995 most people who travelled to and from the island had to visit Kyleakin to use the ferry. Now it is possible to bypass the village altogether. At close quarters most travellers see little more than the Indian restaurant on the outskirts.

Passing through the two largest settlements on the island, Broadford and the capital, Portree, the journey to Breaganish takes up to an hour from the bridge.

On a bright sunny day Jack and Sophie were travelling along the main road which runs parallel to Loch Breaganish when they caught sight on the farthest bank of the speck of a shining white cottage.

"There it is," said Jack. "That's our home".

33

"Wowee," exclaimed Sophie. "It looks so beautiful today."

Within five minutes their car left the main Portree to Dunvegan road and entered on to a narrow lane. A smart sign at the end of the road pointed to the Breaganish House Hotel and another sign indicated a fast flowing stream called Black Burn, which runs in a deep cut at the side of the lane.

The road was rough-surfaced and pot-holed. Sheep and their lambs sitting on the grass verges looked unconcerned as the BMW bumped and scraped along it. As this was to be his regular route, Jack was thinking he should have bought a 4 x 4.

After passing a range of farm buildings and several fields of sheep the car trundled into a stone driveway. Sophie got out and opened a metal farm gate and Jack drove in beside a medium-sized white-painted cottage. A sign attached to the wall proclaimed it to be Glen Cottage.

The former shepherd's cottage, dating from the mid-19th century, was typical of so many of the white-painted Highlands cottages. Outside, it looked very much as it would have done when it was built. But inside its thick walls it had been completely modernised – lounge, dining room and kitchen downstairs, two bedrooms and a bathroom upstairs. Jack had earmarked one of the bedrooms as his writing room. Sophie had chosen the dining room, which had a glorious view over the loch, as her artist's studio.

Jack got out of the car. He had a large smile on his face.

"Come on, over here. There's something I want to do," he said.

"What's that?" asked Sophie.

"Just come over here and give me the key."

Sophie obeyed and handed over the key.

Jack dived at her and lifted her up by her bottom. She screamed.

"I'm going to carry you over the threshold," he said. "It'll be just like when we got married."

"You idiot. You will do your back in," shouted Sophie.

"No, I won't."

He held on to her with one hand while inserting the key into the lock with the other. Having opened the door he threw his "bride" on to a sofa in the lounge, then knelt down and kissed her tenderly.

"Our dream's come true," he said.

"I can hardly believe it," she replied, sitting up straight. "Oh, just look out there!"

Jack looked through the back window and there, on the field beyond the garden, half a dozen lambs were frolicking on a tall dung heap, taking it turns to be "king of the castle". Their temporarily deserted mothers munched grass obliviously at the other end of the field.

Then one lamb gave a mighty skip and ran off towards the sheep, the others in quick pursuit. They each went to their own mothers, tails wagging furiously as they roughly grabbed the teats to gain some sustenance.

Jack put an arm around Sophie as they watched this charming spectacle. Both were thinking that in a few weeks' time these brilliant little creatures would be adorning someone's plate, complemented by mint sauce.

****

After a few days of getting everything in the cottage shipshape Jack and Sophie decided it was time to make friends with the locals.

On their previous visits to the island they had made some acquaintances, but nothing more. Because their holidays had sometimes been no more than annual events many people they met on Skye would nod to them and say "hello". But Jack and Sophie were often unsure whether this was due to recognition or just the friendliness which they had always found in the Highlands. Now it was time to turn some of these acquaintances into real friends.

So they set off one evening for a walk to the nearest hotel with a public bar. There were two ways of getting there. They could walk via the lane on to the main road, eventually reaching the village of Beindow, a distance of around two and a half miles. Alternatively, provided it was not too muddy, they could walk across a sheep field, follow the shoreline of the loch on either side of the Black Burn and then join the main road in the village itself. This was just over a mile.

As it was a fine bright night they opted for the shorter shoreline route.

It was early evening when they entered the Blackhill Hotel, a fine looking white-painted building at the front, let down only by the back yard which was disfigured by discarded beer crates and metal barrels, cigarette ends and dog faeces.

To get to the public bar they had to pass the smart, carpeted reception area, where sitting behind the desk was the indomitable landlady, Mrs Maclean. She addressed them in one of those strange, clipped, half Scots-half "posh English" accents which are a trademark of well-to-do Scottish folk.

"How are you doing today?"

"We're very well, thanks," replied Jack. "How are you?"

"Nothing that a stiff gin and tonic wouldn't put right," replied the hostess. "I've had a deal of buggeration to put up with today."

"Oh, dear," said Sophie. "I'm sorry to hear that."

"Yes, bloody staff, bloody guests. Ah, what a wonderful life. I'm just as happy as a gay bird," replied Mrs Maclean emphatically and cheerily. "Now you just go in and enjoy yourselves. You'll find a rare collection of halfwits, drunks and scholars in the bar tonight."

"We will," said Jack, laughing out loud.

They entered the lounge, where they found a clutch of drinkers standing around the bar, who, although small in number, made up for this by an almost deafening volume. Standing behind the bar was a grey, pinched, insignificant little man - the landlord, Mr Maclean, clearly no match for his spouse.

Jack and Sophie had difficulty getting the landlord's attention owing to the bulging presence of a loud-speaking fat man sitting on a bar stool. His gargantuan bottom prevented access to the bar from all directions, so Jack had to stand on tiptoe behind him to capture the landlord's eye.

Jack ordered two pints of 70 Shillings, the name of the hotel's second best bitter. The fat man turned his head and greeted Jack in his distinctive Highlands accent.

"It's been a while since we have seen you," he said.

"Yes," said Jack. "You will be horrified to learn that we are here for good now."

"Living here? Whereabouts?"

"At Glen Cottage, over at Breaganish. It's where we used to stay on holiday. It came up on the market so we snapped it up. It was always our dream to move up here."

"Aye. Over at Breaganish you say?"

"Yes. You know Glen Cottage."

"Aye. I know Glen Cottage right enough. I hope you'll be happy there. There's some folk wouldn't have chosen it just now."

"Why's that?" asked Jack.

"Did you no hear what happened over there?"

"No. What do you mean?"

The fat man, whose name was Archie Beaton, was talking so loudly that his voice could be heard even above the high volume banter in the rest of the room. Now many of the other drinkers fell silent. They looked over towards the two men at the bar, waiting to hear Archie's reply.

"Iain McConnell was beaten there a few months ago as he was walking along the lochside one night. Left for dead. If it hadn't been for young Jamie Carmichael he wouldn't have survived the night."

Jack had frequently heard the name of Iain McConnell as being a major local landowner. He had never heard him described as the laird, but assumed that he fulfilled that role.

"So did this happen near Glen Cottage?"

"Aye. Just where the Black Burn joins the loch. Young Jamie found him lying unconscious on his back next to the burn, just a few yards from the loch edge."

"So what had happened?"

"It seems he was hit on the head with a club or something. Nobody knows exactly what happened."

"Was he badly injured then?"

"Aye. A badly fractured skull. Young Jamie ran like mad down the road to the nearest cottage. He raised the alarm to get the air ambulance and they took Iain to Broadford Hospital. Then he was transferred to Inverness. He was in a very bad way. They say he was close to death."

"That's awful. How is he now?"

"He's out of hospital. But they say he's still in a bad way. They say he can't remember what happened. He can't remember a lot of things apparently."

"That's very sad. But why was he attacked?"

"No one knows."

At this point a tall, stocky, red-faced, ferocious looking, elderly man, with a bristling black moustache and long, straggly, black hair, lunged forward and pushed himself between Jack and Archie.

"Of course we know," bellowed the man. "It's those wind farm opponents. They will stop at nothing."

The man pushed out his chest and stood with his fists clenched at his sides, defying anyone to disagree with his provocative statement. No- one did. No-one dared.

"Meet Hamish McDonald," shouted Archie to Jack.

Jack held out his hand which Hamish took and squeezed into limp submission.

"Jack Easter."

"Aye. Pleased to meet you, sir," said Hamish. "So you're over at Breaganish?"

"Yes."

"It was a bad business about Iain McConnell," said Hamish. "Someone will pay."

"What's it got to do with wind farms?" asked Jack.

"There are some selfish incomers who are trying to stop Iain having a wind farm built on his land. They don't care that it will bring jobs and money into the community. The bastards should go back where they came from. No- one here would have touched Iain. They would have no cause to. He is a respected man.

"It's my firm belief that it's incomers who have done this. And they will surely pay."

Jack kept his composure but inside he was wincing at the hostility being shown to "incomers" so soon after he had moved to the area. He felt some words of reassurance from him were called for.

"I can't see a problem with wind farms myself," he said.

"I'm pleased to hear it," said Hamish. "I like the English but I will have no truck with people coming here and telling us Skyemen what to do."

"I quite agree," said Jack, in conciliatory tone.

At that point he was relieved that Sophie, who had been patiently waiting at the back of the room, came forward to join him at the bar.

She spoke a few words to Archie and then Jack introduced her to Hamish, who softened and for the first time smiled.

"I hope you will be happy here," he said to her.

"I am sure we will," said Sophie.

Owing to his keen interest in the conversation about the beating of Iain McConnell Jack had forgotten about the drinks he had ordered. He found that the landlord was waiting patiently with two pints of beer poured out. Jack apologised for his ignorance, paid for the drinks and then ushered Sophie away to a nearby table.

He told her the story he had heard, which she took in her stride. She saw no reason why they should worry about local feuding on which they had no particular viewpoint. Jack accepted her assertion, but nevertheless went into a brooding, cogitative state for the remainder of the evening.

He was sensitive about being an Englishman in Scotland but had always found the Highlanders so welcoming and open that he had convinced himself this would not be a problem.

Having met Hamish, a fearsome tower of a man with attitude, he began to have inklings of doubt.

****

The next day it was down to work for Jack and Sophie. Jack spent most of the day and night working on his latest novel in the front bedroom of the cottage which he had chosen as his "office".

Sophie was mainly in the dining room which had beautiful views of Loch Breaganish and the mountains beyond, ideal for landscape painting. She made a start on several watercolours and worked well into the evening.

It was early June, a time on Skye when it hardly gets fully dark at all, even at midnight.

At around 11pm when the sun had gone down and it was gloomy at last, she paused behind her easel, brush in hand, to survey the scene. She saw a man approaching some 50 yards away from the direction of the loch. He had a backpack and was carrying a fishing rod. To Sophie's surprise he opened the small steel field gate which separated Glen Cottage's garden from the sheep field and walked inside the garden.

The man, who looked around 30 but was older, was wearing a tight fitting black teeshirt and olive combat trousers. He was above average height, slim and fit-looking, with tanned brown skin and neat light brown hair. Prominent gold rings in both of his pierced ears gave him a gipsy-like aspect.

Sophie was expecting him to call at the door but instead he passed by the dining room window and walked down the side of the house. She looked out of a side window and saw him open another small steel gate at the front of the property and then head off down the road towards Beindow.

Her first reaction was to be rather put out by the cheek of this man intruding into her property. But when she pondered the matter further she decided that no harm had been done. He was clearly taking a short cut and just giving a broad interpretation to the "right to roam" convention prevalent in the Highlands.

The next night, at around the same time, Jack was beavering away on his laptop in the "office" and Sophie was again at her easel. The same thing happened. The young man with the fishing rod walked through the garden and out of the small front gate.

In the next couple of weeks the procedure was repeated on several occasions, each at slightly varying times of the night. Sophie told Jack about the man. He said the interloper had probably been fishing for sea trout or wild brown trout in the Black Burn. His change of time each night was most likely due to the changing tide times. Loch Breaganish was a sea loch and fish were more likely to enter the Black Burn from the loch at high tide.

On one occasion Sophie was standing up at the picture window at the back of the dining room when the man approached. For the first time she caught his eye and she waved shyly. He nodded to her and gave a faint, almost grudging, smile, and went on his way. For the first time Sophie had seen his face clearly and was struck by how handsome he was. She also noticed that his lissom, quite graceful, walk seemed strangely at odds with his overall Jack the Lad image.

Jack was desperately trying to meet a publisher's deadline for his latest novel and he had been working incessantly for a fortnight to try to achieve this.

One night he was working late and Sophie decided to brave the midges and sit outside to drink a glass of wine and watch the loch. It was getting towards 11pm and she could see the twinkling lights of Upper Beindow over on the far shore.

She sat on a rather uncomfortable canvas chair on what she and Jack called the patio, but what was actually just a few slabs of concrete outside the back door of the cottage.

She heard the clanging of the steel gate at the end of the garden and emerging from the gloom was the usual young man with the fishing rod.

When he got close Sophie smiled and said: "Hello. We must stop meeting like this."

The man raised a hand in acknowledgement: "Hello," he replied. "Bonny evening, isn't it?"

"It's gorgeous," said Sophie. "Did you catch anything?"

"Not a thing tonight," he said. "It's been too dry lately. We need some rain so that the burn is in spate. That's when the bigger trout are about and the odd salmon."

"Oh, never mind. Perhaps next time," said Sophie.

The man started to walk away down the side of the house. Then he turned on his heels and said: "I hope you don't mind me walking through your garden. Fishermen have been using this path for years. But I think that now you have moved in here I ought to have asked your permission."

"It's quite all right by us. It's nice to see some people pass by sometimes."

"Are you here to stay – or are you just holidaying?"

"No. We are here to stay. This is us now."

Sophie got up out of her chair and offered her hand to the man: "I'm Sophie Easter. Pleased to meet you."

"Jamie Carmichael," he replied, shaking her hand firmly.

Sophie thought she would ask him some more about his fishing. But Jamie set off walking again at a brisk pace and was out of earshot within a few seconds.

His reserved, ever so slightly offhand, manner surprised Sophie, who was accustomed to meeting Highlanders ready to have a chat at the slightest opportunity. Perhaps he was shy, she conjectured.

But there was more to it than that. Sophie had been attracted to the stranger, both physically and emotionally. Surprisingly, she had felt herself blushing like a silly schoolgirl as she spoke to him and she instinctively knew that he could sense this and had moved off to prevent her embarrassing herself any further.

Later that evening she told Jack that she had spoken to the fisherman and that his name was Jamie Carmichael.

Jack recalled that he had heard that name before and racked his brain as to when and why. Then it came to him. Jamie had been mentioned at the hotel – the man who had discovered the laird when he had been attacked on the beach and who was obviously considered to be something of a local hero for it.

Sophie was impressed. In the deepest recesses of her consciousness she had already built up the stranger as some sort of hero figure. She was secretly delighted that fact seemed to be confirming her fantasy.

"It's quite reassuring that he is around here most days," said Sophie. "After what happened to the laird you never know who could be lurking around here. We're really quite isolated and it adds a little security to know that someone like Jamie is around. I wonder if he lives nearby? We don't really know who are nearest neighbours are, do we?"

Jack agreed that an important part of settling into their home was to acquaint themselves with the neighbours. He liked to have a Project and he quickly resolved that this should be the next thing on their "to do" list.

The following evening, therefore, the couple set off by car down their quiet lochside lane to look for neighbours. They went north to begin with, in the direction of the smart and secluded Breaganish House Hotel. Set amidst a dense collection of large trees, this imposing old country house hotel, with its associated holiday cottages, was an attractive oasis by contrast to the empty heather-covered hills which surrounded it.

Its most significant features were a long and treacherously potholed stone driveway; croquet lawns which swept majestically down to the loch edge and which were far more frequently populated by rabbits than by croquet players; and a sad, neglected tennis court, with a torn net and a worn red shale surface which had not provided a ball with an even bounce in living memory.

As with many country house hotels the clientele at the Breaganish largely comprised maiden aunts with tweed skirts, sturdy shoes and binoculars, old-before-their-time honeymoon couples and American tourists with too much money to spend.

Jack and Sophie chose not to visit the hotel on this occasion as they had already met the resident proprietors on several previous visits.

Apart from the hotel, only one dwelling-house on the Breaganish peninsular had permanent residents. The other handful of houses comprised either second homes or holiday lets. The one exception was a typical white Highland cottage situated opposite the entrance to the hotel.

It was a neat looking house, immaculately decorated, with its well-trimmed garden dominated by a children's trampoline, and with a recently installed Sky dish on the roof.

As they got out of their car Jack and Sophie could hear someone sweeping a path. Then a woman emerged from the side of the cottage, yard brush in hand.

"Hi there," she said, in a bright, friendly manner. "Lovely evening, isn't it?"

Jack and Sophie agreed that it most certainly was.

Jack explained that they were new neighbours and they had come expressly to make themselves known.

The couple introduced themselves and shook hands with the woman, who announced that her name was Catriona.

She was in her late thirties, blonde and quite petite, with a trim figure and neat hair held in place with bright blue slide. She spoke in a sharp, bird-like, Scottish accent and her face appeared to light up with animation as she conversed.

After the usual mundane pleasantries had been exchanged, she asked: "Won't you come in for a cup of tea?"

She led them inside the house, which was just as neat and clean on the inside as on the outside. Jack and Sophie thought it was typical of many Highland houses they had seen over the years. It had all the mod cons, including wide screen TV, laptop computer and dishwasher, but still had the traditional elements they had come to expect. There were pieces of driftwood fashioned into the shapes of animals, hand-painted stones from the seashore, pictures of lochs and braes, and lots of family photographs, particularly of children. A peat fire burned in the hearth, for even though it was midsummer and a bright sunlit evening, there was still a chill in the air.

Two children, a tousled-hair boy of around nine and a pretty girl of seven with blonde hair in pigtails, were sitting on the lounge carpet. They were watching the TV with their unworked-on homework stretched out on the floor in front of them.

"This is my two, Callum and Kirsty," said Catriona. "They are supposed to be doing their homework!"

The youngsters giggled and shyly, but politely, acknowledged the visitors.

"My two were just the same," said Sophie, laughing. "They always had loads of homework to do but when you went in their bedrooms they always just seemed to be taking a break and playing on their computer games."

Catriona suggested that they leave the children to their arduous chores and sit in the conservatory, which, from its elevated position at the top of a sloping lawn, gave splendid views of Loch Breaganish and the blue-grey-mauve mountains beyond.

Jack and Sophie told Catriona the whole story of how they came to be living on Skye and she in turn opened up about her life. She had been born on the island, the daughter of a Skyeman who typically had half a dozen different jobs – ghillie, painter and decorator, crofter, postman, taxi driver and tour guide. Her mother was an equally typical Skyewoman, a resourceful housewife who combined being a district nurse and midwife with running a bed and breakfast business, raising a large family and taking part in almost every aspect of community life in nearby Beindow.

Catriona's father had died of a stroke in his early seventies. Her redoubtable mother had soldiered on as a nurse until her mid-sixties when she retired to concentrate on running the B and B and helping to look after various of her ten grandchildren.

But, in particular, she cared for Catriona's Callum and Kirsty.

Catriona explained that her own husband had left her for a young filly from Portree who worked in an ice cream parlour and had "tempted him with her nut sundaes and chocolate chip cones".

To make ends meet, Catriona now worked part-time as a barmaid and receptionist at the Blackhill Hotel, made possible through her mother taking on the babysitting duties.

Jack had been looking intently at her from the very moment he saw her in the garden. He felt he had seen her somewhere before but could not recollect where. Now he realised that she had served him from time to time at the hotel.

"Now I know who you are," he said. "You are the helpful barmaid at the

Blackhill. You may not know it, but you probably saved my life once."

Catriona looked at him incredulously.

He continued: "One night - about three years ago – Sophie and I went to the Blackhill for a meal. It was the first time we had ever been there. We had starters – I forget what they were – and then a salmon main course which was to die for, washed down with a great Chardonnay.

"We looked outside and we could see a fantastic sunset shaping up over the loch. Sophie's a complete sucker for sunsets. So, on her suggestion, we decided to go for a walk along the loch and then return to the hotel for our desserts.

"It was a lovely balmy evening outside, the sunset was stunning and the loch was like a sheet of glass. At first the only disturbance on the surface was the ripples caused by rising fish – an irresistible sight for an amateur fisherman like me.

"But then, to our wonderment, we saw something we had only dreamt of seeing before that night – a pod of about ten dolphins leaping gracefully out the water.

"When the dolphins disappeared we lingered, hoping we might see them again. We strolled gently along, looking at the sky and the water and marvelling as usual at the changing colours of the mountains. It was idyllic.

"We continued walking for an hour or so and, almost by chance, found ourselves outside the bed and breakfast cottage where we were staying.

"It was getting dark and so we decided not to bother going back to the hotel for our desserts, but instead to call it a night and go to bed.

"The next morning I woke up early and lay thinking about the previous night, the lovely walk, the dolphins and the excellent meal we had enjoyed. Then a horrible thought dawned on me: we hadn't paid for our meal!

"I checked with Sophie and she confirmed that was the case. We decided that immediately after breakfast we would return to the hotel to apologise and set things right.

"We entered with some trepidation because we had been told that the landlady was a bit of a dragon. Fortunately we found you working in reception and you fetched the landlord, who had served us with our meal. He admitted that he hadn't realised that we had not paid. He laughed about the whole thing and graciously accepted our apology and the cash we owed.

"The next time we set foot in the hotel was earlier this year – three years after the incident I have just told you about. We asked the landlord if we could see the bar menu.

" 'Yes', he said, 'but you are going to pay this time, aren't you?'

"He had recognised us and remembered what we had done all that time afterwards, having never set eyes on us in the meantime! Then he creased up laughing."

Catriona giggled and declared: "All I can say is that you are very lucky I took you to Mr Maclean and not his wife, the dreaded Myrtle. She would have had the police on to you like a shot!"

"Is she a bit of a tartar, then?" asked Sophie.

Catriona replied: "She's the one of the kindest people in the world, but she tries her best to hide it. She terrifies lots of people, until they get to know her and then they realise most of her fierceness and sarcasm is tongue in cheek. It's all an act."

"We'll try to remember that," said Sophie. "She certainly does have a quite scary manner."

Jack and Sophie took their leave from Catriona, feeling well satisfied that they had made a good start in their cultivation of neighbours. She invited them to pop in for a cuppa any time they were passing. They in turn expressed the hope that she would visit them. They were also sure their paths would cross regularly at their new "local", the Blackhill Hotel.

There was no time left for rooting out other neighbours that evening so they decided to pursue the Project on the next evening.

When that time came they set off southwards along the lane, towards Beindow.

In that direction there was only one habitation within half a mile of their home, a former Forestry Commission cottage which for many years had lain uninhabited.

The single-storey white cottage had two small windows to the front and a large chimney in the middle of the roof. Only a small, unfenced, grassed area separated it from the lane. There was a larger expanse of grass at the rear which bordered on to an extensive conifer forest.

At the edge of the forest, only thirty yards from the cottage, was a small glade, a favourite haunt for deer in the early morning and towards dusk.

For many years The Forestry Commission had used the cottage as a bothy for workers and a store for tools and equipment.

Sophie and Jack had looked longingly at this cottage on numerous occasions in the past, wistfully expressing regret that such a desirable property should be so ill-used.

Jack had even written to the Forestry Commission to enquire if they would consider selling it. But they had said it was important for their operations in the Breaganish Forest. And in any case it had no electricity supply.

It had been a cause of some irritation, then, when Jack and Sophie drove past the cottage one day and saw an estate agent's "Sold" board in the garden.

That had been about a year ago. Now there were tell-tale signs that the cottage was being lived in. There were refuse bins at the roadside and a beat-up old car in a makeshift driveway which was merely a section of grass which had been scythed down. An electricity cable led from a pole at the rear of the property. And sometimes smoke could be seen coming from the chimney.

But, as our couple drove up to the cottage this evening, they realised that little or no renovation work had been carried out in the past year. The grass was unkempt and full of thistles, nettles and other weeds. There were no curtains up at the windows – nothing especially unusual in the area – and no external painting had been done.

So it was with just a little sense of foreboding that Jack, with Sophie at his side, knocked on the front door. It was soon opened by a man whom Sophie immediately recognised as Jamie Carmichael. She found herself blushing again.

Jamie was unshaven for several days and wearing a skinny blue teeshirt and denim jeans.

"Hi there. How are you doing?" he said.

Jack explained the purpose of their visit and Jamie invited them inside.

"We don't have many neighbours round here," he said. "It's one of the things I like about it."

Then, realising that might have sounded rather abrupt, he smiled and quickly added: "Please don't take that the wrong way. I like to get on with neighbours."

However, Sophie was not entirely convinced he was being sincere. She guessed that his first statement had been his true opinion.

Jamie showed them into the main room of the cottage which was immediately through the front door. It was a small room, dominated by a roughly varnished wooden table and four equally shabby varnished wooden chairs. There was a grey stone floor with no sign of any carpet or rug, white paint was flaking off the walls and the ceiling was black with damp. There were no mirrors, pictures or ornaments to provide relief from an all-pervading grimness. A black fireplace took up most of one wall. No fire was lit but a pile of firewood in front of it gave a hint of a modicum of comfort in the otherwise unappealing surroundings.

Jamie nodded to the couple to sit down on two of the wooden chairs. He remained standing. There was an awkward silence.

"We were interested to see that someone was living here," said Jack. "I once enquired about buying the place myself. When did you move in?"

"Last autumn," replied Jamie.

"You were very brave. It was a big job to take on," said Sophie.

"I'm only the tenant," said Jamie. "Iain McConnell bought the cottage from the Forestry people. I suppose it made sense. He owns most of the land around here."

"I hope you live rent-free," said Sophie. "You certainly ought to. You more or less saved Mr McConnell's life didn't you? You're quite the local hero."

Jamie stiffened and looked mildly embarrassed.

"The locals like to turn everything into a drama. They tend to exaggerate things. No, I don't live rent-free, but Mr McConnell is a very fair landlord."

Jack was suddenly struck by the idea that a plot for a novel might emerge from the attack on Iain McConnell.

"Did he have enemies?" he asked.

"It's not for me to say," Jamie replied.

He turned his back on the couple and surveyed the loch from the window. Sophie stared intensely at Jack and made a downwards waving movement with her hand to indicate it was time to change the subject.

Jack got the message.

"You're quite a fisherman, Jamie, aren't you?" asked Jack.

"Aye. I certainly like the fishing," said Jamie, turning round to face them again. "But fishing around this loch is not anything like as good as it was when I was a boy."

"Am I right that it's mackerel, pollack and sea trout in the loch and small brown trout in the Black Burn?" asked Jack.

"Aye. That's right. It's mainly wee trout in the burn, but we do get the odd salmon, if the shepherds at the top of the hill don't catch them with their nets first."

Being almost entirely ignorant of the world of fishing, but wishing to make polite conversation, Sophie asked Jamie if he made a living from his catches.

"No. There's no money in it," said Jamie.

"So it's more of a hobby?"

"Aye. Just a hobby."

Sophie would dearly have liked to ask Jamie how he did make his living. But she sensed a sharpness in his replies to her previous questions which she sensed indicated some impatience.

"He probably thinks I'm just a stupid Englishwoman who knows nothing about life up here," she thought.

Sophie decided to keep quiet. But Jack continued to quiz Jamie about the best fishing haunts in the area and the preferred methods for achieving good catches.

Although his answers were largely monosyllabic Jamie replied as usefully as he felt necessary.

While this conversation was going on Sophie had Jamie in her sights. She admired his compact bottom and noticed the smooth, tight and very tanned skin between his teeshirt and his trousers which he exposed as he leant over to reply to some question from Jack. She imagined running her fingers along his lovely back.

Sophie thought of herself as a rational, sensible married woman and yet this quiet, almost sullen, man, who lived in a gloomy, uncared-for cottage, was strangely attractive to her.

Jack considered himself to be a died-in-the-wool heterosexual but even he found himself fascinated by his new acquaintance and keen to turn him into a friend.

He asked Jamie if he might go fishing with him one evening when he visited the Black Burn. Jamie agreed but did not offer a date.

As the conversation progressed Jamie began to gather together various items of fishing tackle which were scattered around the room. He was clearly keen to be off on his evening fishing expedition.

Jack and Sophie took the hint and said their goodbyes. As they thought he would be fishing near their cottage they offered him a lift. But Jamie would not hear of it, saying he liked to walk.

The couple were a little put out by his refusal but not at all surprised. They already had him marked down as a loner.

It enabled them to continue their journey in the direction of Beindow, searching for other neighbours.

As our couple started to drive away they could see him walking – almost gliding - briskly along the lane, rod in hand and tackle bag over his shoulder. He was on a mission.

When the car reached the junction of the main road between the medium-sized village of Beindow and the larger village of Dunvegan it stopped for a minute or so while Jack and Sophie weighed up their options. It soon occurred to them that they had not thought things through. In the Beindow direction there were no dwellings before the village itself. In the Dunvegan direction there was no habitation for at least three or four miles. It was pointless to look for "near" neighbours in either direction.

So their quest for neighbours that evening came to an end. They did an about-turn and headed back towards home. This meant they would see Jamie again as he walked along the lane.

"Do we offer him a lift again?" asked Jack.

"No. He will think we're stalking him or something," said Sophie.

Jack agreed so they limited themselves to waving enthusiastically as they passed by. By way of response he merely nodded seriously.

"Odd cove, isn't he?" said Sophie.

"Yes. But a deep sort of chap, I would wager," said Jack.

They returned home, made themselves a pot of tea, and retired to separate parts of the house.

Jack went to his office, where he wrote a few notes for a novel about a laird mysteriously attacked as he walked along a remote lochside.

Sophie was in the dining room putting the finishing touches to her latest landscape – another view of the loch and the mountains as seen from the cottage. She had completed three others since moving into her new home, all from the same angle. But what set them apart was the colours. One painting showed the loch with calm vivid blue water in front of mountains covered with bright green grass. In the second the loch was brown, broody and choppy and the mountains black and oppressive. In the third picture the water was steel blue, interspersed with white waves, while the mountains themselves were a mixture of several shades of blue. For her latest painting Sophie had shown a suffused light – the loch was a gentle shade of grey while the mountains were soft mauves, lilacs and violets. The changing hues which make Skye magical.

By 11.30pm the painting had been finished to Sophie's satisfaction. It was still not completely dark outside.

Sophie turned the main dining room light out so that she could get a clearer view of the loch at dusk. She left on a couple of small wall lights. She could just make out the dark waters and the white sail of a solitary pleasure yacht which was permanently moored at the far side of the loch. She could see the outline of the large dark mountains which lay beyond the hills of Upper Beindow, where the twinkling lights of cottages gave her reassurance of human contact.

The sheep and their lambs had settled down together for the night.

She gazed at this vista for several minutes, thinking how lucky she was to be living in such a peaceful and blissfully quiet environment.

But this feeling of calm was to be short-lived. She heard the clanking of a gate. She looked towards the bottom of the garden and saw a figure walking towards the cottage. Its lithe movement was by now familiar to her – it was Jamie. Sophie's heart beat quicker and she felt butterflies in her stomach. She flicked back her hair and licked her lips to moisten them.

As Jamie got closer to the cottage he saw her standing in the window and, to her surprise, and pleasure, he blew her a kiss. She waved to him and he went on his way.

Sophie was elated.

Chapter three
Winds of change

OVER the next week or so a pattern began to emerge. On several nights Sophie just happened to be standing near the window when Jamie finished his fishing and walked by the house. Each time she made an even greater effort to look attractive. She groomed her hair so that it looked immaculate and wore her tightest jeans and tops which were either low cut or flimsy and transparent.

One day Jack received a telephone call from their daughter Portia, who was studying at Edinburgh University. She had been sharing a flat with two girl friends but made the surprise announcement that she had found a boyfriend and wished to move into his flat. She needed some help with transporting her belongings.

Jack and Sophie were dismayed by their daughter's decision but felt they had no choice but to accept it. So Jack volunteered to drive over to help with the move.

He expected that Sophie would wish to travel with him as she was always keen to meet up with either of her girls. Both Portia and Cordelia were working as barmaids at weekends and during the university summer vacations so it was unlikely that they would travel over to Skye until Christmas.

However, somewhat to Jack's surprise, Sophie declined to go with him, saying she had arranged to meet a local art gallery owner that day to arrange an exhibition of her works. It was decided that Jack would travel by himself and stay one night in Edinburgh.

The meeting with the gallery owner went well and he agreed to feature Sophie's paintings in a month-long exhibition later in the summer.

After dinner she had intended to complete another landscape, but she didn't. Instead, she took a long bath, washed her hair and doused herself with her best perfume.

She put on a gold-coloured silk dressing gown, turned off the main light in the dining room and stood in the window gazing towards the loch, but also keeping a keen eye on the garden gate.

At about 11.30pm Jamie appeared, fishing rod in hand as usual and with his tackle bag over his shoulder.

As he approached the window Sophie let slip her dressing gown. In the half-light Jamie could see her luscious breasts and he mouthed the word "Wow". She beckoned him with the skill of an accomplished seductress and opened the back door.

Jamie leant his fishing rod and tackle bag up against the outside wall.

He entered the dining room. Without uttering a single word, he clasped Sophie to him, placed his hand on her left breast, and kissed her passionately and quite roughly.

Sophie pushed him away, put her hands on the bottom of his teeshirt and yanked it over his head.

He loosened the belt of his jeans and stepped out of them. Sophie quickly pulled down his briefs and he stepped out of those too.

His penis was already erect and Sophie grabbed it and energetically rubbed it.

As she was doing this he used both hands to caress her breasts and kneed her erect pink nipples.

She leant over backwards and pulled Jamie on top of her on to the hessian carpet. He kissed her again while roughly pushing her legs apart.

She purred with pleasure. Then they made love with wild abandon.

When the passion was eventually spent Jamie dressed himself almost as quickly as he had undressed, went outside, picked up his fishing rod and tackle bag and slid away.

Sophie, still naked, was left prone on the carpet.

Not a word had been spoken.

****

When Sophie went to bed she could not sleep. She was puzzled. She had expected to feel guilt about what she had done. But she didn't. She was proud. She felt like the heroine of a D. H. Lawrence novel. Sophie was a creative person, but this totally unaccustomed act of bravado struck her as the most imaginative thing she had ever done in her life.

Her seduction of Jamie had not gone exactly as she had expected. She thought their love-making would have been a more tender experience – in her bed not on the rough dining room floor.

She had burn marks across her shoulders and on her buttocks which would take a great deal of explaining to Jack. She decided she would just have to keep herself away from him for a couple of days until the sores were healed.

Her over-riding feeling, though, was that she wanted Jamie again – as soon as possible.

She tossed and turned through the short night, getting no sleep at all. She was determined to have Jamie again. At about 5am she got out of her bed, steaming with sweat and agitated. She quickly showered.

Then, without putting on underwear, she slipped into her jeans and teeshirt put on a raincoat and left the cottage by the front door.

The sun was already up as she ran in the direction of Beindow, but a torrential shower of rain gave the morning a refreshing coolness. Sophie felt more alive than she had in her whole life. As she ran along, the rain percolated through her clothing and her luxuriant hair became matted and straggly. In other circumstances she could have felt desperate but instead she felt like an excited water nymph - a brazen naiad about to be despoiled by some rampant Greek God.

Sophie reached Jamie's cottage and banged the door loudly. Jamie opened it, wearing just a pair of black boxer shorts.

She lunged at him, pulled him towards her and kissed him passionately.

"I couldn't sleep," she said. "I want you again."

Jamie did not reply. He pointed to his bedroom door. Sophie dashed past him and into the bedroom. With some difficulty she pulled off her soaking clothes, revealing her wet nude body underneath. She flung herself backwards on top of Jamie's unkempt single bed, opened her legs, clenched her buttocks and leant on her hands so that she presented her quim provocatively towards Jamie. He took off his boxers, revealing his erection. He fell on to her, clutching a breast in each hand, and entered her.

Over the next couple of hours they made love again and again, relentlessly and ferociously. Sophie was thrilled by Jamie's tight body and his nervous athleticism.

After each climax he merely rolled over and lay with his back to her, building up his energy for the next assault. This was a new experience for Sophie. She had not been treated in this way before. Jack was not like this at all. He was tender throughout their love-making and when they had finished he held her hand, caressed her hair and face and told her he loved her.

Before she met Jack most of her sexual encounters had been with teenaged boys in the backs of cars. But even they had been gentler - more romantic even - than this silent, dour and rather rough-mannered Scot.

For the first time she had enjoyed raw animalistic sex. She felt liberated and alive, with a depth of consciousness she had never previously experienced.

The only words Jamie had spoken during this time were "You ok?" after a particularly forceful penetration. That was all.

The next words he said were: "I'm sorry. I've got to go to work."

"I'm sorry too," replied Sophie, smiling.

Jamie, who had hurriedly dressed himself, smiled back.

"Last night was the best fishing trip I've had in a long time," he said.

"You netted a lively one this time, didn't you?" laughed Sophie.

Jamie smirked and kissed her on the cheek.

"I've got to go," he said.

"See you again?"

"Aye."

"I'll get dressed," she said, clambering out of bed, still naked.

"Your clothes are still soaking wet," said Jamie. "You can't wear those."

"I can't walk along the lane naked," she said. "Do you have a car?"

"It's clapped out," said Jamie. "I walk to work."

He opened the door to a broom cupboard and produced a set of green fishermen's waterproofs, consisting of a one-piece zip-up top and trousers.

"Here put these on."

Sophie scrambled into the outfit.

"Allow me," said Jamie. "Let me zip you up."

He could not resist fondling her breasts one more time before pulling up the zip from her navel to her neck.

"You're not just a lively fish. You make an adorable fisherman too," he said.

He foraged again in the broom cupboard and presented Sophie with a plastic Co-op carrier bag.

"Here. Put your wet clothes in that," he said.

She did as he suggested, and then asked: "When can we meet up again?"

"I'm a free agent," said Jamie. "It all depends when your husband's about, I suppose."

"I'll look out for you in the evenings when you come fishing, or I'll drop a note through your letterbox. I'll sort something out."

"Ok."

Jamie opened the front door and looked both ways along the lane to make sure no-one was about.

"Quick. You go out first," he said. "I'll come out separately in a minute or two."

Sophie held his hand and kissed him on the lips and then went on her way home.

When she arrived at the cottage she felt exhausted and decided to spend a couple of hours in her own bed before having breakfast. Jack was not expected home until late afternoon.

She put her hands together and laid them on her soft pillow and then gently rested her cheek upon her hands. She did not sleep. She just lay there in a state of reverie.

She was surprised that she had no feelings of guilt or remorse for what she had done. She felt comfortable with herself and felt an exciting tingling throughout her body.

Sophie had always felt contented with Jack, who was a good, kindly man and a gentle, considerate lover. But she now realised she had never been truly fulfilled, never thrilled to her very bones as she had been with Jamie.

She could not rationalise how she felt and did not wish to do so. She just knew she wanted Jamie again as soon as possible. She wanted this man of very few words, this unknown quantity who had done nothing to woo her, or even charm her.

She wanted his body.

"Is this just recreational sex?" she asked herself.

No. There was more to it than that. It was primeval physical chemistry.

Sophie had had her children and nurtured them lovingly and well. As a rational human thinker she knew she did not wish to have any more offspring.

But as a female animal she still had the need to express herself as a biological entity, even if it was really just a form of mimicry.

When she did rouse herself she spent the rest of the day as a normal housewife, patiently waiting the return of her loving husband. She prepared a special steak dinner with all the trimmings and opened a bottle of Jack's favourite Cotes de Rhone to accompany it.

****

Over the other side of the loch, at Upper Beindow, Hamish McDonald strode purposefully towards a neat white cottage, which nestled comfortably into a niche of a grassy hill and had superb loch views from the front windows.

He hammered on the front door. Big Hamish couldn't just knock. He had to hammer as if trying to bludgeon the door into submission.

A short, crestfallen-looking man with a face made grey by stubble, answered the door.

"Ah, Hamish," he said quietly.

"Angus MacLeod," bellowed Hamish, "I need to see you."

"Well, you have done just that. What can I do for you?"

"I am going round the village to tell everyone there is a meeting in the village hall tonight – about the windmills. Ronnie McColl has called it and he wants as many people there as possible."

"You had better come in, Hamish, and tell me all about it," said Angus.

The two men went into Angus' sitting room, which was as tidy as any room in the Highlands and Islands. It was full of twee ornaments, animals shaped from driftwood and dolls dressed in knitted tartan clothes. It smacked of a woman's touch. In fact sitting in an armchair knitting was Angus' very neat wife, Fiona, a slim grey-haired woman in her late sixties.

She politely acknowledged Hamish and then picked up her knitting and left the room. Clearly he had come for man's talk.

Hamish, with his wild hair, large belly and generally scruffy appearance, looked totally out of place in her carefully arranged room.

"Would you like a cup of tea?" asked Angus. "I'd like to offer you a wee dram, but you know Fiona's views on alcohol."

"No, thanks," replied Hamish. "I understand about your wife. But I'd rather drink my own piss than drink tea. I only drink water, preferably with whisky in it. Now let's get on with the business I am here for. I've lots more folk to see."

Hamish explained that Iain McConnell's planning application for a wind farm on the mountains above Beindow would be coming before the Highland Council in the near future.

There had been objections from a group called SPAT – Skye People Against Turbines. This group, invariably described by Hamish and others as "the fucking incomers", was led by Nigel Tavistock, an internationally known English theatre director who had a large holiday home at Breaganish. In truth only about half of the group were incomers, but that fact didn't suit Hamish's narrative so he chose to ignore it.

Their main objections were that towering wind turbines would spoil the views in a beautiful area, drive away tourists, cause unbearable noise, kill rare raptors, and, perhaps worst of all, devalue their properties. They also feared that work on building the wind farm site would lead to damage to roads by construction traffic and the introduction of undesirable workmen from the mainland into the island.

Supporters of the project, however, said that the wind farm would breathe new life into the area. There would be some direct job creation and also local accommodation providers, pubs and other businesses would benefit from the influx of construction workers and later from maintenance staff. By far the biggest incentive was the promise that the developers would give the village generous annual grants for community projects. And there would be large compensation payments for residents affected by the work.

Ronnie McColl, a community councillor and builder, had put himself at the head of the campaign in favour of the wind farm. In everyday life McColl was a taciturn, sly-looking man, of a spare build and with blue piercing eyes. His normal voice was sharp and terse but at the same time controlled and quiet. But put him in front of an audience and he had the fearsome passion of a Free Presbyterian preacher, unsurprisingly as his father had been that very thing.

The unfortunate result of his overblown rhetoric at public meetings was that what should have been a rational and balanced debate among normally friendly and co-operative neighbours had become a bitter feud between two immovable and angry camps.

Lifelong neighbours had fallen out with each other and were no longer on speaking terms. Some holiday home owners had sold up and returned to the mainland, disenchanted by the sour atmosphere now prevalent in their supposed rural idyll.

The fault for this did not lie entirely with McColl and his supporters.

Nigel Tavistock himself had added fuel to the flames by giving interviews to the national press in which he suggested that the native islanders were not fit to be left in charge of such a beautiful landscape. Several articles had been accompanied by pictures showing indiscriminate fly-tipping, crofts defaced by disused cars and rusting farm machinery, and salmon farms blamed for spreading disease among wild fish.

The normally retiring and phlegmatic "laird", Iain McConnell, had been reluctantly drawn into the fray. He had given a good-humoured interview to The Independent on Sunday, in which he tried to allay the fears of the wind farm opponents. Asked whether the huge turbines could prove fatal to the golden eagles which were quite common in the area, he quipped: "Eagles can see a rabbit from two miles away. So if there's any that can't spot a 100 metre turbine then they should have gone to Specsavers!"

Conservationists were appalled and thousands of photographs appeared on Facebook and elsewhere showing eagles which had been sliced into pieces after colliding with the blades of turbines.

This escalated to an enormous degree. Former wind farm workers started to tell the world that they had been ordered to bury the bodies of hundreds of dead songbirds and other beloved species which had been found dead at the foot of turbines.

It was a PR disaster and Iain McConnell had kept his head down ever since. Even after the vicious attack on him on the lochside he adamantly refused to join in the cacophony of local opinion which asserted that wind farm opponents had been responsible.

However, no such reticence held back Ronnie McColl and his loyal band of followers. Some of them, particularly the younger zealots, egged on by Hamish and a couple of other hotheads who should have known better, started to use the sort of tactics more familiar to the streets of Belfast during The Troubles than the peaceful Isle of Skye.

Cottages owned by wind farm opponents had been daubed with offensive graffiti and stones had been thrown at their windows.

Members of SPAT held their meetings at the Lochside Inn, which provided the main competition to the Blackhill Hotel in Beindow. The owners of Lochside, who came from Manchester, had taken the side of SPAT whereas the Macleans of Blackhill had been shrewd enough to ally themselves to the pro-wind farm lobby.

One night the Blackhill regulars got wind of the fact that a SPAT meeting was in progress. Led by a drunken Hamish, 20 or so of them marched down the lane from the Blackhill to Lochside, chanting various obscenities about "fucking incomers" and "posh English prats".

Along the route various residents emerged from their cottages to see what was going on. Some joined the parade whereas others, even many wind farm supporters, shook their heads in dismay. They were mainly friendly Christian folk who did not wish any unpleasantness and who also deprecated any behaviour which would put off tourists from coming to the island.

The marchers filed into the small public bar and shouted and swore as loudly as they could with the aim of disrupting the meeting which was taking place in a back room.

The landlord, a dour Mancunian with an ill-disguised contempt for all Scots, ordered the protestors out of the bar, but could not make himself heard amidst the hullabaloo. He made a bee-line for one 17-year-old youth who was being particularly aggressive and who was trying to lead a charge out of the bar and along a corridor which led to the meeting room.

The landlord jumped in front of him and barred his way. The young man, by the name of Murdo Ferguson, kneed him in the groin and the landlord fell to the ground in agony.

Two of the protestors dragged Murdo back and then all of them made a frantic exit from the bar and ran off down the street and back into the Blackhill. They realised that things had gone too far.

Archie Beaton was sitting in the public bar. When the door flung open and the protestors piled in looking wild-eyed and panicky he managed with difficulty to shuffle his huge bottom around on the bar stool to face them. He spotted Hamish, more red-faced and hair more straggly than usual. He was out of puff from running.

"What the hell's the matter?" asked Archie.

"That fucking landlord at Lochside got what was coming to him. Murdo Ferguson dealt with him."

"What do you mean, 'dealt with him' ?", said Archie, looking a little alarmed.

"He was being obstructive – wouldn't let Murdo through to the meeting. So Murdo knocked him over. That's it. The fucker deserved it."

"He's certainly an unpleasant man. But I think you may have gone too far this time, Hamish. You shouldn't stir these young lads up like you do. You'll get them into trouble. We don't want them finishing up in prison like you did once."

"Ah, bugger it," said Hamish. "We've got to be strong or these newcomers will walk all over us."

"Look there," said Archie, pointing towards the bar.

Standing at the door was a burly policeman, with a second gangly officer behind him.

"Where's young Murdo Ferguson?" asked the first officer, Sgt John Duncan.

"Yes, where's Ferguson?" said the other officer, Pc Adam Flounce.

Various men in the bar mumbled that they did not know where Murdo

79

was. They had not seen him since they left the Lochside.

The second officer spoke on his radio to other colleagues, informing them that Murdo was not in the hotel and that they should visit his home.

"No-one leaves this bar," said the burly officer. "We shall want to take statements from you all."

While this was going on amid a noisy hubbub landlord Hector Maclean was quietly washing and drying glasses behind the bar. Then Mrs Myrtle Maclean appeared at his side, looking fierce and threatening. One by one as the drinkers saw her they fell silent. The atmosphere which had been hot and unruly became chilled, almost terror-stricken.

Mrs Maclean spoke quietly – icily: "You imbeciles. You cretins. You stupid fuckwits."

She glared at everyone like a latter day Medusa. Some of those present would happily have been turned to stone then and there rather than face any more of Mrs Maclean's fury. Even Hamish looked at the floor, shamefaced.

She pushed past them all to speak to the officers, and her demeanour miraculously changed.

"Good evening, officers," she beamed. "Can I get you anything to drink? A cup of tea, perhaps, if you can't take anything stronger?" she simpered.

The policemen politely declined, saying they had a lot of work to do.

"Well, just tell me if there is anything you need. It's always reassuring to know that the Constabulary are on hand to take care of us," said Mrs Maclean, smiling broadly.

She turned away from the officers to make her way back to the bar. As she passed her "regulars" she spat out various terms of abuse, finishing with the phrase which will stick in their memories for a very long time: "There's more brains in my granny's piss-pot than in all of your heads put together."

That night had significant repercussions. Murdo Ferguson appeared in court and pleaded guilty to assault. He was fined £250.

But what was more remarkable was the fresh spate of national publicity which the case received.

The leader of SPAT, Nigel Tavistock, had alerted all the newspapers and TV channels, telling them about the harassment which he and his supporters had received from the pro-wind farm activists.

The story was that war had broken out in what had previously been a quiet, friendly, rural community. Lots of interviews were carried out with local people revealing the bitterness felt by many.

Nigel Tavistock described the wind farm supporters as "dinosaurs, who think that by putting up a few industrial turbines in a beautiful landscape they can revitalise the economy and bring the population level of the island back to pre-Clearances levels.

"These backwoodsmen are being conned by the developers. There will be no new jobs created for the islanders – just the occasional visiting maintenance men who will spend very little money here.

"And at what cost? Holiday home owners, who bring much more money into the island, will sell up, and tourists, who are the lifeblood of Skye's economy, will stop coming because of the blighted landscape and damage to wildlife resulting from the wind farm.

"Some of the locals have been duped and it is up to SPAT to represent the true interests of the island and its people."

Ronnie McColl told one Sunday newspaper: "People who have no roots here are trying to dictate to the local people what should happen on the island their forebears have lived on for generations.

"These Johnny-come-latelies are more interested in the views out of their windows than they are about the wellbeing of this community.

"The wind farms will help bring jobs and prosperity to the island. The hotels and B and Bs will benefit from the people who come to do work on the site and the community will benefit from the generous grants which the wind farm company have promised to make available annually.

"If the incomers don't like it – they know what they can do."

The entrenched positions taken up by the leaders of the two factions led to increased tensions and bad feeling in the area. Neighbours who had already stopped speaking now became actively hostile to each other, leading to police involvement on several occasions.

It was against this unpleasant background that Hamish had visited Angus MacLeod in an effort to persuade him to join McColl's latest meeting.

Angus listened carefully to Hamish's blandishments, hand on chin. Then, at last, he declared himself ready to attend.

"And what about Fiona?" asked Hamish. "Will she come too?"

"Aye. Very likely she will," replied Angus. "What time is the meeting?"

"Seven o'clock sharp," said Hamish. "But come early as I believe it will be standing room only."

Chapter four
Elephant in the room

ONE OF Jack and Sophie's resolutions on moving to Skye was that they would become well known faces in the community. They were both social animals but the solitary nature of their work made it all the more important that they socialised during their leisure hours.

They both liked the idea of making the Blackhill Hotel their "local" and so they determined to make regular visits there from the start.

A couple of days after Jack had returned from Edinburgh he decided it was time to make an appearance at the Blackhill. He suggested this to Sophie and was a little put out when she said she was tired and would prefer not to go this time.

"But you go. Go and get to know the locals," she insisted. "It's a Friday night. There should be quite a few people in there."

It must be said that her reluctance to join him stemmed from the fact that she would have a chance of meeting up with Jamie as he returned from his nightly fishing trip.

Jack agreed to go to the hotel alone. As it was fine night he decided to walk cross-country to Beindow, following an ill-defined path along the edge of the Black Burn, branching off on to a heavily rutted old cart track and then on to a section of disused highway.

It was 25 minutes later when he entered the Blackhill bar. He was quite surprised to find that none of the usual regulars were there. There was a huge space at the front of the bar which was normally occupied by Archie's bottom. The only customers were two couples, clearly holidaymakers, who were quietly eating bar snacks at opposite ends of the room.

Jack was relieved therefore to see a familiar smiling face behind the bar – that of Catriona.

"Hi there," she sparkled. "It's nice to see you here."

"And very nice to see you too," said Jack. "It's very quiet in here tonight. What's happened?"

"There's a meeting at the village hall tonight about the wind farms. Most people have gone – even Mr and Mrs Maclean. So it's me on my ownsome behind the bar tonight."

Jack had been expecting to chat to some of the "characters" he had met there previously but now he found himself feeling rather chuffed at the prospect of spending the evening talking to the delightful Catriona.

Eye contact is the key to the chemistry of a relationship and the eye contact between Catriona and Jack had been positive, bordering on sexual, from their first meeting.

He loved her chirpy, chipped conversation, her vivacity and her natural friendliness. She liked his kindly manners, his chiselled good looks and his blue come-to-bed eyes.

As they conversed that evening they found an astonishing rapport. On the surface they had nothing much in common. He was academic, fairly serious and a touch lugubrious. She was down to earth, intelligent but far from intellectual, and effervescent without being vapid. But, in spite of these differences, they never stopped talking.

They talked about the island, about people they had met, places they had visited and jobs they had done, about bringing up children and about their dreams and ambitions.

But throughout the evening there was one very large elephant in the room, never spoken of, never even remotely hinted at, but clear as day to both Jack and Catriona. They fancied each other.

Such elephants are very common.

It was 10.30pm before the silence was shattered by the arrival of a crowd of people who had attended the meeting. Archie resumed his dominant position at the bar, which effectively meant that anyone needing a drink had to squeeze in at one side or the other of the counter in order to be seen.

Standing behind him and bellowing into his ear was Hamish, who was over-excited by the meeting and proceeded to repeat to Archie everything that everyone had said, ignoring the fact that Archie had been there himself.

Twenty or so other drinkers were also loudly discussing the proceedings and Mr Maclean quietly slid behind the bar to serve as many of them as he could.

Catriona was now very busy so there was no opportunity for Jack to continue his conversation with her.

Not wishing to get involved in the wind farm controversy, he withdrew to the side of the room and sat alone at a table to drink his beer. He expected to finish his drink and then start the walk home.

But the Highlands are full of surprises. A couple of the young men present opened a cupboard at the side of the room and produced two fiddles. Another man fetched a bodhran – an Irish drum played by hand or a small stick called a tipper – and a fourth took out an accordion.

They sat on stools at the corner of the bar and were soon playing away to their hearts' content, mixing traditional Scottish tunes with wild extemporising. This type of spontaneous music-making had been an important factor in attracting Jack and Sophie to Skye. A musical ceilidh was liable to break out at any time on the island.

Jack would often hold forth to friends about the unbroken Highland tradition of music, song and dance, contrasting this with current English folk music and Morris dancing which he considered a rather ill-starred attempt to resurrect a dead tradition.

The result was that Jack stayed in the bar until closing time at midnight, tapping his feet and applauding enthusiastically at the relevant times.

Before leaving he was keen to say his goodnights to Catriona, who was washing the last few glasses before going home.

"Well, goodnight Catriona," he said. "I'll start the long walk home. It's been lovely to see you again. I'll no doubt be in again soon."

Catriona smiled and said "goodnight". Then, as Jack started to walk away, she called out: "Did you say you were walking? It's dark outside now. I have my wee car. Can I not give you a lift?"

Jack replied: "Why, yes. That would be very nice. Thank you."

"Just a minute, then," she said.

Catriona was wearing tight blue jeans and a pretty bright yellow blouse, decorated at the V-shaped plunging neckline with a multi-coloured flowered border. She looked like a flower herself, a slender but strong little bloom, unlikely to be easily blown over by the wind. She picked up a light raincoat from a peg and beckoned Jack to follow her out to the car park.

They got into her grey Ford Fiesta and sped along the lanes back to Jack's cottage. On their arrival Jack thanked her for the lift. She lightly touched his hand and said: "Any time. I always have to pass your cottage. Goodnight, Jack."

When Jack got to his front door he waved goodbye and Catriona did the same. He caught sight of her infectious smile and felt warm inside.

****

Sophie was fast asleep when Jack joined her in bed. She had had a busy time.

As soon as Jack had left to go to the hotel she had walked down to the pool where Jamie was fishing and arranged to meet him at his cottage later that evening.

She dare not invite him into her own home, just in case Jack should return earlier than expected. If he came home and she was out she would just say that she had been for a walk.

The couple had repeated their frenzied love-making. At one point they got so carried away that they both rolled off the bed on to the floor – where they stayed and made love again.

During this adventure Sophie felt herself in an amoral daze. She was like a child which puts its fingers in its ears to avoid hearing its own voice.

She did not want to *think* about what she was doing. Like a brave novice rider on a young galloping horse she just wanted the thrill without thinking rationally about the risk.

If she was honest she did not even like Jamie. He was uncommunicative, sometimes uncaring in his love-making, and annoyingly enigmatic. She knew nothing about this man's life or about his mind, although she now knew intimately every inch of his sexy body.

But she didn't care. Nice, considerate, safe, middle-aged Sophie had been taken over by a lustful nymph who was a stranger to her. But she liked this stranger and wished she had met her earlier in her life.

She couldn't get enough of Jamie and spent hours thinking of ways of spending more time with him. How could she get Jack out of the way? That was the question she was constantly putting to herself.

In the odd moment she would reprimand herself for having such thoughts. Jack did not deserve this. He was a loving, faithful husband and a great father to their two daughters.

But such thoughts were quickly put to the back of her mind as she looked towards the new major goal in her life – to have sex with Jamie.

Then, a couple of days after Jack's visit to the Blackhill, she hit upon a plan – an unforgivable deception. She was soon to stage her exhibition in an art shop at Isle Ornsay in the south of the island.

She decided to tell Jack that she was panicking because she did not have enough suitable paintings of Skye scenes ready to hang. Therefore she would need to spend most of the next few weeks working non-stop to rectify the situation. She would then encourage Jack to go out on his own as much as possible – on fishing trips or going to the hotel for a drink at night.

When she put her plan into action she found Jack quite willing to go along with it. He hardly admitted it to himself but he was all too pleased to have the opportunity of chatting to Catriona.

****

It was a Tuesday night, probably the quietest night of the week at the Blackhill. Catriona had told Jack that she worked every night of the week except Sundays and Mondays.

So after dinner Jack said to Sophie: "Will you be busy painting tonight, Sophie?"

She confirmed that she would indeed be very busy and so Jack said he might as well take a walk down to the hotel.

When he arrived at about 8pm he was delighted to find that Catriona was behind the bar. There were no other customers. Some holidaymakers had dined there earlier and left and several local men had enjoyed a drink between leaving work and going home for their evening meal. Having finished their work in the kitchen the Macleans were enjoying a quiet night in front of the television.

So Jack spent an enjoyable evening chatting to Catriona, who was worldly wise enough to realise that she was of more interest to him than the beer.

Meanwhile Sophie decided to search out Jamie at his fishing spot. She walked through the field gate at the back of the cottage and along a barely defined grassy path which ran close to the Black Burn.

At dry times of the year the fast flowing burn runs its rocky course through a narrow but very deep valley, fringed by sturdy bushes. The stream is taken to the level of the loch below via a steep waterfall. At the foot of the frothing fall is a large pool, so wide that its centre avoids the strong current of the stream and is as calm as a millpond. It is up to four foot deep, teeming with small brown trout, a few larger brown trout, the occasional sea trout and, once in a while, the odd juicy salmon.

Beyond the pool the tidal section of the stream narrows again and flattens out until it meets with the loch.

Sometimes Jamie fished the pool using earth worms, anathema to the fly fishing fraternity, but the bait preferred by locals to actually catch fish. When the tide came in he would cast a spinner at the confluence of the burn and the loch to try his luck with incoming fish.

The pool was quite remote, and little known, so he would invariably be alone for his evening fishing.

On this particular warm, balmy night he was crouched behind a rock at the foot of the waterfall, trawling an earthworm across the pool. He heard a woman's voice from the grassy bank high above him.

"Hello, Jamie. Caught anything?" said Sophie.

Jamie held up one index finger to indicate the number of fish he had caught. Then he put both index fingers about three inches apart to describe the length of the fish – and shrugged his shoulders.

"No supper tonight, then," shouted Sophie, laughing.

Jamie did not respond.

Sophie scrambled down the steep bank to the edge of the pool. Jamie was wearing wellingtons and had waded through the edge of the water to get to his rock. Sophie did not dare to try to reach him, so she perched on a large rock at the safer side of the pool.

For about half an hour she sat patiently, admiring the scenery and the birdlife and watching Jamie fishing – catching nothing. He said little, apart from cursing from time to time when he had missed a bite.

Sophie began to think that they were wasting valuable time. She was wearing a loosely fitting white blouse with no bra, tight denim jeans and flip flop shoes.

When she saw that Jamie was intensely gazing at his fishing line she removed the blouse. When he looked up

93

he could see what he fancied looked like a mermaid lounging on the rock, her breasts looking even more inviting than usual in the glow of the warm evening sun.

"Come over," she suggested.

Jamie put down his rod, emerged from behind his rock and splashed through the water towards her. He sat down beside Sophie, put his hand around her shoulder and kissed her. He cupped her left breast in his hand and guided it to his eager mouth. He gobbled the breast as if tucking into a delicious meal and then repeated this with her right mammary.

"I've never made love in the open air," said Sophie.

"Then clamber over here, hen," said Jamie.

He beckoned her over to a grassy knoll, sheltered by the high bank. There they made passionate love. The grass was dry but rough and left red scratches all over Sophie's back and buttocks.

When they had finished their love-making she examined these scars.

"How will I explain these marks to Jack?" she said, laughing but somewhat alarmed.

"You'll just have to keep yourself covered up and as far away from him as you can manage," said Jamie, appearing totally unconcerned about her plight.

They dressed, Jamie retrieved his fishing tackle and they walked together in almost total silence back along the track to the cottage.

When they got to the gate at the back of the house Jamie squeezed Sophie's hand.

"See you around," he said.

"Yes. When?" asked Sophie.

"I'll leave that to you," was the reply. And he strode off towards his home.

Sophie was getting used to Jamie's uncommunicative attitude. She could have felt abused but she was all too well aware that she had made all the running. She had become totally obsessed with this man, who gave her nothing in return for her adulation, except sex – wonderful, lustful sex.

This wasn't the woman she knew. Not the grounded, reliable wife and mother Sophie had become. She was a hussy. At the pool she had behaved like some kind of siren, mermaid – nymph.

As she sat in the cottage on her return and contemplated the evening's events, a remembered image gripped her. She recalled a painting by William-Adelphe Bourguereau where the satyr-god Pan – half man, half goat – has been captured at the side of a pool by four naked nymphs, who are intent on dragging him into the water. Satyrs hated water.

It is a painting redolent of sheer uninhibited lust. The god is rough, wild and uncouth looking, but completely vulnerable to the whims of these naughty girls. Sophie knows exactly how they are feeling.

And then a surprising and quite disturbing thought occurs to her. From the beginning of their relationship she had thought of Jamie as a strong, silent, dour type of man. But was he in fact like the satyr being dragged towards the water, strangely vulnerable? *She* had the power over *him*.

She could not banish these thoughts. The result was the firing of her creative imagination. She went over to the table she used for painting and tossed aside a half-finished landscape. Then she took up her palette of oils and her brushes and began to paint at a furious pace.

Two hours later she examined a new half-finished painting. It showed a single naked nymph dragging a struggling satyr towards a pool – the pool at the bottom of the Black Burn waterfall.

The nymph did not look like Sophie and the satyr did not resemble Jamie. She had not become so brazen as to risk Jack seeing such an explicit image. But she now felt she had captured the essence of their relationship. .And she was thrilled.

Jack was kind, considerate and gentle and showed no outward signs of trying to dominate Sophie. But in an unspoken way he had always been the leader in the relationship. She believed she was in the driving seat now with Jamie. His apparently off-hand dismissal of her was perhaps merely acquiescence to her will.

At first this notion gave her satisfaction. But further consideration led to some alarm. Did she really want to be a control freak? Was she cut out to be a lascivious nymph?

Perhaps it was time she asked Jamie what he really wanted out of their relationship. She hoped that all he wanted was sex. She had a loving husband: she didn't need a romantic lover.

But she was new to all of this. In the past she had fallen in love with each of her sexual partners, and suffered the heartache of each break-up. Could she trust herself not to fall in love with Jamie?

She felt surprisingly guiltless about having sex with him. But to fall in love with him would be an unforgivable betrayal of Jack. She determined to remain a nymph, an amoral seeker of pleasure by the pool with her satyr. She stared at her painting and became thrilled by the notion of acting out the imagery in real life.

****

Jack and Catriona had spent every possible moment that evening chatting to each other. She was an easy conversationalist, with lots of views on many subjects, but with a sunny disposition which tended to see the best in everyone and to make the best of every situation. Some cruel locals had suggested that she chirruped like a budgerigar, but these traits endeared her

97

to Jack who had a slightly gloomy attitude towards life and welcomed anyone who could keep him cheerful.

He let Catriona do most of the talking and occasionally felt she must think him boringly quiet. She, though, liked the fact that he listened to her every word intently. She could sense that he was a decent, considerate man. He might fancy her like mad, but she was sure he would not harm her.

At closing time Catriona again offered Jack a lift home and he accepted. As the two of them left the hotel they passed the reception desk where Mrs Maclean was going through a list of breakfast orders. She insisted that all guests at the hotel ordered their breakfasts through a written form filled in the previous night.

"If there's no written order there's no breakfast," she would bark at them.

"Sod it," she shouted in her refined middle class tones as Jack and Catriona passed by. "Two of them have ordered black pudding and white pudding – and we've run out of both."

She looked up and saw Jack and grinned broadly.

"Bloody guests. They only pay a pittance and they make my life a misery."

Catriona laughed: "You know you love them all."

"Get off home with you," said Mrs Maclean.

"Goodnight, Mrs Maclean," said Catriona.

"Goodnight," said Jack.

As they walked to the door together Mrs Maclean looked up from the desk towards them and muttered: "Aha", to herself, in a meaningful sort of way.

It was still daylight as Catriona drove towards home. As they turned the corner off the main road in the direction of Breaganish, Jack said to her quite suddenly: "Would you mind just stopping a moment? Look over there."

Catriona put on her brakes and looked towards a clearing in the forest. There she saw two red deer hinds accompanied by two small calves, calmly grazing in the late evening sunshine.

Catriona had seen such sights many times before on her journey home but she was happy to let Jack have time to take in the affecting sight of these delicate creatures.

As the car eventually pulled away they saw Jamie walking out of his front door. They waved to him and he nodded in return.

"That's Jamie Carmichael," said Catriona. "Have you met him?"

"Yes, we have," said Jack. "We met him the night after we met you, when we were doing our 'meet the neighbours' tour."

"It must have been a short tour," laughed Sophie.

"That's true enough. We only found you and Jamie."

"The only other people usually resident at Breaganish are the Carltons at the hotel, the Tavistocks – for half the year at any rate - and Jamie's mother."

"Jamie's mother?"

"Yes. Sarah. She lives in an old caravan round by the back of the hotel."

"We will have to meet her," said Jack.

Catriona laughed.

"Best of luck," she said.

"Why?"

The car pulled up outside Jack's cottage.

"Well. She's a wee bit eccentric. I suppose you would call her an aged hippy – and you'll be lucky if you catch her sober."

"Should be fun," said Jack. "Anyway, thanks for the lift. I do enjoy our little talks, you know."

"Yeah. Me too," smiled Catriona.

"See you soon," said Jack.

"Aye. I'll look forward to that," said Catriona.

Jack walked to his door with what Catriona noticed was a youthful spring in his step.

It was 12.30pm when Jack entered the cottage. There was no sign of Sophie, who was evidently tucked up in their bed. Her paintings had been stacked neatly away.

After making himself a nightcap he decided to turn in himself. His wife was fast asleep. He noticed she was wearing a pair of pyjamas on what was a balmy night, when she would normally have worn a brief nightie. He thought nothing more of it.

His thoughts were focused on Catriona, for whom he was developing

an attachment. She was a pretty woman –
and a very winsome one, he felt.

If he were single he would try to
seduce her and he felt confident he would
succeed. There were no signs of anyone
else in Catriona's life and she gave slight
hints of being attracted to him.

He felt that on her side there
would never be anything more than very
small hints. She was too much of a lady
and too nice a person to try to break up
someone's marriage.

Jack had recently been reading D.
H. Lawrence's novel "Kangaroo". He had
been thinking deeply about a passage
which dealt with the relationship
between a married couple.

In the novel Jack and Victoria
Callcott have an unspoken understanding
about the limitations of their marriage:

*"She was his wife: she knew it, and he
knew it. And it was quite established and
final. So long as she did not betray what was
between her and him, as husband and wife,
she could do as she liked with the rest of
herself. And he could, quite rightly, trust her
to be faithful to that undefinable relation
which subsisted between them as man and
wife. He didn't pretend and didn't want to
occupy the whole field of her consciousness.*

*"And just in the same way, that bond
which connected him with her, he would
always keep unbroken for his part. But that
did not mean that he was sworn body and
soul to his wife. Oh no. There was a good deal
of him which did not come into the marriage
bond, and with all this part of himself he was
free to make the best he could, according to his*

own idea. He loved her quite sincerely, for her naïve sophisticated innocence, which allowed him to be unknown to her, except in so far as they were truly and intimately related. It is the innocence which has been through the fire and knows its own limitations. In the same way he consciously chose not to know anything more about her than just so much as entered into the absolute relationship between them. He quite definitely did not did not want to absorb her, or to occupy the whole field of her nature. He would trust her to go her own way, only keeping her to the pledge that was between them. What this pledge consisted of he did not try to define. It was something indefinite: the field of contact between their two personalities met and joined, they were one, and pledged to permanent fidelity. But that part of each of them which did not belong to the other was free from all enquiry or even from knowledge. Each silently consented to leave the other in large part unknown, unknown in word and deed and very being. They didn't want to know – too much knowledge would be like shackles."

This passage came once more into Jack's mind as he lay awake at the side of Sophie. It attempted to explain a view of marriage which was initially alien to him. When he married Sophie he had given a total commitment. He had every intention of obeying all of his vows.

But Lawrence's insight into the Calcotts' marriage gave Jack a new perspective. Like Jack Calcott, he trusted Sophie, but did not seek to "absorb" her. There were areas of her life which were peculiarly her own and into which he did not seek to intrude. Her art was a good example. He admired her paintings tremendously and always told her so. And he encouraged her to stretch her creativity to the limits. Beyond that he did not interfere.

Before she began to concentrate on her landscapes she had experimented with a number of genres, including the abstract and portraiture. Some of her pictures had depicted the grotesque and had a quality which reminded him of Bruegel's peasant scenes.

On occasions she had depicted characters so weird that he wondered what was going on in her head. But he never questioned her. What she painted was *her* business and he felt he would be intruding unnecessarily into *her* mind. To quote a cliché, she had to have her own space.

Likewise Sophie did not interfere with Jack's writing. His murder mysteries sometimes contained scenes of such violence, depravity and licentiousness that it seemed incongruous that they should come from the mind of such a gentle, almost naïve, man. But she held firmly to the notion that creativity should accept no bounds.

Jack pondered whether he might be able to adapt his long-held principles of marital fidelity to the Calcotts' model, taking advantage of the "space" which such a relationship provided him to woo, and even seduce Catriona.

He convinced himself that he would be able to live with his conscience if he transgressed, but only if he felt that Sophie might be equally flexible. But that was the rub. He was sure that it would never enter Sophie's head to be unfaithful to him.

He believed that, despite her vivid creative imagination, Sophie's views on marriage and relationships were entirely conventional. Domestically she was ultra conservative. He was convinced that if he went astray she would not understand the betrayal. She was such a thoroughly loyal and decent person that she would almost certainly forgive him, but that would make his unfaithfulness all the worse. He would never forgive himself.

Jack closed his eyes and blanked Catriona from his mind. Then, at six o'clock in the morning, he fell asleep.

Chapter five
Murder and
mystery

TWO hours later he was woken by Sophie standing over him with a freshly made cup of tea. Although he had slept very little he felt as fresh as the tea, alert and positive.

"Thanks, dear," he said. "Sleep well?"

"Not too bad considering all your tossing and turning," said Sophie, cheerfully.

"Sorry about that. I just couldn't seem to get off. But I don't feel tired – in fact I'm raring to go. I've discovered we have a neighbour we didn't know about, and I want to go and meet her."

Jack explained that Catriona had told him about a hippy-type woman, called Sarah, who lived in a caravan next to the hotel. He thought she would be an interesting person to meet.

Jack was gregarious and always liked meeting new people. It was a kind of hobby and it also helped him with the characterisation in his novels. But one reason the couple had decided to leave Stratford-Upon-Avon was that Jack had cultivated so many friends and acquaintances that the telephone would ring too often and people would call round at their house so frequently they seldom had a minute's peace. This was not conducive to the lifestyle of a novelist or of a painter who needed to concentrate for hours at a time.

Jack had a surprise in store for Sophie: "This Sarah woman is Jamie's mother apparently."

"You mean Jamie Carmichael?"

"Yes."

"I hope she's a bit more talkative than her son," said Sophie in a matter of fact sort of way.

Jack suggested that after their normal breakfast of cereal and toast they might take a walk down the road to see if Sarah was at home. At the front of his mind was the fact that to get to the caravan it was necessary to walk past Catriona's cottage.

It was a bright, quite warm morning as they set off. Lambs were gambolling in the field next to their cottage. A dozen of them had broken away from their mothers and were again playing "I'm the king of the castle", this time on a pile of straw bales.

One lamb had somehow managed to get out of the field on to the roadside and its mother was standing inside the field calling to it. It was a pathetic sound and Jack and Sophie were moved by it.

Sophie spurred Jack into action. He chased the lamb along the road and, after a good deal of humorous slipping, sliding and cursing, managed to pick it up. It was heavy and he could not lift it over the fence on his own. Sophie came to the rescue. They grabbed two legs each and tossed the lamb unceremoniously over the fence. It landed awkwardly, but, much to the couple's relief, struggled to its feet and ran off to its mother none the worse for its experience.

It was by no means the first time that Sophie had persuaded Jack to come to a sheep's rescue. She had an extraordinary ability to spot sheep which had rolled on to their backs, a potentially fatal situation. Jack had several times been ordered to stop his car and climb into a sheep field to right an animal. He quite enjoyed it really, as on his return Sophie feted him as something of a hero.

They continued their walk and eventually found themselves outside Catriona's house. Jack looked longingly at the windows, hoping that Catriona might see them but there was no sign of anyone.

So on they went, past the slate grey pillars at the driveway entrance to the Breaganish House Hotel. Here the public road ended and the couple continued along a cart track which led them alongside the small depots of the businesses which operated salmon fisheries and mussel beds in the loch and beyond. A small fishing boat with outboard motor was in the process of being pulled along a concrete jetty by a 4 x 4 vehicle. There was much shouting of directions to the driver by several men involved in the operation.

Jack and Sophie went through a metal gate and behind a stone wall they saw a square enclosure overgrown with bushes and rough grass. Camouflaged among the foliage and under the shade of a rowan tree was a shabby looking caravan. It had obviously once been a white caravan, but it had been attacked so much by algae, mould and mildew that its predominant colour was now a murky green.

Hens were running freely around the enclosure and a goat was tethered to a wooden stake. Several rabbit hutches were scattered around the sides of the caravan.

Jack knocked on the door of the van. It opened and there stood a tall woman in her fifties with long straggly grey hair and a blotchy face, wearing a moth-eaten sweater, a long black skirt and grubby off-white Doc Marten shoes. Her overall appearance was unprepossessing but both Jack and Sophie noticed she had beautiful hazel eyes and an angular bone structure which was a sign she had been handsome in her youth.

"Hello, there. What can I do for you folks this morning?" she asked in a pleasant, lilting, Scottish voice which rose gently into the air like a zephyr breeze.

"We are new neighbours of yours and we thought we ought to introduce ourselves. I'm Jack Easter and this is my wife, Sophie."

Sarah held out a bony hand which was taken graciously by Jack and Sophie in turn.

"I'm Sarah – Sarah Carmichael. Delighted to meet you. You say you are neighbours. Whereabouts are you?"

Sophie explained where they were living, how long they had been there and for how many years they had visited the area.

"Well I have been here for 37 years – more fool me, I suppose you're thinking."

"Not at all. This is our idea of paradise," said Sophie.

"Aye. It is certainly a beautiful place – and the people are beautiful too – most of them. Will you come inside and have a drink with me?"

The couple agreed and stepped up into the caravan. As they looked around the interior of the van they felt they were being transported back into the Swinging Sixties.

Every inch of wall space was taken up with photos and posters of The Beatles, Maharishi Mahesh Yogi, Ravi Shankar, Andy Warhol prints, Allen Ginsberg poems, Legalise Pot posters and covers of Oz Magazine.

There was a large Indian hookah pipe leaning up one corner of the main room and a sitar propped up in another.

On the dining table were a stack of books about herbs and spices and scattered all over the place were wine bottles, mainly empty ones.

A mynah bird was practising its mimicry in a large cage hanging from the ceiling by a meat hook. A disgustingly grotesque hairless elf cat with scary bright blue eyes sat on the carpet, staring like some degenerate alien from outer space sizing up its new home.

"Will you have some chamomile tea, or perhaps something stronger? I have just made some nettle wine. It's rather scrumptious, even though I say so myself."

"I'll try the wine," said Jack. "I once made some nettle beer and that was pretty successful. I've enjoyed nettle soup as well. So let's go for the hat-trick and try some of your wine."

"Oh, go on then. I will too," said Sophie.

"I'll join you," said Sarah.

Judging from the half-empty bottle and the stained empty wine glass at the side of it Jack concluded that this would not be the first glass which Sarah had tried that day,

Forcing her way past piles of washing up – mainly Habitat-ware - in her tiny kitchen, she managed to get to the cupboard where the glasses were kept. She poured out the nettle wine and quickly knocked back her first gulp: "Slange var."

"Slange var," replied Jack and Sophie.

"Slange var," said the mynah bird.

At first Sarah was keen to know all about her new neighbours – where they originated from, what family they had, what they had done in their working lives and how they came to be on Skye. She was particularly interested to learn that Sophie was an artist, having attended art college herself.

She listened intently and empathetically, occasionally totting up their glasses and then insisting on opening up a second, and then a third, bottle of the nettle wine. Jack was loving this unusual sharp brew. Sophie hated it but was too polite to say so.

"So", said Jack. "We've told you all about our dull lives. But what about you? I'm sure you must have had an interesting life."

Sarah's voice was starting to slur: "You don't want to hear about me. I'm just the mad woman of the island. Has no-one told you that? In fact I would bet that that's why you have come today – to have a laugh at the mad woman in the caravan."

There was a new tone to Sarah's conversation, slightly confrontational, almost malevolent.

"Of course that's not why we're here," said Jack. "We're not that type of people."

But that was a lie. As soon as Catriona had told Jack that Sarah was "a wee bit eccentric" he had wanted to meet her for that reason alone. He relished eccentricity in other people and ruthlessly used their strange little ways in his writing. Sophie too liked to meet people she described as "zany". As creative people both of them secretly felt guilty that they were "normal" and so they cultivated eccentric acquaintances in an effort to make up for their own deficiencies in this area.

Sarah took another gulp of wine and then opened up.

"I came from Edinburgh. My parents were doctors and we lived in a posh old town house in New Town.

"My parents were lovely people, tolerant and understanding. Too good for me. I was always an awkward little shit. I didn't take after them at all. My grandmother was Irish, though, an alcoholic who had my mother out of wedlock. When I was naughty my mother used to say that I took after my granny.

"I don't know. I've seen pictures of my granny. She was beautiful but had the devil in her eyes. She married well – her husband was a doctor too. But she took to the bottle after having my mother and was dead by the time she was 40. At least I've lasted longer than that, although I'm buggered if I know why!"

"Buggered," squawked the mynah bird.

112

Sarah stopped talking, giving herself time to take several large swigs of nettle wine. Then she just stared into her glass and it seemed as if she had nothing more to tell her visitors about her life.

Jack decided to prompt her: "So when did you leave Edinburgh?"

Sarah sighed and pulled at her long hair.

"Oh, years and years ago. I went to art college and then to Edinburgh University. Got chucked out in my first year for taking drugs. So I went travelling the world."

She paused, took another gulp of wine, and again fell silent. For a moment she seemed to be drifting out of consciousness in an alcoholic haze. But Jack persisted: "Where did you get to, then?"

"I went to Borneo – lived in the jungle in a hippy commune. Took loads more drugs, ran around in the nude a lot – free love, paganism, drink, rock music – general hedonism. You know the score. I had a whale of a time for a couple of years – until the murder."

She paused.

"Murder?" asked a surprised Sophie.

"Murder," said the mynah bird.

"Yeah. Ruined the whole scene, you know. There was this orgy one night - sex and drugs in the moonlight. We did 'magick' according to the rituals of Aleister Crowley. Have you heard of Aleister Crowley?"

Jack and Sophie both nodded. They too had had youthful fascinations with the Great Beast 666, the notorious English occultist and poet.

"We called our commune 'Abbey of Theleme B'. 'B' for Borneo."

The Abbey of Theleme was mentioned in Rabelais' poem Gargantua. It has been described as an anti-monastery where the lives of the inhabitants were "spent not in laws, statutes, or rules, but according to their own free will and pleasure".

This Utopia was the model of Crowley's commune and also a school for "magick".

Sarah continued: "You know what Crowley's motto was, don't you?"

"Do what thou wilt," said Jack.

"That's right. But someone took that too literally. A young man there got high on drugs. He started raving on about human sacrifice – how it was necessary in order to raise the most important and interesting spirits.

"We all told him to 'shut up, shut up', but he was high as a kite. Just wouldn't listen. He picked up this big knife we had been using for cooking and he just ran towards this young girl. A beautiful girl, pretty and innocent, with lovely long auburn hair. He shouted out 'here's a virgin – that's what we need' and, before anyone could stop him, he plunged the knife into her heart.

"The poor wee girl. She died instantly. The young man - Benjamin he was called - was shocked back into normal consciousness. He just sobbed and sobbed. 'What have I done, what have I done?' he cried out time after time.

"The rest of us were just horrified. Women were screaming. Even some of the men were screaming. We were all drugged up and boozed up, you see, so our emotions were all high to begin with.

"One of the men ran off to the local village and fetched the police. There was to have been a big trial. I would have been called as a prosecution witness. But it didn't happen. Benjamin hanged himself in his cell. Not a nice time."

Jack sat forward, resting his head in his hands, listening intently to all that Sarah said. He could feel a murder novel coming on. He wanted to know more and fired dozens of questions at her. But she was becoming increasingly intoxicated and her memories became muddled and her responses incoherent.

"Ah. It was a long time ago," she said. "A lot of water has gone under the bridge."

Sophie was interested to know what had brought Sarah to Skye.

"A man – a man a lot older than me. At least I thought he was a lot older – 15 years older at least. But good looking. A fabulous shag. Sorry, I shouldn't have said that. Too much wine!"

Sophie laughed: "Don't worry."

"You're broad-minded then? Good. I like to tell things as they are. I was a sexy thing at that time. People said I gave the best head in Scotland. Sorry.

But you're broad-minded. I fucked like a rabbit. Sorry. You don't want to hear all this."

"Was the man from Skye?" asked Sophie, not at all offended.

"Yes. A Skye man. A farmer. But I met him in Edinburgh. After the murder I left Borneo straightaway. I went back to my home city. Worked as a barmaid at a city centre pub. That's where I met him. He was in the city on business and came in the pub for lunch.

"I fancied him as soon as I saw him. Strong, tall, dark man – fit as a fiddle. With a lovely soft Highlands accent. I think he fancied me right away too. I was quite a looker in those days.

"Anyway we got chatting as I served him his meal – about places to go and things to do in Edinburgh. And he asked me if I would show him the best night spots. It was my night off so I said 'yes' and the rest – as they say – is history."

"Did you come to Skye to join him, then?"

"Aye. After only a week or so of knowing each other. But it was not as easy as that. He was married. I knew he was married from the start and I didn't care. I've never believed in marriage. Free love's always been my thing, my dears. Shocking isn't it?

"I came to Skye. He paid for me to stay in the Royal Hotel at Portree for a couple of weeks. Then he bought me this caravan. A friend of his from the mainland had used it previously as a holiday home. We would meet here secretly. Then I found I was pregnant."

"With Jamie?" asked Sophie.

"Hello Jamie," screeched the mynah.

"Aye, with Jamie. Do you know Jamie?"

"Yes. We've met. A nice chap."

"Nice? He's a good looking boy, that's for sure. He's an odd one. Like his mother."

"Did your man accept the baby?" asked Sophie.

"We always kept Jamie a secret between us. Still do. His father always saw us okay for money – up to a point. Then his wife died, of cancer, some years ago. I thought that then he would be able to acknowledge us. People around here are good Christians. They are understanding.

"But, no. He still didn't admit to any connection with us. I said to him a thousand times 'the locals must know. They are not daft. They will have put two and two together years ago. They must have seen your vehicles parked near the caravan.' But, no. He was too ashamed of us.

"Then he presented me with a real bombshell – he was planning to remarry. He had taken up with a woman who lived at the farm next to his house. She had been recently widowed and was ten years younger than him. So that was it for me. The writing was on the wall. He didn't want me."

"Do you still see him?" asked Jack.

"See him? I see him. I see him most days. He says 'hello' – just. And he still arranges money for me. But that's it. 'Hello' is all I get. I don't care. I made my own bed. I've got my animals – and my memories."

"And Jamie?"

"Hello Jamie," interrupted the mynah bird.

"Aye, Jamie."

Sarah said his name in a dismissive way, uttering a quiet sigh. Sophie and Jack deduced that there might be some problem between them. However, the fact that the bird knew Jamie's name suggested he must be a regular visitor to the caravan.

"Have another glass of wine," slurred Sarah.

"No. We really must be going," said Jack, judging that Sarah might soon fall asleep as a result of the drink. "It's been delightful to meet you. Thanks for the wine. You've been more than generous. You must pop in and see us any time you are passing the cottage."

"Thanks," said Sarah, "I don't do much visiting. But I will try and drop by some time. I would like to see your paintings, Sadie."

"Sophie," said Sophie, correcting her.

"So, sorry," said Sarah.

She was sitting forward, supported by her elbow on her knee. Suddenly the elbow slipped. She slumped forward and the glass of wine she was holding slopped out on to the carpet.

"Oh, bugger," she said.

"Bugger", erupted the mynah.

Sophie went over to the sink and found a disgusting looking dishcloth which she used to mop up the wine from the floor.

"You see I'm a fool. I was a young fool and now I'm becoming an old one," said Sarah.

"Nonsense," said Jack, lying again.

Our couple left the caravan to return home. As they closed Sarah's metal gate behind them Sophie gazed up at the mountains to the west.

"Look. There's a new house over there," she said, pointing to a large modern wooden house perched high on the mountainside.

"Some more neighbours." said Jack. "Shall we go and knock on the door?"

"I don't think there's anyone at home," said Sophie. "And anyway we must both stink of drink. Let's try another day."

As they continued their walk home they saw the burly and unkempt figure of Hamish McDonald walking towards them. When he was about 30 yards away he suddenly left the road, clambering up a grassy bank and over the other side, out of view. This tree trunk of a man had unexpectedly shown the dexterity of a frightened sheep in negotiating the steep bank.

Jack and Sophie looked at each other, and laughed. Was he trying to

119

avoid them, or just single-mindedly pursuing a pre-ordained course?

****

Sally McConnell took a cup of tea to her husband, Iain, as he sat in a comfortable chair in his large lounge – a typical laird's room, all brown leather seating, Scots pine panelling, full bookcases reaching to the ceiling – and cold.

"How's your headache now?" she asked.

"Headache? Oh. Headache. I haven't got a headache."

"Good. I'm so pleased," said Sally.

She smiled and shook her head. Five minutes earlier Iain had been complaining of a splitting headache. Now he had forgotten having one. It was early days, though. He had not been out of hospital long since the attack at the lochside.

The doctors had warned Sally there might be after-effects from a fractured skull, headaches and memory loss being just two of them. Dizziness, fatigue, loss of smell, even personality change could be others. And any, or all, of these could last for months or years.

For a man more than seventy years old this was not a good prospect. But Sally was one of those people who can take anything that life throws at them and was philosophical enough to take one day at a time.

Iain himself had been a calm man with a normally cheerful and down to earth view of the world. As a countryman he could reconcile himself to the various stages of his life with the same equanimity as he showed towards the changing seasons of the year.

However, the severe blow to his head had left him feeling panicky and confused. The police had questioned him numerous times about the incident but he could not remember much of use.

He had spent the first part of that fateful evening attending a meeting at the Blackhill Hotel about the wind farm development – a development close to his heart as it would be built on his land. Then he had apparently walked to the Breaganish House Hotel to play snooker and take a dram with the hotel's owner, his friend Robert Carlton. It was one of his regular pleasures.

When he left the hotel he had, as usual, walked homewards towards Beindow along the shore of the loch. He said he had no recollection himself as to what had happened next. It was something which had perplexed him greatly and caused him to have unbearable headaches and some uncharacteristic flashes of bad temper.

In his calmer moments Sally had gently tried to coax some snippets of information from him, but to no avail.

The police had interviewed Jamie Carmichael too as the only other person known to have been in the vicinity of the attack.

Jamie had told them he had been fishing at various points along the Black Burn and Loch Breaganish, finally giving up when the blackness of night overtook him. He had started the walk home when he came across Iain's body. He had taken off his jacket and wrapped it around the man. Finding that he had run out of credit on his mobile phone, and having no landline at his own cottage, he ran like the wind to Catriona's cottage and asked her to dial 999.

With Catriona he had rushed back to the unconscious Iain and waited for the air ambulance to arrive. This took Iain to the accident and emergency department at Broadford hospital in the south of the island.

Detectives scoured the area but found no weapon and no clues as to Iain's attacker. Jamie was under suspicion and had been interrogated several times but the police were satisfied he was Iain's rescuer, not his attacker.

Iain slowly drank his tea and then looked up at Sally dolefully.

He spoke slowly and slightly tremulously: "Sally. I have something to tell you. But I want you to promise me that you won't tell another soul."

"What is it about?"

"It's about the attack. Well, it's about more than the attack really."

"But if it's about the attack why have I got to promise not to tell anyone about it? Surely the police have got to know everything about that."

122

"Sally. There are things you need to know which won't bear repeating outside of this room – at least not if it can possibly be avoided. I need you to promise me that you won't repeat anything I am going to tell you. Otherwise I will not be able to confide in you."

"Very well then, darling. I promise."

Chapter six
Meeting more neighbours

SOPHIE spent the afternoon at home producing another painting of satyr and nymphs at the Black Burn waterfall, while Jack tried to work in his office on his latest novel.

But Jack could not concentrate. He kept thinking of Catriona, trying to find ways of justifying his ardent desire to seduce her.

The passages from D. H. Lawrence's Kangaroo had not entirely convinced him. Now he struck upon a section of Oscar Wilde's dialogue "The Critic As Artist":

"The mere existence of conscience that faculty of which people prate so much nowadays, and are so ignorantly proud, is a sign of our imperfect development. It must be

merged in instinct before we become fine. Self-denial is simply a method by which man arrests his progress, and self-sacrifice a survival of the mutilation of the savage, part of that old worship of pain which is so terrible a factor in the history of the world, and which even now makes its victims day by day and has its altars in the land."

Jack thought long and hard about these words, but found them wanting and shallow. He felt that, like so many of Wilde's observations on life, the passage was merely a self-justification for an irresponsible individuality. And where had that got Wilde? To prison, disgrace and estrangement from the family he professed to love. Jack would have none of it.

He had sworn "forsaking all others" to be faithful to his wife until the day he died and no amount of casuistry could circumvent that oath. He could not deny that "instinct", as Wilde described it, was a prime mover in the thoughts and actions of the human animal. But he totally rejected Wilde's bald statement that conscience must be merged in instinct before man became "fine".

"Fine" – what a ridiculous word to use. Far from producing a "fine" outcome to man's nature, merging conscience and instinct would lead us towards a more bestial condition. Traditional family life would be traduced and children left in broken, dysfunctional homes. Decent, stable society would be overthrown by licentiousness.

If Jack were to seduce Catriona it would be as a result of sheer animal lust, and would be a sign of his craven weakness. He knew this all too well.

His thoughts wandered to another novel he had recently read, Narcissus and Goldmund by Herman Hesse. Goldmund had left the monastery where he had been a pupil for a life of licentiousness and adultery, giving free rein to his libido.

On the surface he was a free spirit but with a "calm" conscience. But on a deeper level his conscience was not at all calm: *"But it was not the adultery and lust that sometimes troubled and burdened his conscience. It was something else. He could not name it. It was the feeling of a guilt one had not incurred but a guilt with which one had come into the world. Perhaps this is what theologians called original sin? Yes, life in itself carried in itself something like guilt..."*

Jack thought Hesse had hit the nail on the head. If he seduced Catriona he would be plagued for the rest of his life with a terrible feeling of guilt.

And yet he could not get this woman out of his mind. She had done nothing to encourage him and yet instinctively he knew that in the right circumstances she would be there for the taking. He was sure that if he willed this strongly enough it would happen.

Equally he was repelled by the Aleister Crowley doctrine of "do what thou wilt". He hated the self-indulgence of the sex, drugs and rock and roll outlook on life. He was balanced, moderate and relatively unselfish.

He could not resolve the dilemma he found himself in, so he adopted the tactic of Prime Minister Stanley Baldwin – "wait and see".

Meanwhile Sophie's head was overtaken by visions of her satyr and nymphs. In each of her recent pictures the satyr bore little or no resemblance to Jamie. But it *was* Jamie, distorted and misshapen to avoid any possible suspicion. The principal nymph was Sophie herself, similarly disguised but there in essence. As for the other three or four nymphs they were mere shadowy copies of figures she had seen in famous paintings by Herbert Draper and John William Waterhouse.

In her present state of mind she could not imagine painting anything other than pictures of satyrs and nymphs with a backdrop of the Black Burn waterfall and pool. Views of the wider sea loch no longer interested her.

Her new-style pictures were the only antidote to a restlessness and impatience for her next meeting with Jamie.

She was revelling in behaviour which would previously have repelled her.

Jack was restless too. They both needed to keep busy in an effort to play tricks with their own minds.

Jack was desperately trying to keep active in an attempt to banish from his mind sinful thoughts about Catriona; Sophie, on the other hand, was frantically painting her satyrs and nymphs so that thoughts of her liaison with Jamie would constantly consume her.

After a silent dinner together Jack sprang up from the table and declared enthusiastically: "Let's go down the road and meet our other neighbours."

"Good idea," said Sophie. "I'll put my boots on."

****

As they approached the wooden house on the hillside Jack was puzzled as to why they had not seen it before that day. After all, they had visited Skye regularly.

The explanation was that this was a "designer" timbered-framed house similar to many others which were going up on Skye at that time. They took only eight weeks to put up. Many locals detested them because they felt they were out of character for the area. They were not thick-walled cottages painted white.

But as Jack and Sophie got nearer to the house they became aware that there was plenty of white paint on show. Chilling, terrible, white paint.

A frisson overcame them as they saw that daubed untidily in foot-high white letters on the front of the house were the words FUCK OFF ENGLISH SCUM.

Jack and Sophie looked at each other in consternation. They both realised that nothing would ever be the same again. In all their years of visiting Skye they had never come up against any overt anti-English sentiment.

Once, when they were travelling on the Scottish mainland, they had seen a poster in a garden saying "Remember Bannockburn". But they only saw it once. The next time they were passing it had disappeared. They had noticed that a holiday cottage on Skye had been called The Auld Alliance – the alliance referred to being the centuries-old one between Scotland and France, against England. But a new owner had since renamed it.

These had been trifling matters compared with the assault to the eyes which the couple now had in front of them.

They saw a Mercedes car parked at the side of the house, indicating that someone was at home. But Jack and Sophie thought this would be a bad time to pay a call and they turned around to make tracks homewards.

As they did so a man's voice called out to them in an instantly recognisable Home Counties accent: "I say there, can I help you?"

They looked round and saw a tall, patrician-looking young man in a light-coloured three-piece suit bounding down the hill towards them.

"I say. What can I do for you?" he said loudly.

"We are kind of neighbours of yours, from just along the road," said Jack. "We had just come to make ourselves known. But we can see that you

129

may have had some trouble and we wouldn't wish to bother you now."

In a quieter voice now as he reached them, the man said: "No. There's no need for you to go. I would appreciate a chat with you anyway. Please come up to the house."

Jack held out his hand and replied: "Oh. Okay then. If you're sure. I'm Jack Easter and this is my wife, Sophie."

"Nigel Tavistock," said the man, shaking Jack's hand and then Sophie's. "Pleased to meet you."

"Oh, Mr Tavistock," said Sophie. "You're the theatre director aren't you? You once directed a play at the RSC at Stratford. I was a set designer there at the time."

"Pinter's The Homecoming", said Nigel.

"Yes, that's it," said Sophie, already feeling she had something in common with her neighbour.

Sympathetically, Jack broached the subject of the offensive graffiti.

Nigel's naturally tanned face turned pallid as he turned towards the house. His stentorian voice faltered slightly as he described the shock he and his wife had received on returning home to see the abusive words.

As they walked towards the house with his new neighbours, he said he was sure this outrage had resulted from his opposition to the wind farm.

Jack and Sophie had heard the locals talk in hostile language about Nigel and his fellow campaigners and were sure his theory about the graffiti was correct.

As they reached the front door it was opened by Nigel's wife, Stella, an attractive leggy forty-something with a deep tan and another pronounced Southern accent. Her eyes were puffed and her mascara had run, suggesting that she had been crying.

She gave Jack and Sophie a warm welcome and, seeing how upset she was, Sophie gave her a reassuring hug.

This touch of human empathy moved Stella to more tears which she desperately tried to wipe away in her embarrassment.

"I'm sorry to be such a wimp," she spluttered, "but to come home and find this – it's just completely knocked me back. I just think we'll have to sell up and do what they want."

Jack had been careful not to take sides on the wind farm issue. In truth he had what he described as "an unfortunate and increasingly worrying tendency to see both sides of an argument". But what he refused to countenance was bullying and barbarity and these were what were symbolised by the graffiti. There was an inherent unfairness here too. Nigel's views on wind farms might be objectionable to people, but in no way could he help being English.

Indeed the whole episode was crazy, he believed. One of the arguments used by the supporters of the wind farm had been that it would help to revitalise the economy, which in turn would make it more attractive to incomers such as the English.

Nigel had argued that wind farms would be ugly blots on the landscape and actually deter tourists and inward investment.

Both sides wanted the same thing – a healthy local economy. They had different ideas on how to achieve this – but why the hatred?

Jack knew that many of the locals hated Nigel. But he was interested to know if the feeling was mutual.

Sophie was also ambivalent about wind farms. She liked the principle of renewable energy, whether it was produced through wind, tides or solar power. But reports of birds getting chopped up by wind turbines had repelled her and she found herself emotionally veering towards the "antis".

Like Jack, she felt deeply sorry for Nigel and Stella over the obscene desecration of their cottage and wanted to offer them as much neighbourly support as she could.

Nigel and Stella showed their guests into their open plan main room, which was ultra-modern, with beamed ceilings, floors and staircase in light brown wood panelling and huge picture windows giving magnificent views of Loch Breaganish and the mountains beyond. Sophie was quite envious of the eagle's eye view the house provided.

Jack and Sophie were invited to sit down on a stylish leather settee and Stella went over to the kitchen section of the large room to make them coffee.

Nigel paced up and down the wooden floor, looking worried.

"It was never meant to be like this," he said. "This was our dream home. Now it's turning into our worst nightmare. It's my fault, all my fault. I should never have got involved in this wind farm campaign.

"You see they wanted someone well known to front the campaign. I am fully on board with it, of course, but now we're brought to this.

"Stella is devastated. It's the hatred, you see. She can't cope with it. When she goes to Beindow people blank her, or they just stare at her. Several times she has had her car tyres let down.

"Once a child of about six shouted to her, calling her an effing bitch. We have had sheep poo pushed through the letterbox.

"I would pack up and put the house on the market tomorrow. But I can't. I really can't."

"Why not, if you don't mind me asking?" asked Sophie.

"Because I would be letting the side down. There are a lot of people in SPAT, our anti-wind farm group, who are sort of relying on me to carry on the good fight. I can't let them down."

Jack began to understand that Nigel's support for his cause was born out of some English desire to do the right thing, a sort of noblesse oblige. He liked him for it.

Stella brought in the coffee on a tray. Her hands were shaking and Sophie could tell at once she was still very upset.

"Let me take that," she said.

"Thank you," said Stella. "I'm afraid I'm being awfully silly."

"No, you're not," said Sophie, forcefully. "It's appalling what has happened to you. I can't believe who would have done such a thing."

"When did you discover the graffiti?" asked Jack, pointedly.

Nigel explained they had gone into Portree shopping that morning, had a spot of lunch there and found the letters on their cottage when they returned home in the early afternoon. So the offensive daubing had been carried out in broad daylight.

Jack was pensive. Since he had started writing mystery novels he had begun to fancy himself as a bit of a sleuth. He desperately wanted to find out who had perpetrated this horror.

A thought had struck him. He remembered that, on their way back from meeting Sarah Carmichael, Sophie and he had noticed an embarrassed looking Hamish McDonald making his way in the direction of the Tavistocks' house.

"Do you know a chap called Hamish McDonald?" asked Jack.

"We certainly do," replied Nigel. "We've had several up and downers with that man. An aggressive sort of fellow. He has sworn at us several times in the street."

"Well," said Jack. "We saw him walking in this direction round about lunchtime today. And he looked a bit shifty to me – as if he was trying to avoid us."

"I got that impression too," said Sophie.

"It'll be him!" declared Nigel. "I can just imagine him doing something like this. He's an oaf."

"Have you told the police about what has happened?" asked Sophie.

Nigel said they had and were expecting them to arrive at any time.

Stella, who was staring out of the window, said: "Look. They're here now."

Alighting from a police car was the sturdy shape of Sgt John Duncan, followed by the lean, willowy and curiously boyish figure of Pc Adam Flounce.

Stella showed them in.

"Bad job this," said a scowling Sgt Duncan. "Not the kind of thing we like to see on Skye."

"Indeed not," broke in Pc Flounce.

"Have you any idea who might have done this?" asked Sgt Duncan.

"Any notion whatsoever?" said Pc Flounce.

Nigel told the officers that Hamish McDonald had been seen nearby. He was supported in this by Jack and Sophie.

"Hamish McDonald!" declared Duncan, echoed by the identical exclamation from Flounce. "He's a rogue and a ruffian, but I wouldn't have thought this of him. As a rule he's more of a loud-mouthed nuisance than a criminal."

"Yes, a loud-mouthed nuisance," interjected Flounce.

"But he did once serve time for violence," said Duncan.

"Aye, he did," said Flounce.

Stella related how Hamish had sworn at them on several occasions. He was passionately in favour of the wind farm, she said, and even more passionately hostile against opponents of it.

Sgt Duncan instructed Pc Flounce to take photographs of the graffiti while he took notes from the two couples. When these tasks had been completed he said he would be contacting them all again to ask them to go to Portree Police Station and sign statements. In the meantime he would be speaking to Hamish.

"Thanks for your help," said a serious Sgt Duncan. "Bad business this. The island is normally very welcoming to everyone. This is completely out of character."

"Aye. Completely out of character for the island," advised Flounce.

After the officers left, Nigel commented: "Funny pair, eh? Like the Old Man of Storr and his very thin shadow. But I liked the way they went about their work. That sergeant appeared to be quite efficient."

Sophie nudged Jack and joked: "That constable reminded me of the mynah bird we met earlier!"

Nigel said: "You haven't by any chance met our neighbour Sarah, have you?"

The couple laughed.

"Yes. I'm afraid we have," said Sophie. "What a character!"

"Did you catch her sober?" asked Stella.

"I think she might have been sober when we first met her at her caravan this morning," said Sophie. "But it didn't last for long. She can certainly knock back the nettle wine."

"I rather think she is either drunk or very drunk," said Nigel.

This reference to drink spurred Stella into hostess action.

"Will you have a glass of wine with us?" she said to Jack and Sophie. "I certainly need one after what's gone on today."

Our couple readily agreed to this plan of action and a bottle of good quality claret was soon opened and dispensed.

There was the normal exchange of information between the two couples, who found they had plenty in common. They were all interested in theatre, literature and art. Stella was the only one who had no professional experience in these areas, but she was keen to write a "chick lit" novel.

She had been an air hostess before her marriage to Nigel five years previously. They were both in their late forties and on their second marriages. Both had two teenage children from their first marriages.

Nigel, ex-public school and Oxford-educated, spoke loudly and confidently and had a natural air of superiority. But he was good-natured and was easy company.

Stella was the daughter of a nouveau riche garage owner from Birmingham, who had used much of his wealth to have her and her two sisters privately educated. Although she was stylish, civilised and normally quite well-adjusted, when things went wrong she became jumpy and emotional and occasionally lost her temper. She had lost her job as an air hostess when she slapped a drunken passenger across the face.

The hostility they were receiving over the wind farm issue was causing her great distress. Sophie did her best to sympathise, but could not help thinking that had she been in Stella's position she would have reacted in exactly the same way.

What could be the pleasure of living in a neighbourhood where so many people hated you?

The couples spent a couple of hours chatting amicably. But, however hard she tried, Stella could not get the image of the graffiti out of her mind and interspersed her conversation with violent expressions aimed at whoever had perpetrated it.

"It's that nasty Hamish. I'm sure of it. I would crucify him if I had half a chance! Nasty, smelly, horrible old man!"

Nigel, Jack and Sophie tried hard to change the subject and Stella kept apologising for her constant references to it.

She repeated her apologies as her guests got up to leave.

"Don't be silly," said Jack. "Of course we understand how upsetting all this must have been for you."

"Thank you for being so understanding," said Stella. "I don't know how I would have got through this evening without having someone sensible like you two to talk to."

Nigel had also been impressed by Jack and Sophie. He had enjoyed their intelligent conversation and was grateful they had helped to keep Stella's emotions under control.

"We are having a dinner party here tomorrow night - just a few friends," he said as he showed the couple to the door. "We would be delighted if you could join us."

Jack and Sophie glanced at each other and were quick to accept the invitation.

"Seven o'clock okay for you?" said Nigel.

"Great," said Jack.

"With a bit of luck we will have the graffiti dealt with by then," laughed Nigel.

****

At the Blackhill Hotel Archie Beaton and Hamish McDonald were dominating the bar. They were loudly exchanging the latest gossip about the wind farms.

Hamish's conversation consisted of little more than a series of angry outbursts peppered with expletives. Mrs Maclean had banned him from the hotel on scores of occasions, but he had always managed to ingratiate himself again by presents of game and fish which he had acquired from sources known only to himself.

Archie, on the other hand, was even louder than his friend, but far less aggressive. Despite his excesses of eating, drinking and extreme opinions he was at heart a gentleman.

"I tell you that these SPAT bastards ought to be driven from the island," roared Hamish.

Archie, who was sitting on his normal stool and facing the door of the bar, tapped Hamish on the shoulder. Hamish turned and saw the contrasting figures of Police Sgt Duncan and Pc Flounce walking towards him.

"Hamish, you need to come with us to the police station," said Sgt Duncan.

"What the hell for?" bellowed Hamish.

"We are investigating a matter which we think you may be able to help us with," said Sgt Duncan calmly.

"What matter?" shouted Hamish.

"We should talk about this at the station," replied Duncan.

"And what if I refuse to come?"

"We will obtain an arrest warrant," said Duncan.

"The devil you will," said Hamish.

Archie grasped his arm.

"Don't get yourself into trouble, Hamish," he said.

"Ok, ok," said Hamish. "I'll come with you. Bugger you!"

The officers left the bar, with Hamish, head bowed and shoulders lowered, shuffling off after them.

Mrs Maclean had joined her husband behind the bar.

"What in heaven's name is going on now?" she demanded of Mr Maclean.

"Don't ask me," was the reply. "Hamish in some sort of trouble again."

"That man!" exclaimed Mrs Maclean. "He'll be the death of us all! Do you know what's going on, Archie?"

"No, I don't," said Archie, sheepishly.

"You must have some idea," snapped the landlady incredulously. "You're practically joined at the hip."

"I don't know. I really don't. It might be something to do with the wind farm. He's been getting very steamed up about it. He was at Ronnie McColl's yesterday. Ronnie gets him all wound up and then he goes and takes things too far."

"So what has he done now?" asked Mrs Maclean.

"I don't know. I don't know. I just know he was vexed after he came back from Ronnie's."

"Vexed! I'll vex him when I get hold of him. We have had the police here too often just lately. Far too often," said Mrs Maclean. "We are a respectable premises. I'll chop his bollocks off."

Having made that eloquent appeal for respectability she was preparing to sweep out of the room in dramatic fashion when the bar door opened quietly to reveal the meek figure of Angus MacLeod.

"My word, Angus," said Mrs Maclean. "We don't see you in here very often. Has your cottage burnt down?"

Angus smiled: "Fiona's having her bath, so I managed to slip away for a few minutes."

"Will you have a whisky with us?" asked Mr Maclean. "It must be years since you were in."

"Ah, no. Better not," said Angus. "I wouldn't like Fiona to think I'd turned into a secret drinker. I just wanted a wee word with Archie.

"Archie, I wondered if you had heard what had happened to the Tavistocks' house."

Archie shook his head.

"I saw Fergus Tobin earlier. He had been over to Breaganish to check on his sheep. He told me someone has defaced the Tavistocks' house – written 'F Off English Scum' in huge letters on the wall. Have you heard about it?"

"No. Nothing," replied Archie.

"Are you sure?" interrupted Mrs Maclean.

"Absolutely sure."

"We had the police in here just now," the landlady told Angus. "They took Hamish away with them."

"Oh, dear," said Angus. "I feared that Hamish might have been up to his tricks."

Archie shook his head sadly.

"I thought he had something up his sleeve."

"The moron," shouted Mrs Maclean. "It will be him right enough. He always goes too far. He will finish up in prison again. And serves him right."

"Oh, come on, Myrtle. That's a wee bit harsh," said Archie. "These damned incomers are the real cause of all this."

Mrs Maclean replied stiffly: "I am as much in favour of the wind farm as the rest of you. I think these SPAT people are a damned nuisance. But there is a limit. We must respect the law of the land."

Archie said: "It's all very well to say that but.."

"There's no buts about it," said Mrs Maclean. "We are civilised in the Highlands. We are not savages."

Angus nodded in agreement: "I don't like the anti-wind farm lobby at all. But we are Christians when all's said and done and should treat people who have a different point of view with respect."

Archie shrugged his shoulders. He knew when he was beaten. He felt a loyalty to his friend Hamish, but recognised he had serious character flaws, including a fearsome temper and a habit of behaving like the proverbial bull in the china shop.

"We don't know it was Hamish who defaced the house," he suggested tentatively.

"That's true enough," said Mrs Maclean. "There are a number of other hotheads in the village. But it is a great coincidence that the police have come for him tonight, isn't it?"

"Aye. I don't dispute that," said Archie. "We will find out soon enough, I have no doubt."

Chapter seven
The Dinner Party

THE ISLE of Skye attracts thousands of tourists every year. Many travel by coach and follow a well-beaten route which includes the island's capital, Portree, the second largest village, Broadford, and Dunvegan, with its well known castle and seal colony.

But the real connoisseurs of Skye find their greatest pleasures elsewhere on the island – at remote mountain lochs, little visited bays and impromptu ceilidhs. There is an abundance of interesting flora and fauna, with even the chance of spotting a family of otters or a passing whale.

Quiet contemplation of the amazing landscape provides many with an overwhelming feeling of peace and wellbeing. And numerous tourists return time after time simply to enjoy the warm and simple hospitality of Skye people.

There are at least as many "incomers" to the island as there are native Skye men and women. But the kindness and tolerance of the local people seems to infect the more recent inhabitants, reinforcing the welcoming atmosphere rather than diluting it.

Skye is not, of course, atypical of the Highlands and Islands. Highland Scots have been noted for their hospitality since long before Dr Johnson's famous visit in the 18th century.

However, there is a much darker story to be told too. Visit the car park next to the ruins of Trumpan church on Skye's most photogenic peninsular, Waternish, and read the interpretative noticeboard. The events recounted there are chilling.

There is a "potted history" of a bitter 16th century feud between the Macleod clan and the MacDonalds, of ClanRanald.

In the spring of 1577 the MacLeods arrived on the island of Eigg intent on bad behaviour. Deep snow covered the ground and no human being was to be seen. This was because the local MacDonalds, having spotted the invaders, had hidden in a cave, the small entrance of which was hidden beneath a waterfall. A strong wind had covered their footprints with freshly fallen snow.

After an unsuccessful search for the MacDonalds, the MacLeods set sail again. But an unwise MacDonald climbed on to a hill to watch their departure and was spotted. The MacLeods returned and were able to follow his prints back to the cave as it had stopped snowing and the wind had dropped.

The MacLeods piled thatch and roof timbers from nearby crofts at the cave mouth and set them on fire, suffocating everyone inside with the smoke.

Several centuries later the bones of the 395 people who perished were given a proper burial.

The MacDonalds of ClanRanald exacted a vicious revenge. One Sunday they sailed in their galleys from the island of South Uist to Skye, and surprised the MacLeods at worship in Trumpan church.

There was a loud shout at the church door, and the MacLeods turned to see the door guarded by men armed with claymores.

The terrified congregation of men, women and children realised that the MacDonalds had set fire to the church. Outside, a piper played wild music to drown the screams of the dying.

Amid the dense smoke, a young girl, the sole survivor of the massacre, managed to squeeze herself through the narrow slit at the corner of the church which served as a window. In doing so she severed one of her breasts. The girl is said to have run ten miles to Dunvegan to raise the alarm.

Before the MacDonalds could return to their boats, the MacLeods

arrived from Dunvegan and a pitched
battle was fought on the shore.

When reinforcements came to
swell the MacLeod fighters, the
MacDonalds fled for the shore in
disorder. They found their boats left high
and dry by the ebbing tide, and it was
impossible to launch them across the
large boulders and slippery stones.

With their means of escape cut off,
most of the MacDonalds were
slaughtered. A few of them managed to
launch one of the galleys and escape,
returning to South Uist.

The MacDonald dead were
dragged to a stone dyke which was then
filled in on top of them, providing their
burial cairn and the name by which the
battle is known, The Battle of the Spoiled
Dyke.

This story is a truly horrific
example of man's inhumanity to man.

On numerous occasions
throughout the years Jack Easter had
stood in the car park near Trumpan
churchyard and read and reread the
interpretative board which summarised
the story of the massacres. The experience
never ceased to move him. He found
himself welling up as he thought about
the terrible ordeal of the young girl with
the severed breast. But his overwhelming
emotion was one of hopelessness for
mankind.

"The people who carried out these
atrocities were Christians, for god's
sake," he said to himself.

Jack had been raised as an Anglican by decent god-fearing parents who had simple unquestioning faiths inherited from their own parents. He had always felt they had lazily taken on the beliefs of his grandparents without really giving serious thought themselves about the nature of man and the universe.

Jack could understand the appeal of such an approach and the end result certainly appeared to validate it. His parents were two of the happiest, kindest people he had ever met and had given him an idyllic childhood.

But such a comfortable cop-out never satisfied him. The more he learnt about Christianity and the behaviour of Christians the less he doubted the assertion that God was good.

He had a wide knowledge of world history and had been repelled by the viciousness displayed by Christians when they persecuted each other over tiny doctrinal differences. He knew about Spanish Catholicism and its notorious auto-da-fe punishment sessions for heretics, which often ended in mass burnings at the stake. And then there were those flayings alive so beloved of the beneficent clergy.

Then he thought about the Isle of Skye he had known and admired over several decades. He had observed church ministers who were gentle, understanding people, a far cry from the austere fire and brimstone preachers of caricature. The churchgoing people of the island were generous and friendly and had a deep sense of community. They looked after their families and, in turn, they cared for and helped their neighbours and their families.

In recent times members of the Church of Scotland, the various other Presbyterian denominations - such as the "wee frees" and the "wee wee frees" - the Episcopals and the Catholics all seemed to get along with each other in a civilised way.

All this was a far cry from the barbarity of Scottish clan history. But Jack gloomily suspected that hidden underneath the modern veneer of civilisation there might remain a wild and intolerant spirit which would never be fully tamed. He had glimpsed it in the behaviour of the pro-wind farm protagonists where it showed itself in a re-arousal of ancient animosity against incomers. Somehow people such as Nigel Tavistock were seen as symbols of oppression – the oppression which followed the defeat of Bonnie Prince Charlie and the Battle of Culloden and the despicable behaviour of landlords at the time of the Highland Clearances.

On the surface the fierce clansmen of old may have been emasculated and turned into the meek and mild churchgoers of modern times. But an aggressive, rebellious streak had been carried on through the genes. Who could know whether this volcano was extinct or merely dormant?

Such were the thoughts which ran through Jack's mind when he returned home from his meeting with the Tavistocks.

****

Jack and Sophie spent the next day at home working. They found it pleasant to have no interruptions.

Around tea-time they talked for the first time about the evening's dinner party at the Tavistocks'. Jack got into something of a flap about what to wear.

"You don't suppose it will be formal wear tonight, do you?" he asked.

"No. I'm sure Mr Tavistock would have said if it was," said Sophie. "There never seems to be much formality up here. I'll just wear a smart trouser suit."

"I think I'll go fairly smart," said Jack. "I shouldn't think anyone will object to a sports jacket, shirt and trousers. What about a tie?"

Sophie, who did not really understand the finer points of men's dress etiquette, shrugged her shoulders impatiently and replied: "Just wear what you like. Nobody's going to care what you're wearing."

"I think I will wear a tie – be on the safe side," said Jack.

Sophie thought that summed up Jack to a tee: "on the safe side". An image of Jamie flashed into her mind. Nothing "safe" about him.

"Should we take a bottle of wine?" asked Jack. "Would they think it was rude?"

"I don't know," said Sophie, meaning "I don't care. I'm getting a little fed up with your petit bourgeois concerns".

With her new-found feelings of liberation she was wondering how she had got herself hitched to this contradiction of a man. He was a free-thinking, creative novelist with the domestic habits and inhibitions of a suburban bank clerk, she mused. What a comparison with the wild Scot she was passionate about!

And yet she felt that in a different kind of way Jamie was a contradiction too. He was certainly wild and uninhibited in his love-making. But in conversation he was guarded and in his actions he was secretive. For example, although she knew Jamie went out to work each day she had no idea what he did for a living. She imagined it was something manual but whenever she asked him about it he either walked off out of earshot or quickly changed the subject.

Jack may have been a man with controlled passions but his lifestyle was an open book. There was nothing secretive about him except in the sacred privacy of his true thoughts. Sophie liked this about his character and it had hitherto made for a happy marriage.

Her relationship with Jamie had rocked the foundations of Sophie's assumptions about life. She was abandoned in love and lust for her young man. But this was not enough to satisfy her womanly curiosity. She needed to know as much about his all-round character as she already knew about every centimetre of his delectable body. She was now determined to find out more.

Later, as the couple arrived on foot at the Tavistocks' house, they noticed a couple of smart new 4 x 4 vehicles parked in the well-lit driveway. Other guests had obviously arrived. They also noticed that the graffiti had been painted over.

Jack knocked on the door where he and Sophie were effusively greeted by Nigel. Jack was relieved to see that the host was wearing a corduroy jacket and trousers and a checked shirt – with tie. He felt even more comfortable when he saw that Stella had on simple black trousers and a top. Half a dozen other guests were similarly attired in smart but informal traditional country-wear.

Nigel introduced the new neighbours to the other guests.

There was George and Penny Saxondale, a couple in their sixties from the township of Cillader, beyond Beindow. A red-faced man with a pronounced beer gut, George had been an auctioneer and estate agent in England before retiring to Skye to indulge his wife in her long-held ambition to start a pottery business on the island. He was announced as being a local Conservative councillor, a rare breed in the Highlands. He was also the secretary of SPAT.

Penny was taller than her husband. She could even be described as statuesque. She was much quieter than her garrulous spouse, somewhat aloof in fact.

But it was clear that she ruled the roost.

Next to be introduced were Edward and Audrey Stafford-Allen, a quiet English couple who owned a holiday home at Upper Beindow, very close to the proposed site of the wind farm. A smart "tweedy" couple in their late-fifties, they ran an antiques business in the Yorkshire Dales and travelled up to Skye five or six times a year. Nigel and Edward had become close friends owing to a shared love of fly fishing and malt whiskies.

The Stafford-Allens were "on the fence" over wind farms. They had no strong views on their merits, but stood to gain several thousand pounds in compensation if the Beindow project went ahead.

The party was completed by two younger guests, an attractive twenty-something married couple introduced as Matt and Natalie Beaton. They both came from old Skye families, and were much richer second cousins to Archie Beaton, the luminary of the Blackhill Hotel's public bar.

The Beatons are one of the oldest and most distinguished clans on the island, having been for centuries medical practitioners for the Macdonalds and later important landowners in their own right.

Matt, a slim, dapper man with an impressive mane of deep brown hair, had inherited many acres of Skye and lived in the house where he had been raised near Dunvegan. Although he was not a member of SPAT he did sympathise with its campaign. He owned a number of holiday cottages in the vicinity of the proposed wind farm and feared the construction work might be bad for bookings. He had also been warned that holidaymakers might think the turbines would spoil the views from his cottages.

His wife, Natalie, was a Macleod, a cousin of the Chief of the Macleods, whose seat was Dunvegan Castle. A leggy blonde with icy Scandinavian-type features, she had been a model in London and had met Stella Tavistock at a fashionable party in Chelsea. She had captivated Stella with her descriptions of the magical island she came from and set the seed which had eventually led to the Tavistocks' buying their house at Breaganish.

In truth the Beatons spent only about four months of the year on Skye, living the rest of the time at their London apartment or their villa in northern Majorca. This fact had not been lost on the local wind farm supporters, who considered them to be "part-timers" whose views should not hold the same sway as fully resident Skyemen and women.

Jack was a little surprised that he and Sophie had never met any of the guests previously, considering how much time they had spent on the island. But then they had mostly socialised at local bars and ceilidh dances and he suspected that evening's diners might be a little "above" that sort of thing.

At recent parties the subject of wind farms had tended to dominate the conversation, but, as Nigel and Stella were unsure of their new neighbours' views on the subject, the other guests had been warned not to harp on about it this particular evening. They had also been ordered not to mention the graffiti incident, as Stella said the thought of it would ruin her night.

As a result, over the starter – cullen skink, a thick Scottish soup containing smoked haddock, potatoes and onions – there was a good deal of small talk and inquisitiveness about what had brought Jack and Sophie to Skye.

The wine flowed and the conversation flowed nicely too. Then a selection of malt whiskies was introduced to accompany the main course of venison haggis with tatties, neeps and gravy.

With each drink he consumed George Saxondale's face grew redder and redder. Jack quietly joked to Sophie that he feared internal combustion might be the end result.

Despite the earlier warnings, George could not resist bringing up the subject of the graffiti.

"I know you would rather not talk about it, Stella, but I just have to say that I hope they catch the bastard who scrawled those obscenities on your wall. They want their balls ripping off."

The other dinners looked down at their plates in embarrassment, hoping that this would shame George into silence. But he persisted: "I think when they find out who did it then we should go and daub his house with some stuff ourselves. I wonder who would...

Stella interjected: "We know who did it."

Nigel jumped into the conversation: "Stella. We agreed not to talk about this tonight."

Stella continued: "Everyone will find out soon enough. In fact I think Jack and Sophie already have a good idea. It was Hamish McDonald."

"Are you sure?" asked Jack. "It was only a hunch on our part."

Nigel replied: "Yes. We are sure. He's confessed to it. We had a call from Sgt Duncan this morning to tell us."

"I hope they've got him locked up," exploded George. "He needs to be hung, draw and quartered."

"No. They've charged him with criminal damage and a breach of the peace and released him on bail," said Nigel.

"Released on bail. Well the soft buggers. This was a hate crime," said George. "That's what he should be charged with. They should lock him up and throw the key away. I think we should go into the village and do something nasty to his house."

Penny Saxondale grasped her husband's arm: "I think we have heard enough from you, George. We agreed earlier on not to bring this subject up. You can see it's upsetting Stella."

"Sorry, Stella," said George. "I was only saying. We've got to take on these ignorant bastards. Play them at their own game. I vote we all go down to McDonald's house right now and make him sorry for what he's done."

"I don't think you're in a fit state to go anywhere. You've been drinking far too much." said Penny. "Just calm down and let the police look after things."

"What do the rest of you think?" persisted George.

"Matt, Natalie – what do you think we should do?"

Natalie shrugged her shoulders and looked towards Matt.

"I think Penny's right. Let the authorities deal with it," said Matt.

"Ah. Fat lot of good that will do," said George. "Nothing will happen, you'll see. And then the same thing will happen again. None of our houses will be safe from these morons. Edward, Audrey, what say you?"

Both agreed that Matt's solution was the correct one.

"You're all a lily-livered lot," snapped George. "We'll never win this wind farm campaign with attitudes like yours. So what about our new friends? You're not as soft as these useless buggers are you?"

"George! Just mind your language," declared Penny. "We're not in the four-ale bar now."

Her husband gave her a black look and turned to Jack and Sophie: "Well. Are you going to support me?"

Jack paused and then spoke slowly.

"It seems to me that by retaliating you would just be sinking to their level – and that wouldn't do your case any good at all."

Sophie nodded her agreement.

"I'm sorry to hear you say that," said George, getting even redder and becoming more irritated and exasperated. "We've got to fight these bloody backwoodsmen on this island. It's the industrialisation of the countryside. They would have power stations with ugly smoking chimneys on the island if they thought it would bring them one job. If there's not enough work on the island they ought to bugger off abroad somewhere to work, like they all used to have to do in the old days.

"I thought at least you two, being new to the place, would back me up. Surely you don't want the buggers to spoil it as soon as you arrive?"

"I'm not sure that wind turbines would really spoil anything," ventured Sophie, cautiously and quietly.

George exploded.

"Wouldn't spoil anything. Give me fucking strength. Have you got a brain in your head, woman? The only people who are going to benefit from all this are the lairds and they're not short of a bob or two."

Matt laughed, taking the remark to be aimed at him.

Penny slapped George hard on the back.

"Now shut up and behave yourself, or I'll take you home. I've never heard the like. Most of us agree with you about wind farms, so there's no need to start swearing and having a go at us."

George would normally have acquiesced to matrimonial governance at this point, but he was so wound up that he could not resist a parting shot.

"Well you say that. But I'm not sure about our newcomers here. I fancy they might be wind farm lovers. I bet *they* think that climate change is man-made too."

"I think it's debatable," said Jack.

"Oh. Now you're showing your true colours. You won't have many friends around this table if you think that crap," said George.

Nigel thought that the conversation had gone too far and he intervened in especially thunderous tones.

"Right! That's enough. No more about wind farms tonight, please. It's what we all agreed – out of courtesy to our new neighbours. And that's an end to it."

Stella looked over to Jack and Sophie, who were obviously discomfited by George's outburst.

She intervened: "Don't get yourself rattled by George. He's an old curmudgeon. George, you'll not see the port bottle on the table tonight if you don't behave yourself."

This was said in a joking manner, but Stella had misread George's mood.

He rose from the table and made towards the door: "I'm fed up with the fucking lot of you. Cowards," he ranted. "I'm going home. Come on, Penny."

Penny looked at him severely: "You may be going home, but I'm certainly not. I *was* enjoying myself. So how do you intend getting home? You certainly can't drive in your condition."

"Then I'll bloody walk," said George.

"You can't do that," said Stella. "It must be at least six miles to your place."

"Oh, let him go – the miserable beggar," said Penny. "Then the rest of us can enjoy ourselves."

George groaned, strode towards the door and let himself out.

Penny turned towards Jack and Sophie and profusely apologised for her husband.

"I'll kill him when I get home. I really will. There was no cause for any of that – no cause at all. He must have got out of the wrong side of the bed this morning. He's been like this all day, railing against the wind farm. Of course the amount he's drunk tonight hasn't helped. He's becoming obsessed. None of us wants to see this wind farm being built, but that's no excuse for his terrible rudeness."

Jack and Sophie felt sorry for Penny and told her not to worry.

They looked round and saw that Stella was standing in a corner with her back to the guests, holding a tissue. She was crying.

Sophie suggested that Jack and herself should leave before they caused any more upset.

But there was a general acclamation from the other guests that this was out of the question.

Nigel sat down at the side of them and whispered to them discretely. At least that was his intention. But Nigel's stentorian vocal cords did not naturally lend themselves to whispering, so the whole room was able to hear him.

"Please don't let George's behaviour upset you. He's drunk. Don't think for a moment that the rest of us take his aggressive line. We are opposed to the wind farm but we are civilised people. Stella and I have never expected our friends to concur with our points of view. We are not like that – and neither are the other people in this room.

"You mustn't think of leaving. You haven't seen the dessert yet."

By this time Stella had composed herself and left her corner: "It's cranachan."

This traditional Scottish dish of oats, raspberry, cream and whisky was Sophie's absolute favourite dessert.

"That settles it," she said enthusiastically. "Wild horses wouldn't drag me away now." The other guests cheered and raised their glasses.

The rest of evening went swimmingly. There was talk of art and literature, the landscape and history of Skye, and stalking and fishing. The fishing was of particular interest to Jack and he was delighted when the idea of a trout fishing excursion to the island's Storr Lochs was suggested. Edward was to take on the role of ghillie, assisted by Matt, an experienced fisherman, with Nigel and Jack being relative novices.

Not to be outdone, the five women planned a trip of their own for the same day. They were to go to lunch at the Three Chimneys Restaurant, an expensive eaterie but one of Skye's greatest assets.

George would be left on his own – to stew.

As they walked home Jack and Sophie talked over what had been a sweet and sour evening. The incident with George had left a nasty taste in the mouth. On the other hand they had met some new people with whom they had been socially at ease and who offered the potential for pleasant friendships.

There was one of those proverbial elephants in the room, though, which Jack referred to during their walk. Their new "friends" were among the most

163

unpopular people in the area owing to the wind farm row. The Tavistocks, unlikely villains though they appeared to be, were the most hated couple on the island.

Jack and Sophie's dream of becoming fully integrated into the community was incompatible with forming friendships with the leadership of SPAT.

"We could have made a big mistake tonight," said Jack. "We said we were not going to get involved in this wind farm business. But now we *are* involved. Up to our bloody necks."

"But we are not involved," said Sophie. "We haven't taken sides on the wind farm. And Nigel made it quite plain that he and Stella don't choose their friends according to their opinions on things."

"I believe him," said Jack. "But I don't think some of the villagers round here will take such a tolerant line. They hate the SPAT people and they will hate us too if they think we are friends with them."

"Well, what can we do about it?" asked Sophie.

"I think we should distance ourselves from the Tavistocks and their friends. I think we should make some excuse for not going on the fishing trip and the Three Chimneys trip. We should stay civil and neighbourly with them, but not get too close."

"Oh, don't be so wet," said Sophie. "It's not like you to be so feeble. I like the

Tavistocks. I think Stella could be a really good friend to me. I'm not going to give them up when they have been so welcoming to us."

"If we do make friends with them I think we can give up any thought of becoming regulars at the Blackhill. We will probably be sent to Coventry when we go to the ceilidhs."

"Oh, now you're being a drama queen," declared Sophie. "Have a few guts."

She was mentally comparing Jack with Jamie again. She was sure Jamie would not be so weak.

"All this could ruin the dream of coming here to live," continued Jack. "Surely you can't contemplate that."

"Of course not," said Sophie, "but it doesn't have to be black and white. I am sure a lot of the villagers are not as extreme about the wind farm as you imagine they are. I am sure if we tell people that we have no strong views on the matter they will accept that. I'm sure they're not going to ostracise us."

"I don't think you realise how strong feelings are," said Jack. "People have been literally coming to blows."

"Well I'm not going to make some feeble excuse for not going to lunch and I don't think you should get out of the fishing trip either. What sort of man are you?"

"Why are you questioning my masculinity all of a sudden. This isn't a question of machismo or lack of it. I am trying to think of a pragmatic way forward."

The couple had been walking hand in hand until this point. Now Sophie wrenched her hand away and stomped off in front of her husband.

"I can see you don't agree with me," said Jack. "Ok. We'll try it your way. I don't want us to fall out about this. We'll go on the trips and play it cool and non-committal with the locals in the pub. I'm not sure it will work, but que sera sera."

Sophie waited for him and took his hand again. She had won.

Chapter
eight
Confrontation

In the early hours of the next morning George Saxondale walked out of Portree police station and got into a waiting taxi. He had had an eventful night

After leaving the Tavistocks' house in a drink-fuelled temper he had walked quickly along the roads from Breaganish to Beindow on his way home to Cillader.

As he passed through Beindow he came upon the cottage of Hamish McDonald, now his arch enemy. Seeing a brick in the grass verge he picked it up, hurled it through Hamish's front window and ran off.

Hamish was sitting in his living room, watching television, when the brick landed on the settee at the side of him. He rushed to his front door and out into the road. It was mid-evening and still light and he could clearly see the portly and ungainly figure of George Saxondale making its getaway.

Hamish was a huge stocky man, but he had a typical Highlander's agility. Being chased by him would be akin to being pursued by a particularly incensed shaggy Highland bull.

And give chase he did. George looked round and saw him coming. A furious Hamish was gaining on him fast. But his prey had a stroke of luck. George came to the open door of the Lochside Inn and he almost fell inside in his panic. Serving at the bar was the landlord, Fred Judd, well-known to George as a SPAT supporter and patron.

"Close the door quick. Please close the door," spluttered a panting and fear-struck George. "Hamish is coming for me."

"Hamish McDonald! He's not coming in here. He's banned", said the landlord.

He dashed to the door, slammed it shut and clicked the lock.

Hamish pounded the door with his fist and swore loudly. But the Lochside Inn was an ancient building with a very sturdy oak door which proved to be an immovable object.

The pounding and swearing attracted the attention of a passer-by, a lean, tallish, grey-faced man, whose chiselled, once-handsome features had deteriorated into a mean, sunken-cheeked visage.

This man was Ronnie McColl, the self-appointed leader of the pro-wind farm campaign.

"Hamish, what's the to-do?" he asked.

"I'm going to kill him. Judd's got him in there. Help me get the bugger."

Hamish thrust his shoulder hard against the unyielding door. He ricocheted back into the roadway, clutching a damaged shoulder.

"You mean Saxondale? I noticed your window was broken. What's being going on?"

"Yes. He broke it. Just now. In broad daylight. Let's go round the back and try to get in there."

"Calm down, Hamish, and tell me what happened."

Hamish could not calm down. Nothing in the world would have convinced him that calming down was called for. But he did manage to splutter out the details of what had just occurred.

Ronnie put his arm around Hamish's shoulder in a matey sort of way and smirked.

"We've got him. Can't you see that? We've got him. There's only one thing to do. I'll call the police straightaway on my mobile. And then in the morning I'll be straight on to the West Highland Free Press. This could finish SPAT – finish them."

Hamish broke away from Ronnie's embrace.

"The police! What fucking use will the police be? A load of tossers. They'll do nothing to him. We ought to deal with this. Give him a beating he will never forget."

169

"Don't be a fool all your life, Hamish," said Ronnie. "Do it my way and we finish off Saxondale and we finish off SPAT. Do it your way and we both finish up in the gaol."

"It would be worth it," said Hamish. "Worth it to see that man in pain. He could have killed me with that brick."

"I'm sure the police will be interested to hear you tell them that," said Ronnie. "It will make the unfortunate misdemeanour of the graffiti seem small fry by comparison. You will be the victim. People will rally round you and they will rally round to our cause in even greater numbers.

"You get off home. I'll phone the police. Put some cardboard up at your window for tonight and I'll send a lad round in the morning to fix it for you."

"Ah, okay then," said Hamish. "Have your way. I can see it's the sensible way. So long as you make sure I am avenged. I don't want people going around saying that you can attack and abuse Hamish McDonald and he will do fuck-all about it.

"But you can be assured I will be having words with that weasel Judd."

"Don't worry," said Ronnie. "His day of reckoning will surely come."

Hamish sloped off to his cottage, muttering blasphemous imprecations as he went. Ronnie was immediately on his mobile phone.

Inside the Lochside, George Saxondale sat, red and perspiring, at a

170

table in the public bar. The landlord and his wife, Enid, were the only other people in the building that night. Trade had been poor at the hotel in the previous few months as most of the local drinking fraternity did not approve of the fact that it had virtually become the headquarters of SPAT.

The Judds had gone to their upstairs parlour to spy on Hamish outside. They had been relieved to see that Ronnie McColl had apparently persuaded Hamish to go home.

They returned to the bar to tell George what they had learnt and discovered that he had quickly sobered up. Nothing sobers up a drunk as effectively as a shock. And few experiences could be more shocking than being chased down the street by a raging Hamish McDonald.

"Has that madman gone?" asked George.

"Yes. He's gone," said Mrs Judd. "What was the cause of all this?"

"I have no idea. We all know the man's a lunatic, though, don't we? You have heard about him daubing graffiti over Nigel's house?"

"Yes. We were told about it," said Fred Judd. "The police should never have let him out. Shall I call them now?"

"No," said George. "No. Not tonight at any rate. I need to get home to my bed. These police matters can go on for hours. I may ring them in the morning."

"But I think we need to ring them now," said Mrs Judd. "That was behaviour liable to cause a breach of the peace. We have to protect our licence. You may not want to ring them now but I think we must do so."

"No, please don't," said George. "I will sort it out in the morning. I can't do with any more trouble tonight. I am already in bad books with my wife. I got into a bit of an argument earlier."

"With Hamish?" said Enid.

"No. I was over at Nigel's. There were some newcomers there having dinner. Arty-farty types. They said some things about wind farms which I didn't like and I lost my rag with them. I walked out. Penny will be furious with me. I mustn't get into any more trouble tonight."

"Well all right then. We'll ring them first thing in the morning," said Enid. "We can't have McDonald behaving like that and getting away with it."

"You haven't explained why Hamish was so furious with you," said Fred.

"I really don't know. He has been abusive to me before and you know how he loathes SPAT. I think he must have been drunk, saw me coming along the road and decided to take out his anger on me."

"But that's intolerable," said Enid. "We must get the police involved – first thing in the morning."

172

George could see that he had warded off the immediate threat of police involvement. But now he determined to try to keep them out of it altogether.

"I am afraid I haven't been entirely honest with you," he said. "You see as I was walking past McDonald's cottage he came running out after me, swearing and cursing. I was not in a very good mood, as I have explained, and I'm afraid I did something rather silly. I threw a brick through his window. It was just to try and calm him down really – a spur of the moment thing. I didn't intend to do any damage, but I did. So you can see I would prefer not to get the police involved."

"I should think not," said Enid. "You must have been off your head to do that."

"I regret to say I was angry at the way he was confronting me. And I also regret to say that I was a little drunk."

"You shouldn't have come here and got us involved," said Fred. "We have our licence to consider. I don't know what we are going to do now."

"Do?" said George. "You don't have to do anything, do you?"

A long debate followed as to the best course of action. Fred and Margaret were tempted to wash their hands of George and tell all to the police.

He began by begging for mercy and forgiveness. Having been unsuccessful on that score he tried to use their loyalty to SPAT as a lever to win them round. Then he changed tack again, relying on their mercenary instincts. He

173

suggested that if they "shopped" him to the police they might find their trade declining even faster as SPAT members took their business elsewhere.

This argument appeared to have won the day and George was feeling a sense of relief, when there was a loud knock at the hotel's front door.

Fred unlocked and opened it and there stood Sgt Duncan and Pc Flounce. They enquired if George Saxondale was there and were shown into the bar.

Sgt Duncan said they had received a complaint that Mr Saxondale had maliciously broken a window at the home of Hamish McDonald.

George immediately admitted that he had done that and did not repeat his lies about how the incident had started. But he did plead that he and his friends in SPAT had been severely provoked by Hamish's aggressive actions towards the Tavistocks.

Sgt Duncan confirmed that they had received a complaint about Hamish from Mr Tavistock, but that whatever he had done did not excuse George's criminal, and very dangerous, action.

"Very dangerous indeed," concurred Pc Flounce, straightening himself up to his considerable full height.

George agreed to go with the officers to the police station.

Fred and Enid Judd were left dumbfounded, having believed every word George had previously told them about the incident. They had always thought of George as a bluff, bullish type of individual, but nevertheless too fundamentally respectable to commit an aggressive criminal act while drunk.

They mused that this event might be another nail in the coffin for their ailing business.

****

A few hours later Ronnie McColl was on the phone to the reporters at the West Highland Free Press telling them about what had happened the night before.

The newspaper in turn contacted the police press office. However, the only police comment forthcoming was that a man had been charged with criminal damage following an incident in Beindow the previous night and released on police bail.

When Ronnie contacted the newspaper again to find out what had been said he was disappointed that George Saxondale's name had not been released. He decided, therefore, to spread the story as far and wide as he was able.

It was Sunday, the busiest day of the week at the Blackhill Hotel. The Sunday lunches there were very popular, especially for people who had been to church in the morning. There was a traditional music session in the afternoon, which drew even greater numbers as the social highlight of the week for the village's drinkers.

Ronnie was in the bar as soon as it opened and was spreading the word, quietly but persistently, of George's misdemeanour to anyone who would listen. And many people did listen. Ronnie was keen to point out that not only had a window been damaged but that the unfortunate Hamish had come within an ace of being killed by the flying brick.

He hinted too that the Tavistocks may have been behind the violence, having falsely accused Hamish of putting graffiti on their wall.

Everything was a SPAT conspiracy to discredit supporters of the wind farm.

Around midday the incredible bulk of Archie Beaton arrived and Ronnie was quick to buttonhole him.

Their mood soon became conspiratorial as they plotted how to use the new turn of events to the advantage of the wind farm scheme.

It would be difficult to imagine a more incongruous pair of allies. The red-faced and lardy Beaton spoke with a booming voice which could be heard all over the hotel, whereas the weaselly McColl conversed in a barely audible whisper, putting his arm around his colleague's huge frame so that he could get closer to him and be more confidential. Every now and again Ronnie would wag his finger towards Archie and mouth "Shush" as he appeared to be desperately, and completely unsuccessfully, trying to keep their conversation private.

But on Ronnie's part this was all a pretence. He was trying to project the image of a quiet, careful conveyor of news which he would really rather not have to pass on, while at the same time being absolutely confident that Archie would announce every detail volubly to the world.

As Archie was declaring that SPAT had at last been revealed as complete "wrong 'uns", Jack Easter walked in. After mixing with the "toffs" of SPAT the night before he had felt he should quickly confirm his solidarity with the down to earth Blackhill regulars.

Archie beckoned him over and told him all about the "attempted murder" of Hamish by the secretary of SPAT.

Jack was flabbergasted and shocked. He had the uneasy feeling that all this had resulted from his difference of opinion with George at the Tavistocks' dinner party.

He decided to keep quiet about his part in the previous night's occurrences because to admit that he was being entertained by the Tavistocks would have put the mark of Cain of him. Quite possibly he would have been ejected from the bar.

Instead he listened incredulously to Archie's accounts of what had happened - accounts which were cunningly embroidered at every juncture by Ronnie McColl. In fact throughout the Blackhill it was now being acknowledged that Ronnie had been the hero of the hour, having saved Hamish from further violence at the hands of George

Saxondale and then having reported the crime to the police in order to have the evil-doer arrested.

Jack was feeling acute embarrassment and tried to get away from Archie and Ronnie as soon as possible. He feared that someone, somehow – he didn't know quite how - might find out that he had been in George's company the night before.

Suddenly he found his escape route: Catriona, who was serving behind the bar, waved to him cheerily.

"Oh. I must just say 'hello' to Catriona – and get myself a drink," he said to Archie.

Archie, by no means an unreasonable man, understood the desirability of both those actions and told Jack to get to the bar. This was none too easy as Archie was flopped in front of it, but Jack bobbed and weaved and manoeuvred a way through a small gap.

"And how are you this fine day?" trilled Catriona, lighting up the room with her smile.

Jack was feeling downcast and apprehensive. But this effusive welcome immediately raised his spirits. Suddenly everything in his garden was rosy!

"I'm feeling great," said Jack. "And all the better for seeing you."

"It's busy today. I've been run off my feet," said Catriona. "But I prefer it that way. Like to be busy."

Jack ordered his pint of beer and decided that propping up the bar, near

Catriona and away from Archie and Ronnie, would be by far the best policy.

Gradually musicians began to arrive for their Sunday afternoon session – two violinists, a bodhran player, two guitarists, a Cumbrian piper and a flautist.

Soon Archie and Ronnie left the room to spread their gossip among the smokers who, as usual, had congregated on the pavement outside. Archie's loud voice had been drowning out the sound of all the musicians put together, so now he had moved outside it became easier for Jack and Catriona to converse.

Their amiable chatter was soon interrupted by the emergence from the kitchen of a flushed and harassed Mrs Maclean.

"Give us a bloody drink, dear – a double Bell's. I'm absolutely knackered," she said to Catriona.

. Seeing Jack, she addressed her next remarks to him: "We've served 70 Sunday lunches today," she said, "and the chef's on holiday. Who would have bloody staff, eh? More trouble than they're worth. It'll be a good day when *I* have a holiday."

"You had a day in Inverness only last week," said Catriona, laughing.

"Oh, yes, hen. At the bloody wholesaler's. A day in a warehouse with Mr Maclean. Better than an orgasm that was, dear."

"Mrs Maclean!" declared a giggling Catriona. "You are a dreadful woman. Cover your ears up, Jack. And on a Sunday too!"

Mrs Maclean took a swig of whisky: "You see, sir, what I have to put up with from my staff. Rampant insolence. I pay them too much, you see. That's the problem."

"National minimum wage," said Catriona, pretending to weep.

Jack intervened in this banter to say: "It's so entertaining here that you really ought to make them pay to work here."

Catriona picked up a bar towel and swiped Jack on the head with it.

"You see how they are with my customers," said Mrs Maclean. "Honestly, the violence we have to put up with in this village."

"Aye. Have you heard about what happened last night?" Catriona asked her.

"Yes, I have indeed," said Mrs Maclean. "Who would ever have believed it would come to this? They will be murdering each other next. That bloody Hamish! He brought it on himself you know. No-one is a bigger supporter of the wind farm than me, but that Hamish is just beyond the pale.

"Well he's banned from here – for good."

With that she downed her whisky and swept back into the kitchen.

Catriona looked over to Jack: "She went over to Hamish's cottage to take him his lunch today. She thought he might not be able to get out because of his broken window."

"Really?" said Jack.

Catriona nodded.

Chapter nine
Doubts and
frustrations

SOPHIE knocked on Jamie's front door several times but there was no reply. As a respectable middle class housewife her natural reaction would have been to accept there was no-one at home, and just turn away.

However, where anything to do with Jamie was concerned she was a wild, free spirit. So she tried the handle and found the door was unlocked. At first she was surprised by this but then she remembered that several islanders had told her that they never locked their doors. It was one example of the quaint innocence which had attracted her to Skye.

Remembering her middle class roots for a moment, she only tentatively looked into his living room.

It was in its usual unkempt state, with a seemingly endless supply of muddy boots and shoes spread across the grimy stone floor and various pieces of fishing tackle strewn around. There were lengths of line with lethal looking spinners attached, knives, bits of rods and a couple of reels.

Sophie was curious. She had been thinking about how little she knew about this seemingly solitary, taciturn man. He had an aging hippy of a mother and a mysterious local farmer as a father, who apparently disowned him, at least publicly. He was a keen fisherman, but this seemed to be just a rather obsessional hobby. He did not even seem to catch very large fish - not enough to sell and make some money from.

So what did he do for a living? She was astonished that she still had not found out. She had been so engrossed in his sexuality that it had not seemed important. She had assumed he must have a job but she had no evidence of it. Full-time satyr?

Perhaps a little peek around his house might give her some more information.

Gingerly she crept around the room, fearful that he might come in at any moment and catch her prying.

She smiled to herself as she thought of the TV game show, Through the Keyhole, with the presenter Loyd Grossman asking in his contorted posh English/Bronx accent "Who'd live in a house like this?"

There was nothing of any interest in the main room – no pictures to look at or drawers to rummage through.

Sophie went into the kitchen, where again there was a bare minimum of what could loosely be called white goods. There was an old-fashioned electric cooker, topped with dirty brown-stained saucepans. A shabby looking fridge had a large dent in it which looked as if it may have been caused by someone aiming a savage kick. The only other objects of any size in the room were a stone sink, full of dirty pots, a washing machine and a rickety cupboard with three drawers.

In for a penny, in for a pound, Sophie opened each drawer in turn. Inside was nothing but pots and pans, cutlery and kitchen utensils.

She went through a small empty hallway and crept into Jamie's tiny bedroom. She had been in there before and already knew there was nothing there but a single bed, a wardrobe and a large wooden chest. She lifted the lid and found the chest was stuffed to the top with a miscellany of items.

There were a few books and magazines, mainly about angling and shooting, some heavy metal CDs, various tools, pens and pencils, string and tape, buttons and belts, discarded ornaments. In fact most of the chest was filled with everyday items which would be found in 99 per cent of homes.

But Sophie's attention was particularly drawn to a dozen or so leather sheaths, carefully stacked together on one side of the chest. She opened one of these and found a gleaming and lethal looking military knife. She shuddered a little. She looked into several more sheaths and discovered more fierce and fearsome weapons. Some appeared to be ornamental, others practical. They all looked vicious. All of them shocked her.

She knew that country people used knives for all sorts of innocent purposes.

But, nevertheless, she wished she had not seen what she had seen.

She decided it was time to leave. There was a small storeroom which she could have explored, but somehow her curiosity had left her. She just wanted to get out of the house as quickly as possible.

She opened the door and went out into the fresh air. It was a warm, quite humid, July evening. But to Sophie it felt fresh – fresh compared with the house she had just been in. She had noticed that Jamie's living quarters had a smell of mildew - a damp smell, redolent of an old graveyard on a late autumn afternoon. A smell of death?

"Now I'm being ridiculous," she told herself.

Earlier that evening Sophie had walked down to the Black Burn pool expecting to find Jamie fishing there. But he was absent. She was aching to see him and so had decided to find out if he was at home.

Now she felt cheated. She realised she was stupid to think like that. After all, there must be more to his life than working, fishing and making love to her.

She sauntered back in the direction of her own cottage. Her feelings of dejection gradually lifted as she took in the sights and sounds of a lovely still evening. She swept back her hair and let the balmy air soothe her.

Contented sheep and fat lambs called to each other without any particular reason for doing so. The Black Burn, which could sometimes be a noisy, raging torrent, trickled along playfully as there had been no rain for several days. She looked up at the sky where half a dozen crows were croaking and hovering and swooping down, pretending to be eagles. A young rabbit scuttled across the road in front of her.

The loch was completely still. It was pretending to be a mirror as it accurately and distinctly reflected every object along its banks.

Over the far side of the loch the mountains, sometimes barely visible in suffused light, were bathed in gorgeous sunlight. Individual trees and single grazing sheep, which would often be invisible, could now be seen in detail.

Only the most depressed of human spirits could have failed to be raised by such surroundings. Sophie loved this place and for a few minutes until reaching her cottage she put Jamie to the back of her mind.

When she reached her door, though, her heart sank once more. She was in love. Erotic love, that madness which afflicts human beings, had taken hold of her. It made her sad. It made her sick. And she wanted it to last forever.

She was desperate to see Jamie now. She knew he had a mobile phone but stupidly she had never asked him for the number. She fancied if she held her breath, closed her eyes and thought deeply enough about her desire then she might be able to summon him up. She tried it. It didn't work.

She stared out of the front window, looking down the road in both directions. Hoping he might pass by. Praying he would pass by.

She would go down to the pool once more, just in case Jamie had taken a different route. She ran through the long grass down to the pool. He was not there. Then she scanned the stretches of beach alongside the loch, again without success.

Dejectedly she returned to the cottage.

She slumped into an armchair, pondering her next move.

There was a knock at the door. Sophie's heart leapt. Could it be him?

She jumped out of the chair, bound over to the front door and opened it.

There, slouched against the door frame was Sarah, Jamie's mother. She looked a mess. Her hair was even more tangled than when Sophie had first met her. She looked drawn and pale and had a large bruise on her cheek. She stank of alcohol – not the stale smell of booze imbibed some hours previously, but the sweet fruity smell of recently consumed drink.

"Hello", said Sophie.

Sarah smiled faintly but did not speak and did not move. There was an awkward silence.

"Won't you come in?" asked Sophie.

Sarah did not answer at first, but then quietly slurred out the words: "Yes. I should like that. I've met you, haven't I?"

"Yes. I'm Sophie. My husband, Jack, and I came to see you at your caravan. Do you remember us?"

Sarah, who was still propped up in the doorway, looked closely at Sophie.

"Oh, yes. I remember. You're an artist aren't you? And you husband writes plays."

"Novels actually."

"Oh, yes. Novels. I remember. You came to see me. You had some of my nettle wine."

"And very nice it was too," said Sophie.

She was now in a quandary. She knew that entertaining this particular neighbour in her current state was going to be very hard work. Yet she wanted to play the good neighbour. And she also wondered if this might give her the opportunity to find out a little more about the son.

"Please come in," she said. "Will you have a cup of tea?"

"Oh, yes – tea. That would be very nice. Could you take my hand, dear? I'm a little unsteady today."

Sophie took Sarah's hand which was shaking and bitterly cold considering how warm it was outside.

"Are you not feeling too well?" asked Sophie, sympathetically, as she guided Sarah to the armchair.

"Pissed, dear. Bloody pissed."

Sophie laughed.

"Yes. You laugh at me. I'm a bloody joke. They all think that around here. The drunken mad woman. I know what they say about me."

The pathetic, wan figure who had staggered across the room suddenly became energised and began to laugh herself.

"And they're bloody right. I'm just a fucking old wino. Chuck me out if you like. I only stopped at your house because I thought I was going to pass out and fall into the road."

"I'll get the kettle on. A cup of tea will steady you up," said Sophie.

Sarah nodded and then buried her head in her hands.

"I know I'm a disgrace."

Sophie busied herself making the tea which she then presented to her guest.

Sarah spilt some of it down the back of the chair, so Sophie steadied her hands and helped her to drink the rest of it.

Before the drink was finished Sarah's eyes closed and she started to snore. She was soon fast asleep.

189

After about half an hour she came round, opened her eyes, looked startled, and asked, pleadingly: "Where am I?"

Sophie smiled and replied: "You're at Jack and Sophie's house. Your new neighbours."

"New neighbours? I can't remember. How did I get here? And where am I?"

"You knocked on the door. We live down the lane from your caravan. Jack and Sophie. We met you at your caravan."

"Ah. I remember. The artist and the poet. What on earth am I doing here? I shouldn't be here. Troubling you. Shouldn't be here. So this is your cottage. What the hell am I doing at your cottage? Have I been a nuisance?"

"No. Not at all. You've just been having a little sleep."

"But what am I doing sleeping here? I must have been at the drink."

"I think you have had one or two," laughed Sophie.

"One or two? I should think it was more than one or two. I'm a disgrace. Just a disgrace."

Sarah put her head in her hands again and started to shake. Sophie could see she was crying.

"What'll happen to me? The drink will sure enough be the death of me."

"Don't upset yourself. There's no harm done. We all like a drink sometimes. Would you like a cup of tea? It often helps," said Sophie.

Sarah wiped away a tear and composed herself: "Aye. A cup of tea would be a help. That's for sure."

Sophie put the kettle on again and then returned and crouched down at the side of the armchair.

"Did you intend to come and see us?" she asked, suspecting that Sarah had merely stopped at any port in a storm.

"I hardly think so, dear," said Sarah. "To tell you the truth I hadn't even remembered you were here."

"Were you on your way home?"

"Aye. That's it. No, it isn't. I remember now. I was on my way..." she paused. "I was on my way to see my son."

"Jamie?"

"Aye, Jamie. I have only the one son."

"I thought he might have been fishing on such a lovely night as this," said Sophie. "He usually comes past here on his way to and from the pool under the waterfall."

Sarah was silent for a few moments.

Then she spoke with some certainty for the first time: "No. He will not have been fishing today. It's a Sunday."

"What difference does that make?" asked Sophie.

"The fishing on the Black Burn is owned by Iain McConnell and he doesn't allow fishing on a Sunday."

"Is that for religious reasons?" asked Sophie.

"Aye. Iain's an elder at the church. They don't hold with carrying on with such trivial pursuits on a Sunday."

Sophie went to finish the preparation of the tea. She returned with a cup for Sarah and then crouched down once more at her side.

Sarah continued to talk in a slow deliberate way, trying to avoid slurring her words. She was beginning to sober up.

"I ought to get on the way down to Jamie's," she said.

Sophie could have told her that Jamie had not been at home earlier but she was sensible enough not to give the game away.

"I haven't seen Jamie for a few days," she said. "I expect he's been busy."

"Busy, yes," said Sarah. "He's been away taking stock to the Black Isle."

"Stock?"

"Yes, sheep, for Mr McConnell."

"Does Jamie work for Mr McConnell then?"

"Aye."

"Is he a shepherd?"

"No. He does sometimes care for the sheep and help to move them around. He does all sorts of things – gamekeeping, forestry. A sort of general factotum."

"He's an important man on the estate then?"

"I don't know about important. He gets paid precious little, that's for sure."

Sophie suddenly sensed a belligerent tone in Sarah's conversation, which she had noticed previously on the visit to the caravan.

"So Mr McConnell's not a particularly generous employer?" said Sophie, with a knowing smile.

Sarah's normally gentle wistful voice took on a bitter edge as she replied: "That man doesn't know the meaning of generosity. He's like all the rest of them, the Scottish Presbyterians. Mean, harsh and cruel. It comes of reading too much of the Old Testament. They forget about the peace and love bits in the bible – and all about Jesus throwing the money-lenders out of the temple. Money is all they care about when it comes down to it."

Sophie was a little taken aback. Sarah's description of the local churchgoers did not fit in with her own experience of meeting people from the congregations. Yes, they could be quite narrow in their doctrines and rather austere in their habits. But Sophie had also found them to be very community-spirited, generous to those in need of help and surprisingly non-judgmental of those who could not live up to the teachings from the Manse.

She had been told about a man from Dunvegan who had been prosecuted several times for illegally distilling and selling whisky and who was a notorious womaniser. He was thought to have sired at least five illegitimate offspring around the island. He had a bike, you see.

When he died the whole village turned out to march behind his coffin, including all the elders of the church. He was a sinner, but he was *their* sinner. They condemned the sin but forgave the sinner.

Sophie's mind turned to this man as Sarah continued to rant on about the hypocrisy of the church-people, her language becoming more extreme and bellicose as she continued.

Sarah was typical of the freedom-loving hippies of the Sixties – tolerant of every sort of debauched behaviour, but totally intolerant of those who wished to promulgate a more innocent, respectful and respectable way of life.

Sophie was quietly tolerant of hippies and Presbyterians, but had none of the certainty of their world views. She loved children and animals, the peace of the countryside and the beauty of nature. She loved domesticity - cooking, cleaning, gardening. But now she had an extra string to her bow. She was a voracious and passionate lover, a nymph of the pool beneath the waterfall. She had discovered a spontaneous side to her nature which had lain buried up until now.

But she had also found that she had a dark side, where the driving force was the will rather than what was moral. Primeval earth forces had welled up inside her and made her reckless. It was a side of herself which was alien to her usual way of thinking. She blushed when she thought of it, but she knew the genie was out of the bottle. She would never change back into quiet, respectable Sophie.

She was scared but excited. It was as if she had travelled to a new country. It was a beautiful country with steep mountains, deep lakes and verdant forests. But hiding in caves on those mountains, resting in the bottom of those lakes and lurking on the edge of those forests were dangerous wild creatures, waiting for their prey. They were waiting for Sophie and she knew it. But the last thing she wanted to do was run away. That was what the old Sophie would have done. She had gone this far and she was thrilled.

Sarah carried on a little more about the evils of Presbyterianism and ended her rant by saying: "And that Iain McConnell – well, he's one of the worst examples of them. Comes over all paternalistic and gentlemanly, but really he's just like Shylock, wanting his pound of flesh from all his workers and his tenants."

Sophie found this description a little hard to believe. There appeared to be genuine affection among the locals for their "laird". People had been noticeably moved when telling the story of the attack on him. Even Jamie, who was hardly effusive about anything, had said he was "a very fair landlord".

Sarah calmed down now, like a suddenly dormant volcano. She smiled at Sophie: "Don't mind me, dear. I'm a silly old woman. They all say so around here."

"I'm sure they don't," said Sophie, knowing she was telling a big lie.

"Well you may say that, dear. But I am not stupid. I know the score. I must away to Jamie's. Not that he'll want to see me."

"I'm sure that's not true."

"I'm afraid it is. He thinks I let him down - and I know I do. But *he* lets me down too."

"In what way?"

"I brought him up to love people, to love animals, to love nature. But he's hard. I don't believe he loves anyone or anything. He certainly doesn't love me. I never get a kind word from him."

Again, Sophie was doubting the woman's judgment. She had heard the regulars at the Blackhill speak quite fondly of Jamie. He was almost a hero for saving the life of Iain McConnell. It must be Sarah who was wrong-headed. That was certainly her reputation.

Sophie did not wish to be seen as jumping too eagerly to Jamie's defence. That would have an element of risk in it. But she could not resist raising an eyebrow and saying softly to Sarah: "The locals seem to think quite highly of him."

"Aye. I know he's the flavour of the month because he looked after Iain McConnell. But that's not really about Jamie. It's more a case of those locals tugging their forelock to the laird. A lot of people around here say they are socialists and want equality and so on. Really they behave like serfs, dear. They haven't smelt the coffee."

Sophie shrugged her shoulders. She was never one for getting involved in political arguments. That was more Jack's area. He was always analysing people's motivations. He did it in his novels. Sophie always skipped those bits.

She decided that discretion was the better side of valour and that she would not mention Jamie again.

Sarah was pulling at her own hair. She wanted to rant and rave. In common with many adherents of peace and love she had an anger bristling just below the surface. She wanted to kill those people who failed to understand why peace and love were not the way forward.

Jamie had come to represent all that she loathed. As a child he had been both dour and rebellious, showing her no affection. These traits had been carried through to his manhood.

Working on Iain McConnell's estate had immersed him into a world where animals were merely potential meat or fish for the table or a passport to pleasure for stalkers and shooters. This world was anathema to Sarah as a vegetarian. She was equally appalled that Jamie never appeared to query the orders given to him by his boss. He always described McConnell as "fair" and "generous", whereas in her eyes the laird was a mean-spirited patrician who exploited the land and exploited those workers and tenants who were in thrall to it.

Jamie's moody demeanour was that of a rebel. But Sarah believed he was only rebelling against *her* and *her* world view. She detected in him a nihilism which she found cold and repellent. Sophie had perhaps come to suspect the same thing.

****

It was nearly 9pm on the same Sunday evening and Jack was still standing at the bar chatting to Catriona. The musicians had packed up their instruments and left about two hours previously. This would normally have been the trigger for Jack to drink up and walk back home. But he was enjoying himself so much that he had no inclination to move on.

By this time he had drunk four pints of bitter and he was on his third glass of Famous Grouse. He was feeling merry and not a little flirtatious.

"You know, this bar is worth coming into for your company alone," he said to Catriona.

"Oh, behave yourself," said Catriona, slapping him on the arm and smiling broadly.

The gesture was not lost on Mrs Maclean who was washing glasses at the other end of the bar. She beckoned Catriona over to her.

"I do believe that gentleman fancies you," she whispered to her barmaid.

"Nonsense," replied Catriona, holding back a laugh.

"Believe me, hen. He's after getting inside your knickers," declared the landlady.

"You're a wicked woman, Mrs Maclean," said Catriona, giving her a similar good-natured slap on the arm to the one she had previously delivered to Jack.

Jack could not hear what was being said but saw the two women looking over at him as they held their whispered conversation.

He smiled at them and raised his whisky glass towards them, so that they would know he that he knew they were talking about him.

Catriona blushed a little, while Mrs Maclean's response was to bustle off without looking in Jack's direction.

"I'm finishing work early tonight," said Catriona. "Isn't it time you were at home too? You usually leave earlier than this. Won't you be wanting your evening meal?"

"You're right," said Jack. "I've just enjoyed talking to you so much I've lost track of time. Could you possibly give me a lift home?"

"Of course," said Catriona.

Catriona washed a few glasses, said goodnight to Mr and Mrs Maclean and then told Jack that she was ready to go. They walked to her Ford Fiesta parked at the back of the hotel and drove away in the direction of Breaganish.

Catriona looked particularly fetching that evening in a short floral cocktail dress with a lace frill topping a low neckline. Her bare arms and legs looked silky and inviting as she sat driving.

As she chattered away Jack was suddenly taken with the thought that she was a life force. And how did he arrive at such a pretentious conclusion? Well, she was effervescent, happy, busy and exuding good health. If this was a mask, then he had never seen it slip and he seriously doubted that it ever would. And yet somehow her cheerfulness never descended into shallowness. Jack sensed she had a strong moral core, which she displayed by being a loving daughter and mother and by spraying with kindness everyone she came into contact with.

This was Jack's dilemma. He longed to take Catriona into his arms and give her a loving kiss. But attempting to do that would be a scary step into the unknown. She might reject him out of hand and that would assuredly mean the end of what was developing into a beautiful friendship.

If she succumbed to his charms then there was a danger she might be riven by guilt and never be the same life-enhancing presence again, at least to him.

And yet as she drove along the lanes in carefree mood an overwhelming desire overtook Jack. He longed to stroke her sinuous and tanned bare arms and to slide his fingers along the inside of her silky thighs. He wanted to press his face against her soft cheek and part those pert smiling lips with a gentle tongue.

How to do it though? He could hardly give her a goodnight kiss outside his own cottage when she dropped him off. He needed a subterfuge.

He remembered the glade behind Jamie's cottage where they had previously seen the deer. He had his plan!

When the car drew level with the cottage Jack shouted out: "Just stop here a little!"

Catriona stopped the car.

"I thought I saw a family of deer just at the edge of the forest. Over there," he pointed.

"I'll pull in a little so you can have a better look," said Catriona.

She pulled the car over on to a grass verge a few yards past Jamie's home.

Jack opened the window and peered out. He pretended to search for deer but in fact he was more interested in whether the car and its occupants could be seen from Jamie's cottage. He discerned that there was no window in the cottage which could provide a view. There appeared to be no human being about either.

"I think they've gone," said Jack, turning to Catriona.

"Aye. I think they must have done. They're fearful creatures," said Catriona.

"Isn't it a lovely spot, though?" said Jack. "I wish we could have bought Jamie's cottage."

"Aye. It's a beautiful wee spot. It surely is," said Catriona.

Jack continued, looking more intently towards the woman: "Aren't I just the luckiest person in the world – in a beautiful spot, on a beautiful evening, with a beautiful young lady?"

He leant over and put his arm around Catriona's bare shoulder. She looked at him questioningly, but soon received an answer to her question as Jack kissed her tenderly on the cheek.

This was the moment of truth, the fraction of a second in which Jack would learn his fate. Would he be rejected – slapped round the face even? Or would he conquer?

The answer was much less clear-cut. Catriona simply stroked Jack's hand, smiled sweetly and said: "I think the liquor may be talking a little, don't you?"

"It's nothing to do with the drink," replied Jack. "I just think you're the most beautiful person I've ever met."

Catriona laughed.

"Nonsense," she said, as she started up the car. "I'll get you home."

Jack was somewhat crestfallen but not totally devoid of hope.

They pulled up outside his cottage and said a friendly goodnight to each other.

"No hard feelings?" asked Jack.

"Oh, get away with you," said Catriona. "I'm not a little girl, you know. I know there's some chemistry going on here. But you're married, so that's it. Goodnight, Jack. See you at the hotel."

"Yes. You will," said Jack.

He got out of the car and they exchanged goodbye waves.

When he got inside the cottage Sophie told him he had been very lucky as Sarah had only just left. She had been in "a bit of a state", being unable to walk in a straight line.

"Perhaps Catriona will see her and give her a lift home," said Jack.

"No. She was going to Jamie's house," said Sophie.

"Oh," said Jack. "We didn't see her along the road."

"I expect she would have got to the cottage by now," said Sophie.

Jack went to bed feeling a little perturbed.

Chapter ten
Son of the
Manse

THE LATEST edition of the West Highland Free Press carried the news that the secretary of SPAT, Mr George Saxondale, had resigned from the post "for personal reasons".

The chairman, Mr Nigel Tavistock, expressed regret at Mr Saxondale's departure and said a special meeting of SPAT would be held to elect a successor. In the meantime the fight against the wind farm would continue "as vigorously as before".

A second article, published elsewhere in the paper, reported that a man had been charged with criminal damage following an incident in Beindow.

Ronnie McColl was cock-a-hoop. His usual demeanour, away from the charged atmosphere of a public meeting, was cold and calculating but on this occasion he could not contain his excitement.

He dashed out of the Portree Co-op brandishing the rolled-up copy of the newspaper in his shaking fist as if it were an offensive weapon. As he was about to get into his Range Rover he spotted the slightly stooped spare figure of Angus MacLeod walking across the car park with his neat corduroy-wearing wife, Fiona.

"Have you seen this?" asked Ronnie, waving the newspaper at Angus.

"No. We're just going in to get our copy of the Free Press now," replied Angus.

"We've got them. They're finished!" declared Ronnie in his usual clipped tones, which made him more reminiscent of a South African than a Highlander.

"Look at this," he said.

Ronnie opened up the newspaper at the page where the story about George Saxondale's resignation appeared and passed it to Angus.

Angus took his spectacles out of his top pocket and slowly read the article.

He paused, lowered his glasses so he could look over the top of them, and said in a deliberate manner: "I think they are in a pickle."

Ronnie took the paper from him, quickly shuffled through the pages and then re-presented it to the older man, declaring: "Now look at this."

Angus took the paper, raised his spectacles and slowly read again, this time the article about the Beindow incident.

Lowering his glasses once more, he said to Ronnie: "It's a pretty pass when things come to this. But it will do the anti-wind farmers no good at all – no good at all."

Angus turned to Fiona and offered her the newspaper. But she was clearly anxious to get on with her shopping.

"No. You can keep it," she said. "No good will come of all this arguing and falling out. Just leave it to those at the council to make the decision. That's what they are there for. Otherwise you will all finish up in gaol."

A wry smile gradually spread over Angus' face as he replied to his wife: "I don't think that is at all likely, my dear. We are not all of the temperament of our dear friend Hamish."

"Well, thank the Lord for that," snapped Fiona. "He's a madman. He's soft in the head if you ask me. He's already heading towards prison again. I just don't know why you tolerate him."

Angus smiled again and turned towards Ronnie: "You can see that Hamish is not the flavour of the month with my wife. She cannot understand why everyone can't be like herself."

"And what am I meant to be *like* when I'm at home?" asked Fiona, tetchily.

"Circumspect, my dear. Circumspect."

"Tsh!" exclaimed Fiona. "Now are we going to get our shopping done?"

"Aye," replied Angus. "You will have to excuse us Ronnie."

Ronnie, who was not to be subverted by this small talk, said: "Well, what do you think? Have we got the SPAT brigade on the run or not?"

Angus paused once more, put his spectacles back in his top pocket, and said: "I would not say as yet that we have them on the run. Let's say they appear to have taken a step backwards."

"More than a step I would say. We will use this to kill them off," said Ronnie, who had no time for half measures. "Good day to you, Angus, and to you Fiona."

Angus politely lifted his battered deerstalker hat while Fiona nodded in a circumspect manner.

****

Ronnie McColl liked to be thought of as a big shot on the Isle of Skye.

His father, the Rev Ronald McColl, had been a well-respected Free Presbyterian minister in Portree for many years before his untimely death from cancer at the age of 55.

The minister's wife had been killed in a car accident when she was only 30 and Ronnie was just seven years old and an only child. Ronnie's maiden aunt, his father's elder sister, had moved into the manse to work as housekeeper and to look after Ronnie.

Although the Rev McColl was a kindly man his way of life was austere and following his wife's death he became increasingly melancholic. He threw himself into his work in the church with a tunnel-visioned vengeance. He spent most of his "leisure" hours on bible study, with the result that his barnstorming Sunday sermons were littered with biblical stories and quotations.

Although he lived in the same house as his son the minister became a distant father, locked away in his study for many hours a week. Most of Ronnie's day to day contact was with his aunt, an even more austere figure than his father. Her favourite sayings were that "Children should be seen and not heard", "Cleanliness is next to Godliness" and "Spare the rod, spoil the child".

The manse was cold and draughty and the meals served up by the aunt were meagre and unimaginative.

While at primary school Ronnie was a shy, withdrawn child, denied maternal affection and showing little emotion himself.

He had few friends by the time he transferred to Portree High School and his shyness and lack of any enthusiasm for sport led to his being ignored by many of his fellow pupils and bullied by others. Being the Minister's son he was also kept at arm's length by some pupils because they suspected he must be a goody-goody and a tell-tale.

Then, in his third year at the school, he became friendly with Billy Rogerson, a sullen streetwise import from

Glasgow, who kept a knife in one pocket and a condom in another. In very different ways they were both outcasts. Billy was something of a bully himself but, significantly, he felt sorry for Ronnie and took him under his wing. He would deal viciously with anyone who crossed his friend.

Under the dubious mentoring of Billy, Ronnie gradually grew in self-confidence and became quite streetwise himself, smoking behind the bike sheds, having exploratory fumbles with girls on the school playing fields and watching the odd pornographic film in Billy's bedroom.

The two of them became the school's leading rebels and their schoolwork suffered as a result. The changes in Ronnie's attitudes and behaviour had gone largely unnoticed by his father, who had become increasingly immersed in his bible. But then Ronnie started to take bad school reports home.

The minister became alarmed. He had harboured the hope that his son would follow in his footsteps and take up the ministry. Despite his growing self-confidence and worldly behaviour Ronnie had not taken his rebelliousness so far as to refuse to sit in church every Sunday and to dutifully observe the Sabbath. Surreptitious youthful smoking, drinking and girling were confined to other days of the week.

The minister now felt it was time to take young Ronnie properly in hand. Each weekday evening when he was

209

satisfied that his son had completed his homework he took him into his study and gave him some intensive bible instruction. He also tried to instil in him the history of Protestantism and the doctrines and practices of the Free Presbyterian Church.

The scheme was a partial success. Ronnie was still at heart a dutiful son and took his father's teaching seriously enough. But his head had already been too much turned by the lures of the wicked world beyond church to give himself over completely to his studies.

He would use all kinds of subterfuge to seek out the company of Billy and the two or three girls who had by now latched on to the pair. For example, he would put his name down for a number of out of hours school clubs but then skive off them to meet up with his friends in the town.

Ronnie passed his time in these contrasting ways until it was time for him to leave Portree High School. In accordance with his father's wishes he enrolled for a theology degree course at the Free Church of Scotland College, near Edinburgh Castle.

Meanwhile Billy took an apprenticeship with his father, a builder based in Portree.

A year went by and Ronnie returned home for the summer holidays. He had found his college studies tedious and did not make friends among the rather other-worldly theology students.

Edinburgh was worlds apart from Portree. By comparison it was fashionable, cosmopolitan and wealthy. He began to envy the men-about-town in the city, with their sports cars, their glamorous girlfriends and their salubrious houses.

Wordsworth famously wrote:

"The world is too much with us; late and soon,

Getting and spending, we lay waste our powers."

Ronnie had memorised this passage in his last year at school and heard his teacher's opinion that it was one of the wisest statements ever made by man.

As he walked the streets of Edinburgh at night he began to question for the first time whether Wordsworth had it right. Surely the world had to be with us. It was the only thing we could be sure of.

On his return to the manse for the first time he felt sure enough of himself to challenge his father about the bible's teachings on poverty.

He quoted Proverbs to the minister: "The poor is disliked even by his neighbour, but the rich has many friends."

His father quoted Timothy: "But those who desire to be rich fall into temptation, into a snare, into many senseless and harmful desires that plunge people into ruin and destruction. For the love of money is a root of all kinds of evils. It is through this craving that some have wandered away from the faith and pierced themselves with many pangs."

Ronnie seized upon this quote and it changed his life: "So it's not money that is the problem. It's the *love* of money. So you can earn money and possess money, but so long as you don't 'love' it you are okay."

His father could not completely demur from this interpretation. But he had a deep foreboding about the way his son was beginning to think.

Ronnie met up with Billy on his first night home. Billy had money in his pocket, not huge amounts as a builder's apprentice, but enough to keep him in beer and fags and enough to be able to take a local girl on a good night out. He had also bought himself a Ford Anglia with a very throaty engine.

Ronnie was envious. If this was "the world being too much with us" then he wanted some of the action.

Then something happened which was to change his life completely. Billy's father died. His company was in the middle of building a sizeable new housing estate on the edge of Portree. Overnight Billy was transformed from new apprentice to boss of the firm.

He admitted to Ronnie that he was "all at sea". He had an experienced foreman and a number of skilled tradesmen to carry out the building work. His mother was busy bringing up his five younger siblings. She agreed that for the time being she would undertake the firm's paperwork and deal with councils and prospective property buyers, but stressed that this could be only a temporary arrangement.

At the end of the wake for Billy's father the two friends discussed this predicament over a pint at Portree's Royal Hotel. Ronnie revealed his disillusionment with theological matters and his new-found interest in making money.

"Then come and join our firm. Come and be my manager," said Billy. "We have always made a bloody good team. We have got a few years' work already planned and there'll be lots of money to be made."

Pound signs started to roll in front of Ronnie's eyes. But, at the age of 18, he had no experience of office work of any kind, let alone dealing with accounts and sales.

"Work with my mum then. She'll soon show you the ropes," said Billy.

Ronnie accepted this was a possibility but he wanted to add something more.

"I could study business management and accountancy in my spare time. Perhaps I could learn something about the building trade too," he said.

And that's exactly what he did.

He went home that night and knocked on the door of his father's study, where the minister was bent over his bible. Ronnie was admitted to the room and, without flinching, he immediately explained his plans to his father.

Although the minister was a bellicose preacher he was a mild-tempered man at home. He did not rant and rave but with quiet precision attempted to show Ronnie that he was making a huge mistake. He was sure Billy would make an unreliable work colleague; he was concerned that Ronnie lacked the necessary skills to take on his new role; and he knew for certain that God would strongly disapprove of his plans.

"I cannot but think that this is the work of the Devil," he concluded.

Ronnie was unmoved by these arguments. He said Billy had ceased to be the young tearaway he had been; he would work hard to complement Billy's skills and be a useful member of the firm; and he would continue to revere God and to attend church as regularly as before. He even promised to do good works in the parish when he became financially self-sufficient and settled.

The two argued well into the early hours of the morning.

Eventually the Rev McColl declared: "I don't approve. I think you are wasting your life when you could have followed me into the ministry of the Free Church. But I respect your right to make your own decision – and I wish you well."

"Thank you, father. I will not let you down," said Ronnie. And he left the room.

When he had gone his father fought back tears. Then he sank to his

214

knees and prayed and was soon becalmed.

Over the following years Billy and Ronnie worked hard and the company expanded so that it was eventually buying land and building houses throughout the Highlands. Ronnie was the front man of the business, while Billy concentrated on the practical side. Billy increasingly came to rely on his friend as the business grew and he eventually offered Ronnie a 50 per cent share in the company, Portree Estates.

Ronnie had various 4 x 4 vehicles which he used for work but his pride and joy was his series of "weekend" cars, usually Porsches. He cut a dash around Skye and attracted a number of desirable girlfriends.

One day his latest girlfriend, Morag, a butcher's daughter, announced she was pregnant. The couple kept this secret and hastily arranged a marriage, conducted by a suspicious Rev McColl. Ronnie was keen to shield his father from any whiff of scandal, but of course when the baby arrived the women of the parish were very quick to make their calculations – and equally quick to forgive the sinners and admire the new arrival.

The couple built a large house with a large garden sheltered by trees and situated on the hills behind the Blackhill Hotel at Beindow. The house had magnificent views over Loch Breaganish.

Within the next five years the family was completed by the arrival of two more children.   Ronnie was a successful man.

He kept his word to his father and the whole family were regular attenders at church. One day the Rev McColl called his son into his study and reminded him of the other undertaking he had made in their previous interview – that Ronnie was to undertake "good works" in the community.

Now Ronnie was not the sort of man to go around giving alms to the poor or caring for widows and orphans. But he hit upon the idea of standing for the local community council. It occurred to him that as a member of the council he could not only serve the local people but also keep tabs on any development and building opportunities which might arise in the area. He stood for the council and was elected.

So, on the surface, everything in Ronnie's life had fallen beautifully into place. The downside was that he did not truly appreciate his blessings. He always wanted more – more money, more recognition of his talents and his worth. He had a mean streak and could be ruthless, scheming and totally uncharitable towards anyone whom he considered might be thwarting his designs.

Ronnie was in his early forties when the proposal to build a wind farm at Beindow was first mooted. He quickly subscribed to the majority view in the area that wind farms could bring economic benefits to Skye. Tourism was all very well but there needed to be more diverse forms of activity if the island's population was to grow. And more people meant more homes to be built!

Ronnie, who never did things by halves, thrust himself enthusiastically into the leadership of the "Yes" campaign. And he soon developed a seething dislike of anyone who took a different point of view.

****

Ronnie drove home from the supermarket and went straight up to a large upstairs room which was the office, conference room and nerve centre of Portree Estates. He opened a drawer and took out a list of around 40 names of the strongest local wind farm supporters. He spent the next hour systematically phoning or emailing everyone on the list and inviting them to a meeting at his house the following evening to discuss the latest developments affecting SPAT.

Thirty people actually turned up to the meeting, made up of some community councillors, a handful of businessmen and a selection of ordinary residents, male and female.

For many of those present this was the first time they had seen the ultra-modern office accommodation. The walls were regaled with photographs and plans of the company's building projects, completed and in progress, as well as various sales graphs and certificates showing both the qualifications of senior members of the company and design and building awards it had gained. On the paper-free desks were computers and printers and a variety of audio-visual equipment.

Suitably impressed by their surroundings and refreshed by the tea and biscuits served by Ronnie's wife, Morag, they took their seats in the smart conference area.

They looked an odd bunch sitting in designer chrome cantilever chairs around the walnut conference table. Half of them had come straight from work – work which included muddy farm-work on the croft and painting and decorating. There was even a sweep, who looked as if he had come straight down the chimney to be there. Some of the elderly men were wearing their Sunday best suits while their wives were in their tweeds. Angus and Fiona were among this number.

Towering over all of them was Hamish, hair as wild as ever and with his legs akimbo and his hands on his knees. He had to sit at one end of the table as he would have taken up three spaces at the side.

Ronnie took his place at the other end of the table and remained standing. As soon as he called the meeting to order there was a rattle of the office door and in lumbered Archie Beaton, who wished everyone a cheery "Good evening".

There was consternation among those sitting around the table. How could they possibly make room for Archie's gargantuan bottom? And, even if they moved up to make more space, the swish cantilever chairs could surely not bear his weight.

Morag immediately understood the problem. Ronnie had a plush red upholstered swivel chair at his own office desk. She quickly brought it over and offered it to Archie, placing it a short space away from the table at Ronnie's end.

Archie gracefully accepted the kind offer and slumped into the chair, where he reclined with a satisfied look on his face.

"Il presidente!" joked a wag.

Ronnie called the meeting to order again. He started quietly enough, painstakingly explaining what had happened to Hamish and the repercussions for SPAT.

Then, as if suddenly recalling his father's sermons in the kirk, he stood up and launched into a furious rhetorical explosion.

"These SPAT people....." he began, literally spitting out the word SPAT as if it were a piece of disgusting gristle..... "These incomers and their toadies want to keep our island as a poverty-stricken backwater. They want us to behave like forelock tugging peasants grateful for the scraps that tourism may bring us.

"But we will not be subservient to a bunch of la-di-da English holiday cottage owners and the Uncle Tom lickspittles amongst us who do their dirty business. We need to be self-sufficient, as we were before the Clearances. And wind farms are just a start along that road.

"We WILL see our island re-populated. We WILL see our sons and daughters and our grandchildren returning to Skye to live and work.

"We WILL defeat the enemy. As the Bible says: 'The Lord shall cause thine enemies that rise up against thee to be smitten before thy face: they shall come out against thee one way, and flee before thee seven ways'.

"We WILL get our wind farm. And then we'll get another, and another, and another, until the Highlands and Islands become the greatest energy providers in Britain – and England will have to come cap in hand to us, as they have done to the Arabs for their oil for generations."

At that point Hamish brought his enormous hand crashing down on the table, causing its legs to shake visibly.

"You have spoken the truth," he growled. "We stand four-square behind you."

There was an eruption of applause from the majority of those present. But a handful of people did not applaud, and, one, Angus MacLeod, tentatively raised a finger to ask to speak.

Ronnie nodded to him: "Angus, let's hear from you."

Angus stretched his arms out in front of him and spoke slowly: "I would just like to proffer the view, in my humble opinion, that as Christians, as I believe most of us here are, we should not be talking about enemies and smiting people down.

"These people you talk of as enemies: they are our neighbours, some of them are our friends. They are all our brethren in front of the Lord. Cannot we disagree with them about wind farms, but still respect their right to a different point of view? Isn't that what Christianity is all about?

"You, Ronnie, have quoted from the Bible – surprising as it is well known that you are not as devout a religious man as your good father. I can quote from the Bible too: 'The Lord's servant must not be quarrelsome but kind to everyone, able to teach, patiently enduring evil, correcting his opponents with gentleness.' "

From his brief spell as a theological student Ronnie recognised these words as being from Timothy 2 in a modern version of the bible.

He was more acquainted with the King James version of the Good Book, and he snapped back: "Aye, and it talks of those opponents as being in 'the snare of the devil, who are taken captive by him at his will.' "

"And who might the devil be in this case?" asked Angus.

"Tavistock! Saxondale! Two devils!" shouted Ronnie.

"What tosh!" declared Fiona MacLeod.

Everyone looked at her, some in anger, others in admiration that she was standing up to Ronnie.

"Behave yourself, both of you. We are not in church now," said Fiona. "There's time enough for quoting the Bible on a Sunday."

"Here, here" came the acclamation from several quarters.

Hamish stood up and pointed his gigantic fingers towards Ronnie: "You should listen to this man. He speaks the truth. They are devils. You should have seen my window the other night to prove that. They are deranged in their opposition to the wind farm."

Hamish sat down.

"You are deranged more like," muttered Fiona, audibly to most in the room, but thankfully not to Hamish.

Ronnie remained as cool as a cucumber during these heated exchanges. For the anger of his rhetoric was not truly born out of passion. It was a calculated, planned anger, designed to arouse the real anger of others.

"Let's get on with the business," he said, calmly.

He proposed that he write a letter to the West Highland Free Press, not specifically mentioning the criminal damage charges against George Saxondale but highlighting the turmoil in the SPAT organisation resulting from the secretary's resignation.

He would also urge all wind farm supporters to write to their local councillors backing the scheme and to sign a petition which would be placed in various shops and other businesses in the area.

Ronnie's audience unanimously agreed to these steps and the meeting ended on a note of harmony.

Hamish nudged Angus as they left the hall and grumbled loudly: "I wonder whose side you are on sometimes."

Angus paused, scratched his chin and replied: "You know, Hamish, there's more than one way to skin a cat."

Hamish roughly ruffled Angus' hair and, grinning broadly, said: "You always were a fucking diplomat."

Chapter eleven

Betrayals

IT WAS a week since Sophie had seen Jamie. Every evening she had found an excuse for walking down to the Black Burn pool. Several times she had walked along the lane and knocked on his unlocked door and peered inside. There were no signs he had been there.

She still did not have a mobile telephone number for him.

Sophie was desperate to see her lover but there was no obvious way to contact him. Desperate times required desperate measures.

At first she thought of asking Sarah what she knew of his whereabouts. She was sure she could make up some reason for needing to know. But she was worried about Sarah's volatile nature. She could turn up drunk at the cottage and spill the beans to Jack.

The only other point of reference she had was that he worked for Iain

McConnell. She waited until one evening when Jack had gone to the Blackhill. She looked up Mr McConnell in the telephone directory, found a number and rang it.

Mrs McConnell answered.

Sophie said she was trying to contact Jamie Carmichael. He had promised to go fishing with her husband but they had been unable to contact him for more than a week. He did not seem to be at his cottage.

Mrs McConnell replied: "I am afraid that Jamie Carmichael no longer works for us. I can't tell you where he is at present. I'm sorry."

Sophie was shocked. She had not expected anything like this.

"Oh, I'm sorry," she said. "I was told a few days ago that he had gone to the Black Isle with some sheep.

"No. That's not correct," said Mrs McConnell, sounding formal and successfully trying to give the impression that that was the end of the conversation.

"Oh. I must have been misinformed then. His mother told me that's where he was."

"Yes. You have been misinformed," said Mrs McConnell, icily. "Goodbye, dear."

"Good-bye. Sorry to trouble you," said Sophie.

She put the phone down and sat in a trance, feeling somewhat shell-shocked but still trying to work out a way of surmounting her problem.

She stared out of the dining room window, hoping for some inspiration.

Then, out of the corner of her eye, she caught sight of a familiar figure walking briskly down the side of the house and carrying fishing gear. It was Jamie!

She scuttled out of the back door and ran up to her lover, tugging at his arm.

"Jamie. Where have you been? "What's happened?"

Jamie pulled her arm away and looked straight into her eyes, with what she took to be a fierce expression.

"I've been away – to the Black Isle."

"Taking some sheep?"

"No."

"I saw your mother. She thought that's what you were doing."

"I told her where I was going. I didn't tell her what for. She would have assumed I was taking sheep. I do that once a year as a rule."

"I rang Mr McConnell's house and spoke to a lady – Mrs McConnell I guess. She said you no longer worked for them."

Jamie looked annoyed.

"Why did you ring them?"

"Because I was worried about you. I hadn't seen you for at least a week."

"What did you say to her?"

"I made an excuse that you had arranged to have a fishing trip with Jack and we hadn't been able to contact you."

"That's all?"

"Yes. That's all. But why didn't you tell me you were going away?"

"My business," said Jamie, roughly.

"That's not very nice, is it?" said Sophie.

"I'm going away."

"Going away."

"Yes. I've got a job working on an estate at the Black Isle."

"Just like that? I thought you were happy working for Mr McConnell."

"I was. He was a good boss. I just felt like a change."

"Your mother doesn't seem to think that he was a good boss. She said he kept you short of money."

"My mother's a drunk. You can't believe a word she says."

"So don't I count for anything? You're just going off and leaving me here?"

Jamie softened a little: "I need a fresh start. I enjoyed my job but I was getting into a rut here. I'm not starting my new job for a few weeks yet. I will have some time on my hands before then. We can meet up as much as you like."

"But what about after that?"

"After that we shall have to see. I'm not going to the other end of the world."

Sophie put her arms around him and kissed him.

"We mustn't lose a second then. Come inside the cottage. Forget your fishing for an hour or so. Jack won't be back until closing time at the Blackhill."

Jamie put his hand on to her breast and kissed her.

"Ok. Let's go inside."

****

Jack was sitting at what had become his usual seat at the bar, next to Archie and a couple of other regulars. They were generally putting the world to rights and Jack was taking every opportunity of including Catriona in the conversation.

She was looking particularly enticing that evening, a low cut elasticated top showing off her pert breasts to best advantage. Her skin tight faded blue jeans gave her a more youthful image than she usually projected.

Jack had a deep longing to seduce her but at the same time a wearying recognition that his conscience and her decency would never let it happen.

The conversation turned to Jamie.

Archie told his fellow drinkers that he had heard that Jamie had left his job with Iain McConnell. It was all a mystery as no-one Archie had seen could explain why that had happened.

The other drinkers were surprised to hear this news, particularly as Mr McConnell owed such a debt to gratitude to Jamie for saving him.

"You all know, Jamie," said Archie. "He's a man of very few words. But he has told one or two people that he wants to make a fresh start and that he has got a job on an estate in the Black Isle."

There was much shaking of heads and looks of disbelief.

228

Catriona was the first to speak: "I'll never forget that night when Jamie came knocking at my front door to tell me about the attack."

"He came to YOUR house?" said Jack.

"Yes – on that terrible night."

Jack always liked to hear a good yarn and was keen to know more about what had happened. He encouraged Catriona to tell him the whole story.

She said that she had been in bed when there was a loud banging at her front door. She felt scared but ventured downstairs. Before opening the door she had shouted: "Who is it?"

Jamie shouted that it was him.

Catriona opened the door and saw Jamie sitting on all fours in front of her, out of breath and obviously in acute pain.

He told her that Iain McConnell had injured his head and was lying next to the Black Burn. He was unconscious, maybe even dead.

Jamie implored Catriona to dial 999 for an ambulance as fast as possible. She rushed into the house and did that and then returned to look after Jamie. He told her he had been running along the loch shore towards her cottage when he tripped over a large piece of driftwood, badly twisting his ankle. The pain had been so bad that he had literally crawled the last 200 yards along the beach, rocks, grass bank and road to the cottage.

Catriona helped Jamie into her car and she drove to the then empty cottage now occupied by Jack and Sophie to get as close as possible to the track which led to the Black Burn pool.

She grabbed a rug from the boot of her car and ran down to the pool, with Jamie dragging himself as quickly as he was able behind her. She came across Iain McConnell's motionless body, covered with blood and sand, with a deep red gash at the top of his head.

Catriona covered Iain with her rug and she and Jamie knelt over him as they waited for the ambulance to arrive. She was shaking with shock and Jamie held her hand and consoled her, even though the pain from his ankle was excruciating.

"He really was a hero that night," she said.

The air ambulance landed on the stony beach at the lochside and the police arrived at the same time and took charge of the situation. They took photographs of the scene as the air ambulance crew tended to Iain. He was stretchered on to their helicopter, bound for Broadford Hospital.

Having made sure that Catriona had recovered her composure and been assured by the ambulance crew that Jamie's ankle was only sprained, police officers drove both of them to the police station for questioning.

As he had been first on the scene Jamie was interrogated for many hours on what had taken place that night. There was clearly some suspicion that he might have been involved in the assault, but the police could discover no evidence or motive. He was eventually hailed in the press as a hero without whom Iain McConnell could have died. Although Iain had no recollection of the incident, his wife was fulsome in her praise of Jamie's actions.

Catriona said general opinion in the area was that Iain had made enemies owing to his wind farm proposal and that someone had taken revenge.

Archie and his friends at the bar fully endorsed this theory, which had been vigorously fuelled by people such as Ronnie McColl and Hamish McDonald.

Jack was intrigued by this story. He felt a crime novel coming on.

He was interested as to why both Iain and Jamie had been on the Loch Breaganish beach so late at night.

Catriona said Iain had a regular practice of walking from his home alongside the loch to the Breaganish Hotel. There he took a few drams with his friends, the hotel's owners, Robert and Gina Carlton, and played the odd game of snooker with Robert. He would then return home via the lochside.

Jamie often went down to the Black Burn pool to fish, staying until dark. That was what he had been doing that night. The police had found his fishing tackle near to the spot where Iain had been assaulted.

While Jack was digesting Catriona's narrative the bar door burst open and a rough-looking unshaven youth appeared. It was Murdo Ferguson, the hero or villain according to one's taste of the evening assault upon the Lochside Inn.

"Hamish has been arrested!" he shouted.

With difficulty Archie turned his head to look at him.

"What for now?"

"He's daubed graffiti all over that shit Saxondale's house and the coppers caught him red-handed."

Archie sighed: "He's heading back to gaol, I'm afraid. The fool."

"Saxondale had it coming after what he did to Hamish's cottage," said Murdo.

"Hamish does go rather overboard though, doesn't he?" suggested Jack.

"You're talking crap, you are. What do you know about it?" said Murdo.

"Calm down, lad," said Archie. "That tongue of yours will get you into trouble too one day."

"I'm just fucking saying. That's all," said Murdo.

· "If you want to do something useful, go up to Ronnie McColl's and tell him what's happened. He might stand bail for Hamish," said Archie.

Murdo agreed to do that and quickly left the bar.

Inevitably much talk followed about Hamish's latest plight before the drinkers eventually went home to their beds. Equally inevitably, Jack was left alone in the bar with Catriona until closing time. By now this had become a regular twice-weekly occurrence.

As had also become the norm, Catriona offered Jack a lift home, noticed as usual by an all-seeing Mrs Myrtle Maclean. This time she could not resist a comment as they passed her at the reception desk.

"Goodnight you two. Don't do anything I wouldn't do."

"Shut up," said Catriona playfully. "You're wicked."

The landlady waved her away.

The journey home was uneventful, leaving Jack to go to bed feeling horny and sad.

He cuddled up to Sophie, hoping to make love to her. But she was sound asleep – again.

****

It was late August and Skye was experiencing one of its rainier periods. Carried over the island by very strong Atlantic winds, the rain hardly ever stopped, morning and night. It was heavy and enveloped the Cuillin mountains in a permanent mist. The so-called Misty Isle was at its mistiest.

This posed little in the way of inconvenience to the Skye people. They knew it would pass. It might rain and blow for two or three weeks, but it would pass. In the meantime the rivers were in full spate and fishermen braved the elements to take the chance of some trout or even a salmon or two.

Jack and Sophie were just as philosophical about the weather as the locals. They both had largely indoor jobs and they actually enjoyed the claustrophobic feeling which the low cloud and mist brought to the island. The cottage was cosy and they felt safe.

The pair were no strangers to working at home together, albeit in separate rooms. They had no problem with giving each other "space". It was one of the strengths of their marriage.

But they had always thoroughly enjoyed their "together time" too. Either Jack or Sophie was likely to break off from work at any time and suggest a shared cup of tea or coffee. They would talk about their future plans and the interesting excursions that each would like to go on.

In the last few weeks, though, a change had come over them. They were still in love with each other. But they were both in love with another person too.

Their outward pattern of behaviour when they were together did not change one iota. Neither had a clue that the other was thinking most of the time about someone else.

They continued to stop work for their tea and coffee breaks, for their meals and for a glass of wine in the evening. They had continued to go off on walks or car drives together, exploring various "undiscovered" parts of the island.

It was their work that was changing. Jack's fantasising about Catriona was altering the nature of his writing His crime novels were becoming laced with far more love and sex scenes. Every woman in those scenes was Catriona, under the guise of several different names and physical characteristics. He found it increasingly difficult to write about anything else.

It has already been recorded that Sophie's paintings had become predominantly ones of nymphs and satyrs. They had become more sexual and violent in content in recent days. In truth the satyr was always Jamie and now there was only ever one nymph in the picture, instead of the group as before. The nymph was of course Sophie herself. It was as if she could not bear the thought of sharing Jamie with any other nymphs. SHE would pull her unwilling satyr into the water unaided.

Jack had never asked Sophie to read any of his novels before they were published. For a fairly self-confident man he had a reticence when it came to letting family and friends read his work before someone more independent and objective had had the opportunity to judge it. He could not have borne any censure or ridicule from someone closer to him.

Because of this there was no chance of Sophie reading his current work and noticing the great change that had taken place.

But for Sophie it was more difficult. She produced large canvasses which could not be hidden away. Jack had several times expressed surprise about the new direction her work was taking. She explained this by saying that she had become totally fascinated by mythological stories and images. She claimed she would produce a set of paintings concerning nymphs and satyrs and then move on to some other myth.

The sexual content of the images did not disturb Jack in any way. In fact they turned him on. They were no worse than orgiastic scenes depicted by many of the Great Masters.

In particular he had studied Nicholas Poussin in connection with a novel he had written about a fraud connected with the Holy Grail. He had noted that Poussin's paintings contained dozens of erotic intertwined bodies, mostly depicting mythological tales.

He expressed some doubts as to whether the tourists to Skye would like Sophie's new subject matter. They had already lapped up some of her landscapes of the island and she had been confident she would make a decent living through that genre.

Sophie assured Jack that she would still paint landscapes to pay for their "bread and butter". But she was content she could find markets off the island for her new mythological studies. If Poussin could do it, she could!

Jack was always keen to encourage her creativity and so said no more on the subject.

Jack and Sophie were a successful, happy, compatible, loving couple, completely at ease in each other's company, with two lovely, bright daughters and presenting a kind, respectable and amiable aspect to the outside world.

So what had gone wrong?

From one perspective nothing had gone wrong at all. Their respective cravings for Catriona and Jamie were a direct result of the "space" they gave each other and of which they were proud. They could have carried on for a long time in the present vein without any trouble – so long as neither of them suspected the other of infidelity. For the "space" in the relationship was conditional on the trust between them.

So far Sophie had betrayed that trust absolutely, both by her thoughts and her actions. Jack had betrayed it by his thoughts and his intentions. His actions had been constrained only by his strong sense of conscience and by Catriona's own respectability.

****

Towards the end of the rainy spell Jack received a telephone call from Nigel Tavistock, who gave news of the fishing trip which had been proposed at the dinner at his house. It was suggested that Jack, Nigel, Edward Stafford-Allen and Matt Beaton should make the trip early the next day. The weather forecast was better than it had been for several weeks and the plan was to fish at the Storr Lochs, renowned for providing the best trout fishing on the island.

Edward had arranged to buy four day passes which would cover both the

237

Storr Lochs and a number of other good trout waters nearby.

Jack readily agreed to the plan, so next morning Matt turned up in his new Range Rover to collect him. Nigel was already on board and Edward was picked up along the way.

When the party arrived at the extensive Storr Lochs, next to the sea to the north of Portree, they first went to collect the rowing boats they had hired for the day.

As a beginner, Jack was to share a boat with Edward, the most experienced angler, while Matt, whose fishing had been lifelong but spasmodic, was to accompany Nigel, who had fished only half a dozen times before.

Although the weather forecast had been promising, it did not live up to expectations. It was cloudy and dry, but there was a very strong wind which made it difficult to control even an anchored boat and made casting inconsistent.

The party gave it their best for three fishless hours before Edward declared they were wasting their time. They all agreed with his suggestion that they should move on to a more sheltered spot.

So it was all aboard the Range Rover for Loch Cuithir, a hidden gem of a loch enclosed on three sides by mountains.

The route from the Storr Lochs was north along the main Portree to Staffin road, passing the impressive Lealt

Falls, which were in a deep cut between the main road and the shore, then taking a metalled track past the tiny settlement of Lealt to follow the meandering Lealt River.

The track went past ruined concrete buildings which were once a diatomite factory. No, not dynamite – diatomite.

Edward, who had made himself an expert on local history as well as local angling, explained that diatomite was a clay-like floury grey substance. It was found in certain freshwater lochs and supplied minerals used in the manufacture of many products, ranging from beverages, sugars and cosmetics to chemicals, industrial oils, paint – and dynamite.

Work had begun at Loch Cuithir in 1899 and come to an end in 1960.

The former industrial site there is now deadly quiet and deserted, but over the years saw a great deal of activity, with a large factory building, an aerial ropeway and even a three-mile-long light railway with embankments to take the product to the shore.

The diatomite was taken to the coast at nearby Invertote for the drying and grinding processes and then the finished product was transported by boat to the mainland.

The industry, unique in Skye for its modernity, employed up to 80 people.

But the Skye diatomite industry had a story behind it which might well have provided a plot for one of Jack's novels. It all revolves around the fact that the drying factory at Invertote was owned by Germans.

Although the industry was closed down during the First World War the Germans were surprisingly allowed to stay on.

A rumour began to circulate that the area was haunted and that a ghost from a recent tragic death at Lealt Falls had appeared at the factory.

But it appears that the rumour was started by the Germans, with the intention of keeping locals away.

It turned out that the Germans were spies and that the area was being used as a German base, with submarines surfacing in the sea bay. Jack imagined a James Bond-type scene, with a British secret agent donning diving gear and going underwater to scupper the German subs.

Skye does that to you. It is often difficult to separate the truth from the myths that you would so much like to believe.

The Range Rover passed by the old diatomite factory and was soon at the end of the track.

As the party alighted Jack looked around. He had often thought that the pool at the bottom of the Black Burn was the nearest he would ever get to paradise.

But the scene in front of him was utterly awe-inspiring.

The small loch itself, as still as a millpond, was beautiful enough, but the mountains towering around it gave the impression of a large goldfish bowl.

Some may have found the atmosphere oppressive, but to Jack the proximity of the mountains produced a perfect peace. His companions, who had visited the loch previously, seemed similarly impressed. They just stood silently looking around them, soaking up the solitude.

Then Jack noticed something which made him smile. Tucked in a corner adjacent to the loch was a well-constructed picnic table. This was typical of the Highlands and Islands. There are times when you think you have arrived at somewhere truly remote, only to find that you are in fact at the end of a well-worn path, recently visited. This is often the cause of a tinge of disappointment, usually quickly dispelled by the sheer beauty and scale of the landscape. Jack knew this only too well, hence the wry smile.

He was a practical poet. The picnic table was a useful place to sort out the fishing tackle and to eat his sandwiches later.

Edward was pleased that his fellow anglers were being quiet. He put his finger to his lips and said: "Let's stay very quiet and the fish may not notice we are here."

They looked over to the still loch and noticed the tell-tale bubbles and ripples which indicate the presence of fish. An odd jumping fish breached the surface. It was an exciting prospect for any angler!

The foursome positioned themselves strategically on the nearside of the loch. And straightaway their silent approach paid dividends. Each of them caught a decent sized brown trout within seconds.

"This is heaven," whispered Jack.

But then – nothing. Not a single fish was caught for the next hour. Edward decided it was lunchtime. They gathered around the picnic table to eat their smoked salmon sandwiches, game pies and oatcakes with cheeses, washed down with a bottle of Chianti from Matt's cellar.

Jack expressed his surprise that after such an exhilarating start to their fishing at Loch Cuithir the catching had stopped so abruptly.

"It doesn't surprise me in the slightest," said Edward. "Maybe no-one has fished here for months and then suddenly a selection of juicy flies presents itself. Exciting! We'll try a bit of that.

"But the rest of the fish probably notice the commotion of fish getting caught and then see us standing there. Something's up, they think. Better lie low for a bit."

The others laughed. They had full confidence in Edward's knowledge, but how did he really know what trout were thinking? In fact, did trout think at all?

"And anyway," continued Edward. "You wouldn't want to be catching fish all day, would you?"

"Oh, I don't know about that," said Nigel, with a novice's enthusiasm.

The other novice, Jack, nodded in agreement.

"Let me tell you a story," said Edward. "A very keen angler died and went to the next world. He was delighted to be met at the gate by a man who looked very much like one of the Scottish ghillies who had been so helpful to him during his fishing career.

"This 'ghillie' confirmed that he had been assigned to look after our friend on his arrival. He pointed to a beautiful loch and beckoned the man to follow him.

"He handed over a rod and suggested the angler cast his fly to a particular swim. The man cast and immediately caught a fat brown trout. The ghillie told him to cast again, which he did, and again he caught a big fish. For the next hour every time he cast his fly he caught a good-sized fish. The man couldn't believe his luck!

"The ghillie then took him to a second pool – and the same thing happened: he caught a fish every time he cast out. Then he went to a third pool, a fourth, a fifth and a sixth. Every cast produced a fish.

"After six or seven hours of this our angling friend had become fatigued and, quite frankly, bored by the whole process.

"'I've had enough of this," he said to the ghillie. "This is Hell."

The ghillie replied: "Yes, sir. And where exactly did you think you were?"

Edward's listeners appreciated the joke.

Nigel said: "Ok. We get the point. We have been lucky already. We have caught a fish each and we are in this completely lovely place."

Matt concurred: "You will learn that just being on Skye is enough. The fish are a bonus."

When they had finished their meal Edward got up from the table and indicated that the others should take up their rods and follow him.

He led them a few yards along the track and pointed out another separate small pool. And looking into the distance they could see two other small lochans.

Edward was not quite sure if these waters had separate names, or if, together with the main loch, they were collectively Loch Cuithir.

"Let's try these pools," said Edward, "and give the main loch a rest for a while."

The party fished for the next couple of hours. Matt and Edward caught a small trout each. Nigel and Jack caught nothing.

They returned to the main loch for the last hour of the trip. But the fish were still hiding. None had been large enough to be taken home for the pot, but all agreed they had enjoyed the location and the experience.

The party decided to round off the day with dinner at the Cuillin Hills Hotel, the best hotel in Portree. At the hotel reception they were passed by none other than Ronnie McColl, who was just leaving. There was a chill in the air. Ronnie nodded to them and they nodded back.

Chapter twelve
Paradise lost

THREE hours earlier Sophie and Jamie had lain on the bed at his cottage. They had held their longest ever conversation.

Sophie had pleaded with Jamie to reconsider his decision to move away from Skye to the Black Isle (which is not an island but a peninsula), but he was immovable.

He said he was in his mid-thirties and if he did not move on and better himself now he never would.

Sophie tried her best to find out more about her lover. Had he ever been married, engaged, or even had a steady girlfriend?

Jamie's answers were "No", "No" and "Yes". Nothing more.

She asked him how long he had worked for Iain McConnell. He said since he had left school.

She asked if Mr McConnell had been upset that he was leaving and whether he had asked him to stay on.

Jamie said he did not know what Mr McConnell felt. He did not recall whether he had been asked to stay on.

Every question Sophie posed received little more than a one-word reply. And the replies contained as little information as Jamie could contrive to provide.

When she returned home that night Sophie wondered, as she had many times in the last few weeks, why she had become involved with this monosyllabic man. She almost thought "boring" man, but inexplicably she found him the most exciting person she had ever met.

She could converse with Jack until the cows came home. She loved his company and felt comfortable in their intimate moments. But she had never felt the same passion or the same thrill as she found with Jamie.

She felt sick to the pit of her stomach every time she thought of him or caught a glimpse of him. She was hopelessly in love with someone she knew little or nothing about.

What she did know about him she did not very much like. He was undemonstrative, unromantic, a little uncouth and quiet to the point of being unfriendly. Lots of "un" characteristics. Nothing very positive, except his wonderful, athletic body and his seemingly unquenchable virility.

As she considered herself to be a rational human being, she tried to explain their relationship intellectually. But she found that was impossible.

She fell back on the non-intellectual – the vacuous world of the spiritual. She recalled studying Zen Buddhism when she was a teenager and remembered that an important part of the teaching was that one should not grasp on to things. That was the answer! She must not try to "grasp" Jamie or "grasp" her relationship with him. She must just let everything happen, without feeling guilty, without feeling at all.

She searched the worldwide web to remind herself what Buddhism taught about grasping. She came across the teachings of a guru, Satya Narayan Goenka, who said: "Grasping at things can only yield one of two results: Either the thing you are grasping at disappears, or you yourself disappear. It is only a matter of which occurs first."

"Very wise," thought Sophie. "Very wise."

Deep down she knew that she was desperately looking for an excuse for her morally indefensible behaviour. She had looked to mythology and now to Buddhism. What next? Mind-changing drugs? What was she doing to herself? To her self-respect? To Jack? To her family?

She sobbed. She would never see Jamie again. It had to end. Now.

She showered. Symbolically. Like Lady Macbeth she was trying to wash away her guilt.

She went to bed. She calmed down. She thought: "Jamie is only here for another few days. No harm can come if I just see him a few more times. Then it's over. Back to Mrs Respectable Married Woman for the rest of my life. I promise. Three or four days and it will all be over. Time and space are great healers. When he goes to the Black Isle, I may never see him again. His mother lives just down the road, so perhaps he will visit. But I am a strong woman with willpower. I will not succumb again. I will still fancy him like mad, but I will treat him as a memory - partly a good memory, partly a memory of which I am deeply ashamed."

****

The next evening Jack walked into the Blackhill bar and the usual company was assembled. Catriona, as he knew she would be, was serving.

He said "Hello" to Archie and Hamish who were dominating the bar. Archie was pleasant and welcoming as was his custom. Hamish usually offered a perfunctory but perfectly civil "Good evening" in return. But this time he just grunted and turned his head away.

Jack looked at Archie, who said: "Don't mind Hamish. He's in a bad mood, I think."

Hamish swung round: "I'm not in a bad mood."

"Aye. Okay," said Archie.

Hamish turned away again and began to talk to two other men at the bar.

"Is he all right?" asked Jack.

"The thing is that there's been some blather about you in here tonight."

"About me?" said Jack, surprised.

"Ronnie McColl was in earlier. He was talking about the writer who lives over at Breaganish. He said you were really friendly with Tavistock and his SPAT cronies. He had seen you at the Cuillin Hills. That's all. You know what Hamish is like. He thinks everything is aimed at him."

"That's ridiculous," said Jack. "We'd just been on a fishing trip together – four of us. Only two of the party have anything to do with SPAT. We didn't even mention wind farms all day."

Hamish had been listening to the conversation and chimed in angrily: "A man is judged by the company he keeps. And you keep some shitty company, my friend. Bloody incomers."

Jack was mild-mannered and pacific by nature. But he did not stand for nonsense.

"That is the most ridiculous thing I have ever heard. I don't choose my friends according to their views on wind farms. Personally I have nothing against wind farms."

"Aye. That's what you say. I would advise you to stay away from those parasites," said Hamish, growing redder in the face.

"I will choose my own friends, thank you. I will not be seeking your permission. What you did to Nigel Tavistock's house was disgusting. You're a bully boy, Hamish. You will turn people against the wind farm by the way you are carrying on."

Hamish slammed down his lager glass on the bar, swore a terrible oath, and stormed out.

Jack pretended to keep his cool, but as he picked up his whisky glass to down his drink his hand was shaking. This was partly through fear of the enemy he felt he had just made, but mainly through anger at the injustice of what he had been subjected to.

Archie was sympathetic.

"That was uncalled for," he said. "We are all pressing for the wind farm to go ahead, but Hamish does not know where to draw the line. I would not wish to make a friend of Tavistock and his gang myself because I believe they are a selfish bunch. But there's no way Hamish should have gone on at you like that.

"Come on, have a drink on me and let's forget what's happened."

Archie turned to Catriona, who was well aware what had been going on and was already pouring out a sympathetic glass of whisky for her friend.

"Take no notice of Hamish," she smiled. "He has a notoriously short fuse."

At that moment Mrs Maclean walked into the bar from the direction of the reception desk.

"What on earth's the matter with Hamish now?" she asked. "He just slammed the front door and I thought it would fall from its hinges."

"Something or nothing," said Archie. "He was getting a little hot under the collar about the wind farm."

"Well, he needn't take it out on my front door," declared Mrs Maclean. "The man's a complete lunatic."

Jack was beginning to feel a little guilty that he had caused an upset.

"I'm afraid it was me he took exception to," he said.

"You?" said the landlady.

"Yes. I went on a little fishing trip with some new acquaintances of mine, and one of them happened to be Nigel Tavistock."

"Oh, that man," said Mrs Maclean.

"Yes," said Jack. "I know he's persona non grata around here. But I have found him a perfectly decent sort of chap. We can't all have the same views, can we? "But Hamish obviously doesn't think that way and we had a few words. I'm sorry if I have caused any ructions."

Mrs Maclean looked at him sternly.

"You have to be careful what you do and say when there's Neanderthals like Hamish around," she said. "It's a good thing that he's not his younger self or you would probably be lying in a heap on the floor by now.

"He's been banned from this hotel on dozens of occasions before now, both by my husband and myself and by the previous owners. But we're all soft as shit and let him come back in again. You see he can't help being a total wanker. He was just born that way. They say his father and his grandfather were famous wankers too and his mother was three sandwiches short of a picnic. So he never had a chance really.

"I'll be giving him a piece of my mind the next time he dares to come in here."

Catriona laughed: "If he hears that you're on the warpath, he'll probably leave the island!"

"Let's forget about the miserable old bugger. Cos that's what he is, even though he's one of my best friends," said Archie.

"They should tie Hamish McDonald and Nigel Tavistock together, fasten lead weights to their legs and drop them into the loch," said Mrs Maclean. "Then we might all have a bit of peace."

She strutted out of the bar, happy that she had propounded the complete answer to the wind farm controversy.

Jack smiled at Catriona. Mrs Maclean had put everything into its proper perspective and he was calm again.

The rest of the evening at the Blackhill passed pleasantly enough. Several of the regulars who had heard about the spat between Hamish and Jack came over to sympathise with Jack and tell him not to take Hamish too seriously.

One or two others huddled in a corner talking darkly about incomers and the trouble that they always seemed to cause.

Closing time arrived and Catriona offered Jack his lift home. He was in his usual dilemma as to whether to make another move on the barmaid, but had again come to the conclusion that discretion was the best policy. He told himself that he was playing a long game. In fact he was held back by a mixture of conscience and fear that any precipitate move might spoil a lovely friendship.

As the car approached Jack's cottage he let out a groan: "Oh, no!"

Catriona declared: "Oh my god."

The front wall of the cottage had been daubed in black paint with the highly original slogan: "FUCK OFF ENGLISH SCUM".

The car stopped and both Jack and Catriona got out.

"This is terrible, really terrible," said Catriona. "This is Hamish's doing. I'm sure of it."

"I wonder if Sophie knows about it?" said Jack.

"I should come in with you. If she's upset I might be able to help," said Catriona.

"Yes. Please do," said Jack, opening the front door.

They looked around the cottage and Jack decided that Sophie must be in bed. He went into the bedroom and turned on the light. She was awakened by that and greeted him.

"Now don't get upset, my love," said Jack. "But something not very nice has happened."

He explained about the graffiti and Sophie, who was in her nightdress, leapt out of bed, dashed past Catriona and went outside.

"That's horrible. Absolutely horrible," she said. "We must call the police."

"I'll call them now," said Jack and he went straight inside to the telephone and dialled 999.

While he was on the phone, Catriona explained to Sophie what had happened in the hotel earlier that night. She said she was sure that Hamish was the only person who would have done something like this.

"That horrible, horrible man," said Sophie. "He wants putting away. Poor Nigel and Stella. I can understand now how dreadful they felt when it happened to them."

Catriona said: "It's all down to this wind farm business. But you two have got nothing to do with that."

"We've been so careful not to take sides," said a tearful Sophie.

The two women went back into the cottage where Jack had completed his call to the police. He had been told that someone would be with them soon.

Catriona asked where the kettle was and insisted on making a cup of tea. When that job was done the three of them sat down as they waited for the police to arrive. Catriona was at her most empathetic. She instinctively knew that it was necessary to express high dudgeon about the enormity of the deed that had been done and the wickedness of the man who had perpetrated it. But she was unable to banish totally the essentially sunny side of her nature and made skilful efforts to convince Jack and Sophie to look on the bright side.

"They will surely put him away this time and that should put a stop to a lot of this nastiness. No one will agree with what Hamish has done and you will get a lot of sympathy in the village.

"We are a Christian island and actions like this will not be tolerated."

Jack had not seen this earnest side to Catriona before and it further endeared her to him. She was the full rounded package that a human being should be. He felt rather ashamed that his main interest in her so far had been about her bright face and pretty body. Now he was in love with her whole person.

There was a knock at the door. Jack opened it to the redoubtable duo of Police Sgt John Duncan and Pc Adam Flounce.

"A rum business this, sir," said Duncan.

"A rum business indeed," echoed Flounce.

"Come in," said Jack.

"Didn't we meet before?" said Duncan. "At Mr Tavistock's house?"

"We did," said Jack.

"Aye. It's a rum business. And the same words on the wall."

256

"Exactly the same words," said Flounce.

"And we may be thinking it may be the same culprit."

"Aye, the same culprit."

Sgt Duncan asked Jack when and in what circumstances he had discovered the graffiti. Were either Jack or his wife members of SPAT and did anyone bear any grudges against them?

Jack related the story about his very own spat with Hamish at the Blackhill.

Sgt Duncan took down statements from Jack, Catriona and Sophie, while Pc Flounce busied himself taking photographs of the crime scene.

At the end of the interviews, Sgt Duncan explained that there were already matters outstanding regarding Hamish. He faced charges over the graffiti incident at the Tavistocks' house. As a result of a fracas during his arrest he had been further charged with assaulting a police officer, the unfortunate Pc Flounce.

"He's got a bad record," revealed Sgt Duncan. "He has seen the inside of a prison before because of his vile temper. He could go down again this time."

"Aye. He's heading for prison again this time," commented Pc Flounce.

Jack and Sophie agreed that this was no more than Hamish deserved.

Even Catriona, who served Hamish in the Blackhill several times a week, nodded her approval: "Aye. He's had it coming for some time, I'm afraid."

The officers took their leave. In a quaint sort of way they were a very reassuring couple – throwbacks to an age when the "service" in "police service" still meant something.

Having received heartfelt thanks for her support and kindness, Catriona left shortly afterwards.

The feelings of reassurance felt by Jack and Sophie, though, were short-lived. They both felt as if they had been hit in the stomach. They had this sinking feeling that their dream of a happy life on Skye had been brutally taken away from them. And it was all so unjust.

They had both tried to be diplomatic about the wind farm, which had been quite easy as neither of them had any strong views or axe to grind on the subject. And yet they had managed to upset people from both pro and anti-wind farm groups with spectacularly dramatic results.

Within the space of a few days Jack had managed to upset the former secretary of the anti-wind farm group - making him so angry that he had smashed someone's window and got himself arrested. Then they had so upset the victim of the window smashing incident that he had felt furious enough to daub their cottage with obscene graffiti.

"It's all over," said Jack. "We might as well sell up now and go back to England. There's no way we can be accepted in this community after all this."

"It's so unfair," said Sophie. "We've done nothing to deserve this. I'm feeling as bad about it as you are. We may as well pack it all in now."

They were side by side on the settee. Jack put his arm around his wife to comfort her and they sat in sad silence for half an hour.

Secretly they were having very differing thoughts. Jack could not contemplate leaving Skye because it would mean leaving Catriona. Sophie knew that Jamie would be leaving the island in a day or two, so Skye would not have such a hold on her.

But then, as they lay in bed later, an intriguing idea presented itself to her. At one time they had thought about living in Inverness. Could she perhaps suggest a compromise move to there? It was not far from the Black Isle, opening up the possibility of carrying on her affair with Jamie.

Such are the wild thoughts that go through people's heads in the feverish turns of the night, usually to be dismissed as idle fantasies in the cold rational light of day.

****

Morning came and there was no time for idle speculations. The priority was to clean the graffiti from the front of the house.

No practical man, Jack rang Nigel Tavistock to ask how he had removed the offensive words from his property.

Nigel was shocked to learn the news. He knew full well that Jack was ambivalent about wind farms and was mortified that people should have been attacked who had only a slight friendship with him.

He was even more upset when Jack told him he was contemplating selling up and going away.

"We can't let them win," said Nigel. "We must fight these bully boys."

Nigel, noted for being urbane and measured, though loud, in his manner of speech, said this with such a force of conviction that it had the effect of putting the mettle back into Jack. He was no wimp. He must not give up either.

Nigel gave Jack the phone number of the painter and decorator who had removed his graffiti and Jack was straight on to the man to make the arrangements. He stressed the urgency of wiping the shame from the cottage and the painter had the job completed by lunchtime. This was unusual for Skye where workmen's "today" can often mean next week, or next month.

During the morning Nigel and Stella came round to show solidarity and express sympathy with their neighbours.

At first it appeared that their kind errand was not being exactly helpful, as Stella became almost hysterical as she ranted about what she would like to do to Hamish and what she thought about Skye people generally.

She began to beg Nigel that they should sell up and leave Scotland for good. Nigel tried to comfort her. He told her not to worry and that everything would change once the wind farm planning application had been determined. But his slightly patronising manner made her angrier and even more distressed because she thought he was not taking her seriously enough.

Jack and Sophie listened quietly as the couple argued about their own future on the island. However, Stella's emotional pleadings had the opposite effect on them than might have been expected. She might have convinced them that leaving the island was the only alternative for both couples. But in fact they were much more impressed by Nigel's argument that most of their troubles would be over once the planners had decided on the wind farm.

Nigel was becoming increasingly embarrassed by Stella's behaviour and decided it was time to leave.

"I'm so sorry," said a tearful Stella to Jack and Sophie. "You didn't need this from me when you have your own problems. I apologise."

Sophie put her arms around Stella and kissed her, telling her not to worry.

Jack shook hands with Nigel and thanked him for coming round. He told him he would keep in touch with any news about Hamish.

Not long after Nigel and Stella had left Pc Flounce arrived at the cottage.

Jack showed him in. The constable appeared to be in an excitable, rather nervy, state.

"Just come to put you in the picture," he said. "Terrible night last night, terrible. Sgt Duncan's at the hospital. Broken nose. Really terrible.

"Anyway you want to know what happened.

"We went from here to Hamish's house and he came out of the front door fighting. Called us all the names under the sun and thrashed about with his fists when we tried to put the cuffs on him. His arms were flailing about and he caught Sgt Duncan on the nose. Probably didn't mean to do it but he did it. He's going to get the book thrown at him this time. Could go down for six months, I should think. Poor Johnny – Sgt Duncan I mean. I should have done more to help him. But Hamish is a big man. He gets uncontrollable. Anyway he'll get his comeuppance this time. We'll throw the book at him – criminal damage, breach of the peace, assault on a police officer. It's not fair on you folk. Not fair on Mr and Mrs Tavistock. Nice people. Don't deserve this. You neither."

Sophie thought Pc Flounce needed to calm down. She offered him a cup of tea.

"Aye. I'll take a cup of tea," said Flounce.

The excitable but dedicated constable gave a detailed explanation of what would happen next from the legal standpoint and politely took his leave.

"I rather think that Hamish is in a spot of bother," concluded Jack sardonically.

Chapter thirteen Revelations

SALLY McConnell opened her door to the dishevelled figure of Sarah Carmichael.

Sarah looked drawn and black around the eyes, her hair even more straggly than normal and her pink tie-dye teeshirt and white jeans stained with the remains of several meals and a few bottles of red wine.

By contrast Sally looked like the stereotypical Scottish country lady, dressed in sensible tartan jacket, a white blouse and black trousers.

Usually a friendly and homely soul, she gave Sarah a frosty, disapproving look.

"I suppose you had better come in," she said.

Sarah thanked her.

Sally led her into the sitting room where Iain was in his armchair. He beckoned her to sit in an identical chair facing him.

"You're not to upset him," said Sally. "He's still not at all well."

"I'll try," said Sarah. "But I can tell you that I'm not happy – not happy at all. How could you do this, Iain? Send Jamie away like this?"

"I'm sorry. Truly sorry," said Iain. "But after what happened what else could I have done?"

Sarah started to become agitated: "It wasn't all his fault, you know. There's two of you in this story."

"I know. I know," said Iain. "But what was I to do?"

"You should have done the right thing all those years ago," snapped Sarah. "But, no. You put your sacred reputation before anything else. Before me. Before Jamie."

Sally stood silently in the background, holding back tears.

She had found out just a few days previously that her husband had a huge skeleton in his cupboard. He had revealed that years ago he had fathered a love-child - Jamie Carmichael.

Sally had not been on the scene at that time – she was his second wife. But he had been determined his affair with Sarah should not wreck his first marriage to Norah, a woman he dearly loved. She was to be kept completely in the dark.

He had secretly paid for a plot of land next to the Breaganish House Hotel and bought Sarah a caravan where she could live with her son. Only his best friends, the Carltons, from the hotel, were privy to what was happening.

Iain had agreed to pay all Sarah's living costs on the condition that she kept the arrangement secret and did not reveal to a soul who Jamie's father was.

She had kept her word, even though on occasions when she had been on drink or drugs she had come perilously close to letting the cat out of the bag. Even Jamie was not told about Iain. He was led to believe that his father was a man his mother had met briefly at university and lost contact with.

Nevertheless Iain had had many a sleepless night worrying that Sarah would let him down.

However, this had not stopped him from continuing to visit Sarah while Jamie was out at school. He could easily slip out of the hotel grounds and into her caravan.

Everything changed when Norah died of cancer at the age of 35.

Sarah thought her time had come. She was fully expecting that, after a decent interval, Iain would take her and Jamie into his home as his wife and then publicly acknowledged son. And Iain had done little to dispel this belief.

But he prevaricated. He had become an elder of the church and had a reputation for respectability which he was desperate not to lose.

The "decent interval" of time stretched to two years and then he had news for Sarah which left her feeling bereft and bitter. He had met a homely and pleasant widow called Sally at church and he had proposed to her.

Sarah had always taken drugs and drunk too much. Now she doubled her intake and her behaviour became increasingly erratic.

She was still attractive in a dissolute sort of way and had a strange witch-like allure. Although her behaviour was a source of raised eyebrows and gossip she was nevertheless a popular figure in the area. Her free spirit made people laugh. Some churchgoing women secretly envied her highly individualistic lifestyle. Some of their husbands secretly fancied her.

Highland people can take anyone to their hearts if they have integrity – and they felt Sarah had that in spades.

As soon as Iain told her he was intending to remarry he had a permanent dread that she would beat a path to Sally's door and tell her everything.

But Sarah, a highly intelligent and shrewd woman beneath her scattiness, managed to contain her bitterness. She was too proud to go grovelling to Iain in an effort to persuade him to give up Sally and she had a depth of humanity which held her back from revealing her situation to Sally herself.

So she came up with a plan. Jamie was about to leave school, where he had under-achieved, being more interested in girls, fishing and films than in schoolwork. He needed a job and Sarah hit upon the idea that Iain was the obvious man to give him one.

Although he had a tendency to be selfish, Iain was at heart a decent man. When Sarah suggested her scheme to him he clearly stated he did not need to be cajoled or threatened to give Jamie a job. He genuinely wanted to help his son and to do so would lift some of his feelings of guilt.

So Jamie went to work for his father, although he still had no idea of the relationship. Iain was kind to him and gave him a responsible job on the estate. But Sarah was at least correct in one of her observations: Iain was the proverbial careful Scotsman and was rather parsimonious when it came to pay packets.

Iain tried hard to befriend Jamie. He took him fishing and shooting and taught him the skills of gamekeeping. He spent so much time with him that there was even a scurrilous rumour among other farm staff that Iain was grooming the young man for a homosexual relationship.

But the friendship was largely a one-sided one. Jamie was cold and morose and Iain found it difficult to engage him in any conversation beyond the immediate requirements of work.

Life went on in much the same way for 18 years.

Iain had become accustomed to visiting the Carltons at the Breaganish House Hotel every Thursday night. Occasionally he would sneak out the back of the hotel to visit Sarah in her caravan.

There was no sex now, just financial arrangements.

On one fine night Iain had made one of those visits and found Sarah in a drunken and aggressive mood. She loudly complained to him about the poor wages he paid to Jamie, especially remembering that he was his father.

Iain protested that he already paid Jamie more than anyone else working for the estate. If he were to increase his pay any further it would arouse the ire and suspicions of other workers. It might even resurrect the rumours about a homosexual relationship which over the years had become discredited.

Worse still, suggested Iain, it might lead Jamie himself to question why he was being so generously treated compared with his colleagues.

This infuriated Sarah. She raged at Iain, saying that he should have acknowledged Jamie as his son from the very start. He had treated them both cruelly.

Iain stepped out of his normal character and lost his temper, telling Sarah that a man in his position could not afford to be associated with "a drug-taking, drunken slut".

Sarah screamed and then writhed on the floor, wailing uncontrollably. Iain left the caravan and dashed back to the hotel. He went straight to the toilets, tidied up his smart countryman's attire, composed himself and then went into the bar to suggest a game of snooker to Mr

Carlton. He told his friend nothing about the row with Sarah.

It was midnight by the time that Iain set off along the shore of Loch Breaganish on his homeward journey. It was a beautiful fine night, with the moon and stars shining brightly. The lights of distant houses at Upper Beindow could be seen clearly. Iain still used a torch to find his way along the path which was a mixture of grass, large stones, shingle and sand, severed at intervals by rivulets of water.

He woke up a day later in the trauma ward of Broadford Hospital.

Sally, of course, was told the story of how Jamie had found her husband and run for help. When she was told that he was being interviewed by police as a suspect she was incredulous. Although she had never particularly liked Jamie, she had no reason to doubt his loyalty to Iain and knew of no reason why he should wish to attack him.

The local people she spoke to were adamant that Jamie would not have done such a treacherous deed. He was popular among the women of the area who were more than willing to overlook his dour demeanour and instead quite happy to gossip about his good looks and manliness. A number of fathers had had reason to complain about his callous casting aside of their daughters. And one or two husbands bore him ill-will as a result of past relationships with their wives. But because Jamie had been born in the neighbourhood and attended the local schools he was very much "one of their own".

The supporters of the wind farm were quick to jump to the conclusion that "outsiders" opposed to the scheme were responsible for the attack on Iain, as the landowner who would primarily benefit from it.

Sally was soon made aware of these suspicions and she believed them.

But then came the turning point – Iain's confession to her about his relationship to Jamie.

As he related the story about what had happened that night, immediately prior to the attack, a dreadful thought began to form in Sally's head. His attacker must have been either Jamie or Sarah.

When she suggested this to Iain, he had paused for what seemed like minutes and then replied: "That is exactly the conclusion I have reached myself."

"Then we must tell the police," said Sally. "Straightaway."

"No," said Iain firmly.

"Why on earth not?" asked Sally agitatedly.

"For the same reasons I have kept my secret all these years," said Iain. "I could not bear the shame of it all."

"But your shame pales into insignificance compared with what has been done to you," said Sally. "You were very nearly murdered. Even now you will never be the same man again.

"You wanted to keep Jamie a secret from me. But now you've told me you're his father. There's nothing more to fear from me. I'll not be leaving you. You may have humiliated Norah by what you did, but not me. It's too long ago to have much effect on me.

"I can't say I'm happy. I thought I'd married a respectable, decent man, a much better man than my first husband and a much better man than most others around here. But I was wrong. You are no better.

"But you're no worse either. Just another sinner, like we all are, I suppose. At least that's what the Bible tells us.

"But there's a much bigger sinner here – the sinner who nearly murdered you. You must out them. It's your civic duty if nothing else. If they could do this to you they could do it to someone else.

"If it's that Sarah who did this – well we all know she's a madwoman, addled with drink and I don't know what else. She needs locking away before she does kill someone.

"If it's Jamie, then he's a danger. I never did like that boy. Always so taciturn. Always going about with a knife or a gun in his hand. I know he's a gamekeeper, but I've always thought he goes about looking like someone out of a Wild West film. I've told you so before, but you just brushed it aside.

"What was he doing hanging about on the lochside at midnight? I know what he said. He'd just finished fishing. From what I've been told there's seldom a fish of any size to be caught in the Black Burn, or in the loch for that matter. No fish big enough to keep a man out of his bed at midnight. There's much bigger fish to be caught in your own lochans, which he had access to. It doesn't make sense.

"I see it now. I would bet they were both in on it - Jamie and his weird mother. You've got to tell the police. Bring them to justice."

"They will have justice enough when they meet their Maker," said Iain. "We surely don't want our dirty linen washed in public. No - not *our* dirty linen. *My* dirty linen. You certainly don't deserve all this. You have truly been a godsend to me.

"Call me a coward if you like. Because that's what I am and always have been.

"I should have accepted Jamie as my son from the start, confessed everything to Norah. But I was too scared. Even when Norah died I was still too scared. About my reputation.

"Many round here still think of me as the laird. They probably never use that word, but that is in truth how they see me. They look up to me, just as they looked up to my father and my grandfather before me. I felt I could not besmirch their good name – the good name of McConnell, which has been a good name for centuries here.

"I know I was wrong and I know I'm wrong in what I'm going to tell you now. I'm not going to the police. I daren't have all this come out. And I feel deep down that I have deserved what happened to me that night. If Sally or Jamie, or both of them, attacked me then I think that was what the Almighty wished to see happen. It was the wages of my sin and they were just the agents chosen to bring my Retribution.

"No. I won't go to the police."

"You're a stupid pigheaded man then, Iain McConnell," chided Sally. "It's not for you to decide what is or what isn't God's will. I'm as religious as the next woman but you're just using this Old Testament stuff to justify your lack of backbone.

"I know you've been through an awful lot these past months. But even I didn't know you'd become this weak in the head. However you try to wrap it up, you know as well as I do the difference between right and wrong. And what was done to you that night was wrong. Far more wicked than anything you have done to them.

"Yes, you will have to answer to God for what you have done. But they must be made to answer to Man first, and then their Maker later. That's the law of the land. And we are the sort of people who obey the law of the land."

"You are right. I know you are right. But I can't do it. I can't do it because I am scared about the consequences for myself. And I can't do it because I have wronged those two people, Sarah and Jamie, enough already. When all's said and done, I'm not absolutely sure who hit me that night. It might not have been either of them."

"But who else could it have been?" asked Sally.

"There are those who have said it was the anti-wind farm brigade," replied Iain, weakly.

"I did once fall for that idea," said Sally. "But when you think more about it, it doesn't make sense does it? Killing you wouldn't have put an end to the wind farm, would it? The electricity company would have approached me as your widow and I would have signed up for it. It doesn't add up. But revenge by Sally and Jamie – that adds up."

"I fear you are right, dear," said Iain, wearily. "But it makes no difference. I will not go to the police. Please let that be the end of it. I couldn't bear it if we were to fall out about this."

Sally knew it was time to withdraw. She shrugged her shoulders and walked towards the door through to the kitchen.

"I'll start to prepare dinner then," she said, in an irritable tone.

But she did not prepare dinner. She walked through the kitchen and out of the back door, across the crew yard of the farm which was adjacent to the house and towards the shed where Jamie kept his gamekeeper's equipment. It was approaching 5pm and she knew that this was the time when Jamie was about to finish work for the day. His routine was to visit the shed to drop off any tools or other materials and park up whatever farm vehicle he might have been using during the day, usually either an old red

Ford Escort van or a smart new quad bike.

He drew up in the van just as Sally reached the shed and he got out.

"Hello, Mrs McConnell," he said.

"Hello, Jamie," said Sally. "Come inside the shed a minute. I need to talk to you."

Jamie could see from her manner that she had serious business to discuss.

Once inside the shed she looked at him hard in the face.

"I know that you are Iain's son."

Jamie winced ever so slightly.

"I am pleased you know," he said.

"I also know that it was either you or your mother who attacked Iain."

It was Jamie's turn to stare into Sally's face, his pupils strangely dilated.

"Not my mother," he said.

"You then?" said Sally.

"I loved that man. I thought he was the only real friend I had ever had. Sometimes I thought that he treated me like I imagined a father would treat a son. I wasn't sure about that, because I had never had a father. But he was good to me.

"But then I found it was all a lie. He was good to me because he had a bad conscience. I hated him then and I needed to take my revenge. I could have left him for dead that night. But then I thought of my own skin. I didn't want to spend the rest of my life in prison. Like father, like son, eh? Both too scared to take the consequences of their actions.

"I've thought about that since. We are really no better than each other. Both afraid to face up to what we've done."

"You could have killed him," said Sally. "You are little short of a murderer. It was only through the grace of God that you are not a murderer."

"I know," said Jamie. "But I had to do something. For my mother's sake, but most of all for my sake. No-one crosses me. No-one."

Jamie's countenance changed as he said this. The look of a flawed human being, a wounded animal even, suddenly changed to the face of a cold-blooded killer. Sally sensed it and felt herself shudder.

But she was a strong woman, this homely churchgoing widow and second wife. She was not going to be intimidated. She ploughed on with the purpose of her meeting.

"How did you find out that you were Iain's son?"

"It wasn't until that night. I was calling on my mother. When I got to her caravan I heard noises from inside – a row going on. I listened at the door and I heard my mother pleading with Mr McConnell to do something to help his – his son Jamie. She was screaming and he was shouting at her to 'shut up'. Then he flung the door open and charged past, walking towards the hotel.

"I was behind the door as he flung it open and he didn't see me. He was in too much of a temper and a hurry to get away, I guess.

"I went in to see my mother and she was lying flat on her back, crying her heart out. When she composed herself she told me the whole story, about how Mr McConnell had abandoned us both. I was angry and full of hate. I wanted to make him pay. I went to the hotel and looked through the windows to see if he was there.

"For a while I didn't see anything. But then I saw him and Mr Carlton in the snooker room, playing snooker. It made me hate him even more. Poncing around playing snooker with that toffee-nosed Carlton bloke - the laird at play - while my mother was left in her shitty caravan crying her eyes out. And me, who was I? A low-paid lackey grateful for a tiny cottage and a few crumbs from the master's table."

Sally butted in: "So you are jealous of Iain? It doesn't surprise me. Your mother once accosted me in the Co-op when she was drunk. She started to tell me we landowners were all wicked capitalists and that come the socialist revolution it would all change. We would be 'for it'."

Jamie said: "No. My mother talks crap. I want to be the laird. I want to inherit Mr McConnell's estate as his rightful son and heir. I want to make more money out of the estate than he has ever done. Fill it full of wind turbines for all I care. If it's money in the bank, then that's what I want."

Sally wished that she had not mentioned the Co-op incident. It had deflected Jamie from his confessional.

"So you saw Iain at the hotel," she interjected.

"Yes. I was livid. I was determined to hurt him – to fucking kill him if I'm honest."

Jamie did not say any more for a while. Sally had been surprised by the uncharacteristic animation and passion in his conversation so far. She did not want him to go back into his usual shell until he had told her everything.

"So what did you do?" she asked.

"I knew he would walk home along the lochside. I had seen him there several times and he told me he had been playing snooker at the hotel. So I went home, found a piece of heavy wood which used to be part of a fence post and went down to the loch's edge. I took my fishing tackle with me so that if anyone happened to see me it would appear that I was innocently fishing.

"I waited for him. When I heard him walking along I came up behind him and whacked him on the back of the head. He went down on the ground, unconscious.

"Mr McConnell was lying quite a distance from the pool, too far away for me to have seen his body if I had been fishing from there. So I dragged him to the burn, nearer to the pool. Then I used my landing net to scuff up the sand and pebbles so nobody would notice any tracks through them."

Jamie paused again.

Sally became impatient.

"So then what did you do?"

"I ran for help – to Catriona's."

"And you told the police you had found Iain there when you were fishing?"

"Yes.

"What happened to the piece of wood?" asked Sally. "The police said they couldn't find any weapon?"

Jamie grinned an evil grin.

"I went back to my cottage straightaway and threw the piece of wood way into the trees at the back of my house. I had thought of throwing it in the loch, but I knew it would get washed up by the tide and the police might find it."

Sally erupted in fury: "So you are telling me that you left Iain unconscious while you went back to your cottage and got rid of the weapon. He could have died five times over while you were doing all that!"

Jamie replied coldly: "I did what I had to do, to save my skin. Covered my tracks. Just like Mr McConnell would have done. Like father, like son."

Sally was repelled by this argument. How could anyone have behaved so callously? This had not been genuine anger. It had been a cold and calculated act. She told Jamie so.

"Was it not cold and calculated when Mr McConnell abandoned the mother of his child and his new-born son and kept them secret for decades? That wasn't anger was it? It was a plan that was hatched in cold blood with no remorse ever shown. And it has left me as I am – unloving, cold, friendless and, yes, I admit it, ruthless.

"But if it were to come out – all of this. Who would gain the most sympathy do you think? The heartless landowner who had abandoned his mistress and baby, deceived his two wives and had the hypocrisy to set himself up as an elder of the church - or the poor baby himself, abandoned, robbed of his rightful inheritance and then, in a moment of unaccustomed anger, avenging his poor abandoned mother who he had seen on her back screaming after being abused by that landowner?"

Sally fell silent. She believed that what she had just heard was a travesty. How could any sane person put the cold-blooded near murder of a respected, largely decent, human being on an equal footing in the scale of morality with the everyday dilemma of a man fathering a child out of wedlock and keeping it secret?

But notwithstanding this revulsion, her easy solution of going to the police suddenly did not seem as straightforward. This young man was dangerous and wicked and yet he had some legitimate claim of grievance.

"I'll talk to Iain," she said to him. "And then I'll talk to you again."

"I hope you are going to see me all right," said Jamie.

"After what you have done?" replied Sally sharply.

"I am his only son," said Jamie. "I was his only son before you were his wife. I am owed some inheritance. Ask Mr McConnell to think about that."

Sally did not answer. As she was leaving the shed she thought she heard Jamie mutter: "I have plenty of pieces of wood in my garden."

This chilling message sent her head into a spin. She thought she was going to faint as she made her way back to the house. But she managed to get to the sitting room and slump into an armchair.

Iain, who was sitting in his accustomed chair opposite, said: "My dear, you look as white as a sheet. Whatever is the matter?"

Sally told him what had occurred. At first he was inwardly annoyed that she had taken it upon herself to tackle Jamie. But his concern for her shocked state over-rode that feeling and he listened patiently to her story.

The couple spent several hours going over the facts and debating what should be done.

Eventually they agreed a plan of action.

Iain was to give Jamie a sum of £100,000 as a recognition of their kinship. On Iain's death he would receive a further sum of £100,000. The residue of the estate would be left to Sally. There would be no recourse to the police.

Sally was adamant that Jamie should no longer work for the estate. She said she would never feel comfortable again to have him close at hand. Therefore Iain would use his landowner contacts to find him employment elsewhere. Jamie would be asked to swear to keep secret his relationship to Iain and the financial settlement that had been offered.

He would tell his mother that he and Iain had had a heated argument about pay, during which Jamie had revealed that he knew Iain was his father. He would say that Sally had overheard this conversation and demanded that Jamie be sacked and sent away so that no-one else would ever know the truth about the relationship.

Jamie was called to the house and agreed to these terms. He was soon found a job on the Black Isle.

This was what had happened in the days before Sarah paid her visit to the McConnells.

As she drunkenly berated Iain for his treatment of Jamie – "sending him away" – Sally could hold her tongue no longer.

"You stupid woman!" she scolded. "Jamie is the luckiest man alive. He could be spending a very long time in prison now if it wasn't for Iain's forbearance."

Sarah swung round to face her, bared her teeth and cried out: "What are you talking about woman? What's this rubbish?"

"You know exactly what I'm talking about," replied Sally.

"Prison? Why would Jamie be in prison? That boy's a good boy."

"He nearly killed my husband. That's how good a boy he is. And he has all but threatened to do the same thing again."

Sarah slumped against a sideboard and put her head in her hands. She was in tears.

"What do you mean 'nearly killed' Iain. When? How?"

"The attack by the loch. You must have known that Jamie did it," said Sally.

"You're saying that was Jamie. You cow."

"He admitted it to me."

"I don't believe you. Jamie wouldn't do such a thing. You're just trying to blacken his name because you're jealous of me – because I've had a child with Iain, something you could never have."

Sarah's voice became increasingly shrill and threatened to descend into hysterics.

Iain held her by the shoulders, firmly but gently.

"It's true, my dear. You can ask Jamie yourself."

Sarah looked up at Iain and beat him on the chest with her clenched fists.

That released the tension which had been building up inside her and she became calmer.

"Say, for a moment, that what you're saying is true. Why does he have to go away? I'm sure he could be persuaded not to tell anyone about any of this. He certainly wouldn't go around telling people that he had attacked you."

Iain explained that Sally was frightened of Jamie and would feel uneasy if he continued to work for the estate.

Sarah protested that Jamie was not a violent person and the attack – if he was the attacker – would have been a "one-off".

Sally intervened: "He's threatened to do the same thing again."

Sarah burst into tears and screamed: "Not my Jamie. He wouldn't. I know he wouldn't."

"I can't risk that," said Iain. "He nearly killed me once. If he loses his rag he could have another go."

Sarah pleaded: "Please, please, don't send him away. Let me talk to him. Let me make him promise that he will behave. I know he's not the most loving person in the world. I know he can be cold and heartless sometimes. But he's all I have. I can't live without him. Please, please, let him keep his job."

Iain replied in measured tones, which suggested he would allow no further argument: "I am sorry – really sorry. But I can't have Sally living in a state of fear. I owe that to her."

Sarah had composed herself by now. The shock of what she had been told had sobered her up.

In a controlled and deliberate manner, equal to that of Iain's, she said: "Very well. I see that, yet again, all the fucking cards are stacked against me. You have beaten me again. I just ask one further thing of you, Iain."

"What is that?" asked Iain.

"That you buy me a proper house, somewhere near where Jamie is going to work. I know he would never want to live with me. I don't think anyone would want to live with me. But find me somewhere nearby and I will never bother you again."

"More money," snapped Sally. "How much are you two going to get out of Iain?"

"We are his son and his son's mother. Why shouldn't we have our dues?"

"What about the injuries which Jamie inflicted on Iain? Is there to be no compensation for that?"

"Some would say he deserved those injuries. Being a pacifist I could not agree. But there were, as the courts would no doubt understand, extenuating circumstances. Just grant me this one last wish and you need never see me or hear from me again. The madwoman would be out of your life forever."

Iain looked over to Sally with a look of withering desperation. She shrugged her shoulders and mouthed the words: "It's up to you."

"All right, all right, Sarah. I'll do what you wish," said Iain.

Chapter fourteen
Appeasement

TWO DAYS after the graffiti incident, Jack was driving through Beindow on his way to Portree when he saw Hamish standing at the front gate of his cottage. This took him a little by surprise as he had naively thought his tormentor would be in jail somewhere.

When he later gave the matter further thought he realised it was likely that Hamish would have been released on bail.

What really disturbed Jack, though, was that through his driver's mirror he saw Ronnie McColl's Range Rover pull up outside the cottage.

As Jack drove along he turned over in his mind the events surrounding the graffiti attack. He remembered what Archie had told him about Ronnie's visit to the Blackhill Hotel. It had been Ronnie who had told Hamish about Jack's fishing trip with Nigel Tavistock and his friends.

Now Ronnie was visiting Hamish so soon after his release from the cells.

The two of them must be in cahoots, he deduced. He pondered on the idea of telling the police about this theory, but by the time he pulled up in the main square at Portree he had talked himself out of this course of action.

He knew Ronnie was something of a big cheese in the area. To make an enemy out of him would alienate many other people in this close-knit community.

Jack had strong principles and a clear perception of right and wrong. But he disliked confrontation and was inclined to be one of life's appeasers – more of a Lord Halifax than a Winston Churchill.

In his youth he had read Lateral Thinking by Edward De Bono and it had transformed his outlook on life. He often applied its principles to everyday problems, i. e. if digging one hole deeper and deeper does not achieve the result you are looking for then give up that hole and start a new hole somewhere else.

Applying this technique to his present predicament he believed it would be futile to keep upsetting those local people who were fanatically wedded to the wind farm project. It would be far better to persuade them of his true views on the issue, i. e. he had no strong opinion at all.

Jack decided his new hole would be a fox-hole. He would try to fix up a face to face meeting with Ronnie McColl.

287

After doing some shopping and visiting the public library which is shared with Portree High School, he made his way back to Beindow. He drove up the well maintained tree-lined private road which led to Ronnie's home and office.

He parked up and then approached a door at the side of the house which bore the silver lettering "Portree Estates". He walked inside and there found Ronnie's wife Morag sitting at her husband's desk.

The hospitable lady flashed him a welcoming smile and asked what she could do to help. Jack nervously explained that this was not exactly a business call, but it did indirectly concern the wind farm scheme and it was important that he saw Mr McColl as soon as possible.

Morag started to explain that her husband was out at present when there was a crackling noise from the gravel car parking area and Ronnie's Range Rover arrived.

Ronnie, looking smart in a sharp dark suit and wearing designer sunglasses, entered the office. His wife explained that a gentleman wished to speak with him.

Ronnie smiled weakly and offered his hand to Jack: "You're the writer from over at Breaganish aren't you?"

"Yes. Jack Easter."

"What can I do for you, Mr Easter?"

"I expect you have heard about what happened at my cottage a couple of days ago."

"I did hear something about some rude words being daubed on your cottage. A nasty business."

"I have the strong belief that this was something to do with the wind farm and a mistaken view that we – my wife, Sophie, and I – might be among the opponents of the scheme."

"Is that so?" asked Ronnie.

"You probably know that Hamish McDonald was arrested," said Jack.

"I had heard so," said Ronnie.

"He was aggressive towards me in the Blackhill on the very same night that my cottage was attacked."

"Is that so??"

"Yes, it is. And I was told that he was angry with me because you had been telling people that I was friendly with Nigel Tavistock and some of his friends."

"I did mention that I had seen you with Tavistock at the Cuillin Hills."

"If Hamish hadn't known that I don't think he would have attacked my house."

Ronnie paused and folded his arms. Then he said calmly: "I am not sure that Hamish has admitted to that. He gets blamed for a lot of things around here, but he is not as bad as he is painted. And don't forget that he was assaulted himself by the secretary of the anti-wind farm group."

Jack continued: "I'm a great believer in 'innocent until proved guilty' but I have strong reasons to believe that Hamish attacked my home and Nigel Tavistock's as well. But that's not what I am here to talk about.

"What I wish to make clear is that neither Sophie nor myself have anything against wind farms. It is not something we are particularly interested in. Nigel Tavistock is merely a neighbour of ours who has been very welcoming to us. We are happy to make friends with anyone who is friendly to us, whether they are pro-wind farm, anti-wind farm, or, like us, sitting firmly on the fence."

"On the fence, eh?" said Ronnie.

"Yes. Until the iron enters our souls," joked Jack.

Ronnie did not get the joke.

"Why are you telling me this?" he asked.

"Because I understand that you are very prominent in the pro campaign. I would very much appreciate it if you would spread the word among your followers that we are not in any way opposed to your position. Otherwise I fear that life could become hell for us here – a place we love very dearly."

Ronnie replied: "I believe you over-estimate my influence. However, I will be happy to tell people what you have said to me. I can do no more."

Jack thanked him and added: "You know, Skye is one of the most beautiful places in the world. But another reason for its attractiveness is the friendliness of the people here to visitors. I would hate to think that people would be put off from coming here because they heard about disharmony between the people who live here and a mistrust of incomers."

Ronnie looked irritated by that remark.

"You are not suggesting, I hope, that the pro-wind farm campaign is in any way hostile to tourism. It is the mainstay of our economy. We want more people to visit here and more people to live here. You may not have noticed, but I build houses. I want new people to come to the island and buy my houses. The wind farm will be part of an economic regeneration of the island. It will create more economic activity.

"No. It's the Nigel Tavistocks of this world who would hold the island back. They have already got their posh holiday homes with their brilliant views, but they don't want to share the island with other people – not even with the locals who have lived here for years. They would be willing to see our young people leaving the island for good because there are no jobs here – so long as nothing spoils the view from THEIR holiday homes."

Jack was tempted to ask whether it was possible that too great an industrialisation of the countryside might not actually make Skye less attractive to tourists and potential home buyers. But he kept quiet, realising that putting forward such a view would lay himself open to new suspicion that he was in the "anti camp".

Instead he commented weakly: "I think you have a very good point."

"Is there anything else I can do for you?" asked Ronnie, looking at his expensive watch.

"No, thank you. I just wanted to make my position clear in the hope that we can continue to live our lives in this community without any hostility towards us."

Ronnie nodded and then turned to Morag, who had been sitting quietly at his desk.

"Give Mr Easter one of our brochures. He will find them interesting."

Morag handed to Jack a glossy brochure entitled "The Economic Case for Beindow Windfarm".

Jack thanked her, shook hands with Ronnie and left.

As he drove home he had a feeling of some satisfaction. Although he considered Ronnie cold and untrustworthy he thought at least the visit might take some of the pressure off Sophie and himself.

But he realised Ronnie bore such a hatred towards Nigel Tavistock that further friendly contact with the latter might jeopardise the couple's future on the island.

****

When Jack opened the front door of the cottage he immediately heard a familiar patrician voice in conversation with Sophie. The visitor was Nigel Tavistock.

He had come to ask a great favour from Jack.

He explained that, with the resignation of George Saxondale, the SPAT organisation had been left without a secretary. They had also lost the principal propagandist for their cause. SPAT therefore needed a new secretary and publicity officer. Jack's ability as a writer made him an ideal candidate for the role.

Nigel appreciated, of course, that Jack did not share his members' passionate opposition to wind farms. He also fully understood that the graffiti attack might make him unwilling to associate himself with their cause.

But the group was desperate not to lose any momentum in its campaign as the decision on the wind farm could be just a few weeks away.

Nigel's request was Jack's nightmare. He believed that his meeting with Ronnie just might have wiped the slate clean as far as the pro-wind farm group was concerned. If he agreed to be secretary of SPAT all that good work would be undone.

He politely declined Nigel's offer, saying that the graffiti incident had been so traumatic that he would do nothing to encourage further attacks.

Nigel was disappointed but said he understood Jack's qualms.

Sophie, though, incensed by the rape of their home, urged Jack to be brave and stand up to the pro-wind farm bullies. She saw this as yet another example of her husband's tendency to take the line of least resistance, a trait which, in her new feeling of liberation, she found increasingly irritating.

Jack, though, was firm in his policy of appeasement. He was determined not to take sides.

Nigel tried a different tack. He said that Matt Beaton, the wealthy landowner who was backing the SPAT campaign, had expressed a willingness to provide financial support if and when it was necessary. He was sure that Matt would agree to pay a generous honorarium to a suitable new secretary.

Sophie urged Jack to seriously consider that offer. She was not a mercenary person but she had come to like the Tavistocks very much, particularly in view of the support they had shown in the previous few days.

Jack liked the Tavistocks too and his resolve began to weaken slightly. He suggested a compromise. He would not attend SPAT meetings to take the minutes and send out the correspondence etc. But if Nigel would brief him about any publicity that SPAT would like to be issued he would write press releases and other material, which would then be sent out under Nigel's name.

Nigel was satisfied with this suggestion and the meeting ended very amicably over the glass of claret.

When Nigel had gone Jack told Sophie about his meeting with McColl and of his suspicions that the builder had at least stirred up Hamish against them. He thought Sophie would be pleased with the initiative he had shown. But because she was now firmly in the Tavistock camp she was intensely annoyed with him.

"For God's sake show some backbone," she said. "Where has all this 'turning the other cheek' stuff come from? McColl and his gang are a bunch of criminals and here you are sucking up to them. I don't believe you sometimes."

Jack was mortified. Throughout their marriage Sophie had rarely spoken to him in such an aggressive way. The bit about "turning the other cheek" had particularly hit home.

One of the reasons he had always given people for his not being a Christian was that he could not stomach the notion of "turning the other cheek". He thought it flew in the face of human nature. Now he was being accused of the very thing he despised.

Appeasement, which he did advocate, was something different. It meant the cynical realpolitik of accepting where superior power actually lay and accommodating it. But "turning the other cheek" was a pathetic denial of using the power which one had available.

The couple argued vehemently, but not for long. That was not their way. What was done was done and that was it.

****

Jack felt nervous when he next went on one of his regular evening visits to the Blackhill. He was unsure of the reception he might receive. Would Hamish be there? And would others take a similarly aggressive line in view of Jack's friendship with Nigel Tavistock?

As he went past reception Mrs Maclean was perched on her usual high stool poring over some accounts and made some grumpy remarks about local traders being slow in presenting their bills. But then when she looked up and realised it was Jack she was talking to, her demeanour changed.

"Oh, be quiet, woman," she said. "You'll not be wishing to hear about my problems. It appears you may have plenty of your own."

Jack knew this was a reference to the graffiti, but not wishing to appear to be a drama queen, he merely looked at her in a questioning way.

"I've heard about what that moron Hamish did to your cottage. I've banned him, of course – for this week anyway. I expect he'll be back."

Jack would normally have found such inconsistency difficult to fathom out. But he knew Skye people well enough by now to realise that they had a limitless capacity for Christian forgiveness.

He told Mrs Maclean that he and Sophie were made of sterner stuff than to be dwelling on the graffiti incident. This was hardly the truth but he knew it was what a tough cookie like Myrtle Maclean would like to hear.

When he looked around the bar on his entrance, Jack at first thought that his worst nightmare had come true. For not only were all the usual regulars in the bar, including the voluminous figure of Archie Beaton, but sitting in one corner talking together were Ronnie McColl AND Hamish McDonald!

Ronnie nodded seriously when he saw Jack, while Hamish just stared into his whisky glass.

Archie and his drinking companions at the bar welcomed Jack in the same friendly manner as usual, although Archie kept throwing nervous glances in Hamish's direction as if expecting some eruption from that body.

Behind the bar was the chirpy presence of Catriona accompanied by the quiet, businesslike Mr Maclean.

Catriona looked as alluring as ever in a bright flowered blouse and tight white slacks. She greeted Jack cheerfully and immediately started to pour his accustomed tipple – a pint of Black Cuillin beer.

After exchanging a few pleasantries with her, Jack whispered that he had been told that Hamish had been barred from the hotel.

Catriona whispered back that Mrs Maclean had indeed banned the big man but that her husband had turned a blind eye when he saw Hamish arriving with Ronnie McColl.

Jack was angry when he heard that. It seemed that no-one was willing to get on the wrong side of Ronnie. As he pondered on whether to leave the bar, partly in protest at the management's weakness, and partly because he was frightened of what Hamish might do next, Mrs Maclean appeared.

Her husband looked sheepish and pretended not to notice she was there. But all that was in vain. Mrs Maclean declared loudly: "I told you I did not want that man in my bar!"

Then she strode over to Hamish and shouted: "Out!"

Hamish grumbled and looked over to Ronnie in a plea for him to intervene on his behalf.

But Ronnie just said: "I think you had better go, old man."

Mrs Maclean stood hands on hips waiting for her command to be obeyed. Hamish hastily finished his drink, uttered an expletive and made his exit.

Mrs Maclean shouted over to her husband: "I'll deal with you later" and exited herself in the direction of the reception.

An unnatural silence had descended upon the bar as the drinkers had waited with bated breath to see what Mrs Maclean would say and what Hamish's reaction would be.

Now the normal hubbub resumed and everyone seemed relieved that the anticipated showdown had come and gone. The most relieved person there was Jack. Even though he sensed throughout the evening that a slight reserve was being shown towards him, his worst fears of ostracism subsided.

Ronnie had left the bar shortly after Hamish without making any comment and the atmosphere had become noticeably more relaxed.

In fact Jack began to feel even more sociable than usual and was drinking faster than was his habit. By the time closing time came around he was feeling decidedly "merry".

Catriona noticed that he was slurring his words and that he had told her on at least four or five occasions how attractive she looked that night.

"I think you'd better have a lift home with me," she said, and he readily agreed.

"I can't think of anything I would rather do."

Catriona shook her head and laughed.

"What a sport she is," thought Jack.

As they drove along towards home he told her in gushing terms how grateful he was for the support she had given to *him* (he didn't mention Sophie) on the night of the "graffiti incident".

Catriona said she was just being a good neighbour, as was the normal thing in the Highlands.

Jack told her she had gone far beyond the call of neighbourly duty and she was surely the most beautiful person, both in mind and in body, that he had ever met.

As the car approached Jamie's cottage he shouted out: "Look the deer are out at the edge of the woods. A whole family of them. Please let's stop and have a look at them."

Catriona laughed, as a sense of déjà vu came over her: "I'm not falling for that one again!"

But Jack insisted: "Just stop the car for a moment, please. They're over there. Look."

Catriona brought the car to a stop and looked over towards the clearing.

"I can't see anything" she said.

"Sorry. I was joking," said Jack, who put his arms around her shoulder and brought his lips to hers.

This time Catriona responded and they kissed deeply.

Eventually she pushed him away.

"What are we doing?" she asked. "You're a married man!"

Catriona's words were spoken as if in anger, but Jack detected a playfulness around her lips which belied that.

"I'm sorry," he said. "But I'm smitten. I can't help it. I meant it all – about how beautiful you were."

"Let's just forget that happened," said Catriona.

Jack grinned: "I should have thought of some better excuse than that. I mean, if I'd been driving I would have probably run out of petrol!"

"Aren't you meant to be a writer?" Catriona chided. "I would have thought you would have come up with something a tad more imaginative."

They both laughed. The moments of tension had passed.

As they arrived at Jack's cottage he bravely suggested a goodnight kiss. But Catriona refused.

"Not tonight," she said.

Those two words surprised Jack, and filled him with hope. But, as he lay in bed that night next to Sophie, they also frightened him. He had started something which he did not know how to finish. He had shocked himself by his own bad behaviour and he could not sleep for worrying about it.

****

Over breakfast the next morning, Jack and Sophie took stock of their situation.

Despite the misgivings about his behaviour with Catriona the previous night, he had woken up feeling unusually bright and cheerful.

He believed any threat from Hamish and/or Ronnie had diminished and that he was still being accepted by the rest of the locals.

He told Sophie this and argued strongly that they should not give up on their dream. They should stay put on Skye and play their full part in community life. The unspoken but predominant reason for this view, though, was that he wished to stay close to Catriona.

Sophie, on the other hand, began gently to articulate the notion that people might never forgive them for appearing to side with the SPAT leaders. They would always be outsiders treated with suspicion. Foremost, but equally unspoken, in her thoughts was the fancy that they might move nearer to the Black Isle – and Jamie.

She said how nice it might be to live in another, less remote, rural area of Scotland, perhaps on the east coast, not far from the capital of the Highlands, Inverness.

Jack poured cold water on this idea. He reminded Sophie of their tours in Scotland in past years. Could she not remember how flat they felt when travelling down the east side of the country and how their spirits were immediately lifted when they started to go west, into higher and wilder countryside?

Sophie could not for the moment counter this argument. But an irrational determination was beginning to build up that she wanted to be wherever Jamie was.

If Jack would not move from Skye, then her next move would be to persuade Jamie to stay. As she worked on her latest nymph and satyr painting that morning it came to her that an extraordinary, imaginative, and extremely passionate act was what was needed.

During the afternoon she took a stroll along to Jamie's cottage but discovered he was out. She left a previously prepared note asking him to go fishing at the Black Burn pool that night, where she would meet him.

Chapter fifteen
Desperate measures

IT WAS 8pm when Sophie set out from her cottage to walk down to the pool. Jack had gone to Nigel Tavistock's to help him to prepare a press release for SPAT. The organisation had uncovered some statistics from Scandinavia which indicated the devastating effect that wind farms were having on the birds of prey population.

It was a beautiful evening, the sky was cloudless, the air was balmy and still and the loch waters were as blue as anything to be seen in the Greek islands.

Sophie was wearing a white blouse, a red sarong and blue sandals. Her hair was hanging loose across her shoulders.

As she looked down from the top of the hillside she could see Jamie standing, fishing rod in hand, immediately to the side of the waterfall which plunged into the pool. He was naked from the waist up, his spare, bronzed body glowing in the sunlight. He had tight-fitting blue jeans and brown sandals.

Sophie ran along the top of the hill and then scrambled down the steep grassy bank towards the poolside.

She stood on a large flat stone and shouted over to Jamie, who was some 30 yards away. The rocks he was standing on, below an overhang comprising a steep rock face and a variety of creeping plants, could only be reached by a difficult route, partly through shallow water and partly by jumping between slippery boulders He waved to her and continued fishing.

Sophie unbuttoned her blouse from top to bottom and then flung it on to the grass. She was wearing no bra and so exposed her lovely breasts with their erect pretty pink nipples. She leant backwards and unfastened her sarong, again throwing it on to the bank. She was now completely nude. She stood with legs akimbo, pointing her neat quim provocatively towards her lover.

"I'm coming in," she shouted, and then dived into the clear water of the pool.

She squealed as she hit the water, which was very cold even after a warm summer, splashed a little and then managed to scramble a few breast strokes. When she reached the far side of the pool she grasped hold of one of the rocks near to Jamie and hung on to it in front of him.

Jamie, who was not amused by Sophie's antics, put out his hand to help her out of the water, but instead she clung on to it and then pulled him towards her.

"Come on in, come on in," she cried.

"Don't be stupid," he replied. "Come out!"

Sophie let him pull her up out of the water. But then she grabbed both his hands and again pulled him towards her.

"You're my satyr. I'm your nymph," she said, "We're going to make love underneath the waterfall."

Jamie screamed: "Don't be fucking stupid. Let me go."

"Don't be a wimp," she said, struggling with him.

She pulled him hard and he lost his balance, doing the splits as he tried to stay on the greasy rocks. She jumped towards him and grabbed one of his legs, desperately trying to pull him into the water.

"You're a madwoman," he shouted angrily. "Get off me!"

But Sophie just laughed and continued tugging.

"I have to do this. I'm a nymph devoured by lust."

Jamie stretched out an arm and managed to grab his fishing knife from a rock. He waved it at Sophie and screamed menacingly: "Let me go or you'll get this!"

Sophie laughed and tugged at his leg again. He leant forward, pulled her towards him and lunged with his knife at her stomach. The blood spurted out and turned the water red. Sophie flopped down on the bank screaming in terror and pain.

Jamie ignored her pleas for help and traversed the slippery and rocky path back towards the grass bank at the loch-side of the pool. His foot continually slipped off the rocks into the shallow water at the edge of the pool, causing loud splashes and sending out waves across the surface of the normally calm water.

Having reached the grass he went charging off and soon disappeared over the brow of the hill.

Sophie was left sobbing and panicked as the blood cascaded from the deep open wound in her tummy. She struggled along the same path as Jamie had taken, often losing her balance and finishing up on all fours as she slipped off the stones and hit the water's edge.

Eventually she made it to the rock where she had left her blouse and sarong. She picked up the blouse and clasped it as tightly as she could around the gaping wound. Then she clambered up the bank and ran along the rough track which led towards her cottage. Several times she fell over as she tried to run too fast along stretches of the route where the grass was very long.

Along the track she came to a metal gate which prevented sheep from straying out of their field. To open it Sophie needed to pull open the heavy spring bolts. She tried to do this with one hand while clutching the blouse to her bloody wound. But the effort was too much for her and she dropped to the ground screaming in pain. She shouted for help as loud as she was able.

She was losing touch with reality. Her shouts and screams appeared to be strangely separate from her weakened body - like an out of body experience.

****

At around 8.30pm that same night the Rev John Grimmond was in his study at the Beindow manse preparing his Sunday sermon when there was a rattle at the front door. He sighed, stood up and went to open it to his unexpected visitor.

"Miss MacInnes," he declared. "What can I do for you this evening?"

The old woman looked flustered and distressed.

"May I come in?" she asked, nervously.

The minister showed her into the study and sat her down.

"It's happened again."

The minister, who was seated behind his desk, put his head in his hands.

"Tell me, Miss MacInnes."

"Well, Minister, you remember a few months ago I had that terrible vision – of that couple and their terrible goings-on and that poor baby that was promised to die…

"I remember, Miss MacInnes. I remember."

"It's happened again. The poor baby - it turned into a man in front of my eyes and it was falling… falling into hell - into the everlasting bonfire. Just falling, falling – and then there was the spark from the fire – and then I came to myself again. But I am left with this awful foreboding. I am so scared this time, Minister. The poor baby… it means something awful has happened. I'm sure it does."

"Miss MacInnes, I believe that you had a terrible nightmare and then you woke up. It's not uncommon. Please, calm down and don't worry yourself."

Miss MacInnes replied: "I know you don't believe me. But it's all happened before so many times on the island. The spark from the fire – and then someone dies. It's the second sight. I know it is."

"Miss McInnes you will be believing in devil worship next. This is unChristian – a silly superstition. I have told you this before and I thought you believed me."

"I do want to believe you. I'm a good Christian woman. I really am."

"Last time we said a little prayer together and I think it helped, didn't it?"

"It did help. I was hoping we could do the same again."

We will Miss MacInnes. We will."

"But before we do, can I just ask you one thing, Minister?"

"Of course."

"Should I tell the police about what I have seen? Just in case something terrible is going to happen."

"No, Miss MacInnes. The police are very busy and they will not thank you. What evidence could you give them that would be any use to them?"

"I could tell them the name of the local man who I recognised in my vision."

"No, Miss MacInnes. I think they would laugh at you."

"Laugh? Oh, dear. I hope not. What if I went to see the man himself?"

"I think you would be worrying someone unnecessarily."

"Very well, Minister. I know I will never convince you."

"Let's pray then, Miss MacInnes. Then I will get the car out and take you home."

****

Jack had walked home from his meeting with Nigel Tavistock and arrived at his cottage. He walked through the front door and expected to find Sophie inside the house. When he could not find her he went outside the back to look for her there.

It was a still, becalmed evening. At first the only sounds Jack heard were the gentle bleatings of lambs as they chased each other around their field.

But then he heard another, more distant, noise – a woman's voice, making a repetitive high-pitched sound. He sensed something was not right and he raced over the field and through one metal gate.

He was then about 100 yards from the second gate where Sophie lay and he could now clearly hear her gradually weakening cries for help.

As he approached the gate he came to an abrupt halt and gasped for breath. He had seen Sophie's still body, doused with blood. For a few seconds he stood motionless, horror-struck, trying to take in exactly what he had seen.

Then he roused himself and his adrenalin started to flow. Somewhere from inside a business-like strength took him over and impelled him to action.

Jack went over to Sophie, knelt down and looked at her closely. She was still breathing. He was wearing only a light teeshirt and jeans. He took off the teeshirt and wrapped it around the top half of his wife's body as far as it would go.

He took his mobile phone out of his jeans pocket and dialled 999. In calm tones he described to the emergency control what he had found and his precise location, stressing the fact that there was no easy access from the road to where they were.

He was asked if there would be a convenient landing area for an air ambulance. He explained that there was a flat area of stony beach nearby – ironically the same spot where the air ambulance had touched down a few months earlier when Ian McConnell had been attacked.

When he completed his telephone call Jack gently put his arm around Sophie's shoulder to cradle her head and sat there for about 20 minutes until the air ambulance arrived.

Sophie was stretchered and put aboard the helicopter and Jack accompanied her to Broadford Hospital accident and emergency department.

He spent an agonising night while doctors treated Sophie's wound. She had lost so much blood that a transfusion was needed.

Jack had several hours to think about the horrific circumstances of the night. Who would have inflicted such an injury on his innocent, decent, wife? Because he had found her almost naked he assumed that her attacker had a sexual motive. She may have been stabbed as she tried to resist rape.

Could her attacker have been the same madman who had attacked Ian McConnell in the same area?

His mind was in turmoil. A huge feeling of guilt descended over him like a black cloud as he thought about his kiss with Catriona. He was so ashamed of himself.

Early the next morning the doctors informed him that Sophie had needed numerous stitches to her stab wound but that there was no reason why she should not pull through. A few inches either way and the knife would have ended her life. She would have a very nasty scar on her stomach, but beyond that she should have no further complications, the doctors said.

At last Jack was told that he could go into Sophie's room. She was conscious but distressed when she saw him.

She started to sob and say "I'm sorry. I'm so sorry" over and over again.

Jack took her hand and whispered to her that she had nothing to be sorry about.

Sophie was sobbing uncontrollably now and was not be to comforted.

"Do you know who did this to you?"

She nodded.

"Who was it?"

"Jamie – Jamie Carmichael."

"Jamie!"

Jack paused, hardly daring to mouth his next words: "Did he … try to rape you?"

"No."

"He just stabbed you for no reason?"

"Oh, Jack," she sobbed. "I'm so ashamed."

"You're ashamed. But why?"

Through her tears and in a barely audible voice, Sophie whispered: "I saw Jamie by the Black Burn pool. Under the waterfall. I was messing about, having a bit of fun. I tried to pull him into the water. Then he turned nasty on me. He picked up this knife and just stabbed me. Then he ran off."

Jack fell silent. He found it unbelievable that his sober, respectable, wife should have been behaving in such a way and have provoked such a cold-blooded response from her attacker.

Sophie continued to weep as he churned over the matter in his mind. A thought then hit him like a hammer. If Jamie had stabbed her and immediately run off then why had he found her nearly naked?

"How did you come to lose your clothes?" he asked.

"There's something terrible I have to tell you."

She paused and wiped away her tears with the flat of her hand.

"I was having an affair with Jamie. I was cavorting about in front of him naked because we were lovers. I'm so sorry."

Her sobbing became more intense and louder. Jack merely shook his head once in disbelief. He was not by nature an angry man and had an ability to stay calm when all around him were losing their heads. But even Sophie was shocked by his lack of emotion on this occasion.

The hurt he felt at what he had heard was tempered by an element of relief. He suddenly thought he was "off the hook" as far as his feelings towards Catriona were concerned. A large amount of the guilt which had been troubling him was lifted from him. He knew this was not what he should be feeling at such a traumatic time. But that was exactly how he did feel – relieved.

Sophie was almost angry with *him* for not appearing to be beside himself with anger.

"I don't expect you will ever be able to forgive me," she said. Then she winced in pain and put her hand on her stomach.

"I do forgive you, my darling. I may never be able to forget. That's beyond what any human being could possibly do. But I do forgive you. All I want is for you to get better."

Sophie smiled and said: "I love you so much. How could I have been so selfish?"

Jack smiled too and replied: "We are all selfish. Some of us get away with it unscathed. You haven't done.

"But let's hear no more of this now. You mustn't upset yourself even more. You must tell the police about Jamie."

"They have seen me already," she said. "But if they catch him things will be even worse for us. There will be a court case – and the shame of it all. I can't bear to think about it."

Jack took her hand again. "Don't worry about that now. We are strong people. We will get through this, I promise."

****

314

At around 9pm the previous evening the doorbell had rung at Ian McConnell's house. As usual it was answered by Sally.

The hunched little figure of Miss McInnes stood in the porch. She was warmly welcomed and invited inside.

Having established that Iain was at home, Miss McInnes surprised Sally by saying that she needed to see him in private.

"Is it some church business?" asked Sally.

"Aye. Church business. A wee problem we have at the church."

Iain was watching television in the sitting room but he politely turned off the set on seeing his visitor. He too reacted with surprise when told that Miss McInnes wished to see him alone. He knew her to be a decent woman with a rather timid nature, so put her strange request down to some reticence on her part.

Around 20 minutes later he showed her to the door, thanking her for her visit.

"What was all that about?" asked Sally when she had gone.

"Oh, something of nothing," answered Iain. "A little problem to do with the church – nothing more."

"Why the secrecy then?" asked Sally.

Iain hesitated and merely replied: "I'll tell you later. Now I have remembered that I had promised to go to

315

the Breaganish tonight to have a game of snooker with Robert. I'd forgotten all about it. I should be there by now."

He started to put on his sports jacket which he had left hanging in the hallway.

But Sally showed immediate concern. The last time he had visited the Breaganish House Hotel had been on the fateful night when he had been attacked.

"You're not going to walk over there, are you?" she asked. "It's getting quite late. And I don't want you walking along that beach again – not while that maniac is still living around there."

"No, I'm late already so I had better drive."

Sally was even more alarmed to hear that. Iain had only driven once since his accident and that had been against doctor's orders. Two weeks previously he had insisted on driving just a couple of miles along an isolated lane to see how he coped. Sally had reluctantly travelled with him in the passenger seat. She had noticed how nervous he had seemed and how he had broken into a sweat.

She now saw a similar look of agitation on his face. The old Iain never looked agitated, but since the blow to his head his personality had changed and he quite often had a panicked expression.

"I'll get Fergus to take me. I saw him walk across the yard just a few minutes ago so I guess he'll be at home. I must be off. My fault – forgetting what I was meant to be doing tonight. You know what I'm like these days."

316

Sally nodded and sighed a little.

"Well, don't forget to come home," she said, smiling.

Iain strode off in the direction of the estate cottage where a young farmworker called Fergus Mackinnon lived. But as soon as he was out of sight of the main house he veered off to the crew yard, got into his Range Rover and drove off at speed.

As he travelled along the Breaganish road he heard a helicopter overhead. Then he saw two police patrol cars parked at the side of the road. It was a narrow single track road and he had to drive very gingerly to get past them.

He parked on the grass verge just beyond them and got out of the car. He ran across the grass towards the loch for about 30 yards. This brought him to a rock face, the steepest of all the descents to the loch.

He stared down into the water and saw below him a small motor boat manned by three police officers. They were pulling a blood-stained half-naked body out of the water and over the side of the boat.

Iain's blood ran cold and he stood perfectly still peering at the horrific sight that confronted him.

He heard some rustling of the grass behind him and when he looked around he saw the familiar faces of Police Sgt Duncan and Pc Flounce. Sgt Duncan put his arm around Iain's shoulder.

"I'm afraid it's young Jamie," he said.

"It's what I was afraid of - the old lady. She knew you see. She told me…"

Sgt Duncan gave Pc Flounce a puzzled look. Pc Flounce looked even more puzzled himself.

Iain felt his legs give way underneath him. The next thing he knew he was sitting upon the grass with a police officer holding each of his arms.

"Don't worry. You just passed out. It was the shock," said Sgt Duncan.

"Yes, the shock," said Pc Flounce.

"We have radioed for the doctor," said Duncan.

"Aye, the doctor," said Flounce.

Iain looked at them pleadingly: "Is Jamie all right?"

"I regret not," said Sgt Duncan. "I'm afraid that Jamie has passed away."

It was still a warm, close, evening but Iain started to shiver uncontrollably. His face was expressionless except for a slight quiver of his lips as he tried to fight back tears.

Pc Flounce came to him with a blanket and covered him.

****

Television news the next morning was full of the story. A woman had been stabbed and seriously wounded. Her attacker, a 36-year-old local man, had later been found drowned in Loch Breaganish, having suffered a stab wound himself.

Rumours about what had "really happened" spread like wildfire through the area. Jamie Carmichael had sexually assaulted the writer's wife and then stabbed her. He had then stabbed himself and jumped into the loch where he drowned.

Most rumours turn out to have some approximation to the truth. It was only after a few days that the story took a new twist, with the revelation that Jamie and Sophie had been having consensual sex at the time of her stabbing.

"Ah", thought some, who still regarded Jamie as a local hero and Sophie as an anti-wind farm outsider. "Perhaps she stabbed Jamie and pushed him into the loch and then tried to cover up her crime by stabbing herself."

This story appealed to people's prejudices and it became the accepted version of events in Beindow and district.

When Sophie emerged from hospital and returned to her cottage with Jack the couple did not venture out of the house.

In the next few weeks there were lots of interviews by the police. But apart from genuinely sympathetic visits from Catriona and the Tavistocks there was no other friendly human contact during that period.

Jack and Sophie gave nothing away to their friends, merely accepting their sympathy and confirming that Jamie had stabbed Sophie. They hid behind the assertion that the police had instructed them to say no more.

There were two less than friendly incidents.

A kind-hearted local scrawled the word "Murderer" in large letters on the cottage wall. Hamish was in jail and so not responsible this time. Some other unidentified well-wisher had been at work.

And there was an even scarier incident one night as Jack and Sophie were preparing for bed.

There was a fearful hammering on the front door. The couple were extremely frightened and even more panic-stricken when they heard Sarah's shrieking voice. This got louder and louder and then there was a sound of glass shattering as Jamie's mother smashed an empty sherry bottle against the outside wall.

"Come outside, you murdering bitch," was the much-repeated shout from Sarah.

She moved her attack to the back door, which she battered and kicked so hard that Jack and Sophie feared she would soon be through it. They had already telephoned the police and so stayed inside the bedroom hoping they would soon come.

Sarah shouted all kinds of accusations about Sophie, but there was a repeated outburst which struck Sophie to the core.

"He couldn't swim. You pushed him into the water and he couldn't swim."

Suddenly Sophie had a dreadful thought. That was why Jamie was so upset when she had tried to pull him into the pool at the foot of the waterfall.

"He couldn't swim!"

Jamie had been scared of the water and that was why he attacked her, she thought. The whole tragic business could have been avoided if she had not been so selfish and stupid. Everything was *her fault*.

The police came and took Sarah away before any material damage was done. They warned her on pain of arrest not to harass the couple again.

But for Sophie the visit had been devastating. Any future happiness for her would be superficial.

The next morning a For Sale sign appeared at the cottage. Jack and Sophie left Skye bound for a rented house in Cornwall. Anywhere would have done, so long as it was a long way from the island.

The newspaper headlines followed them for several months yet.

The most sensational of them came out of Jamie's inquest, with the whole sordid story of Sophie's affair with him coming to light.

****

The private funeral of Jamie Carmichael had taken place at Inverness Crematorium.

The only people present were Sarah, Iain and Sally McConnell and Fergus Mackinnon, who had worked alongside Jamie for several years.

Predictably, Sarah arrived late, smelling of drink, with a deathly pallor broken only by black circles around her bloodshot eyes.

She sat alone on the front row of the chapel, with the other three mourners on the second row. Iain looked old and ailing. Bright red eyelids protruding from watery eyes highlighted his deterioration.

As they left the chapel and made their way through the car park, Iain asked Sarah how she was getting home.

"Do you care?" she snarled at him. "I've got my bus pass."

"I was going to offer you a lift," said Iain, pointing to his Range Rover.

"Don't be ridiculous. I've been an embarrassment to you for years. You know you don't really want me to travel with you. I'm surprised you even came to the funeral."

Iain turned to Fergus Mackinnon and gave him the Range Rover keys, hinting that he might get into the vehicle so they could have some private words with Sarah. Fergus took the hint and left the other three together.

"I've come to my son's funeral," said Iain. "There's nothing terrible about that is there?"

Sarah snarled again: "He wasn't your son."

Iain looked astonished.

"Don't be ridiculous. You've been drinking."

"He wasn't your son. As if it makes any difference."

"Of course it would make a difference," said Iain. "What are you talking about? I'm not listening to your nonsense any longer."

But Sally intervened: "No. Let her explain what she meant by that."

"Jamie was Benjamin's son."

"Benjamin?" said Iain.

"Yes, Benjamin. Jamie was conceived in Borneo. His father was Benjamin. I've told you the story about Benjamin often enough."

"You mean the fellow who murdered that young girl?"

"Yes. He stabbed a young girl through the heart and then hung himself. That was Jamie's dad. He was obsessed with knives and stabbed someone. Does that remind you of anyone?"

Iain stood open-mouthed.

"So you were already pregnant when you came back from Borneo."

"I was a bad girl, wasn't I? I got bar work in Edinburgh hoping to find some gullible mug as soon as possible. And I found one, didn't I?"

Sarah pointed at Iain, laughed, and then struck him on the shoulder as a symbol of irony.

"I've kept you all these years – and looked out for your son. You're a disgusting woman!"

Sarah laughed again: "You did the least you could get away with. I felt sorry for you to begin with. But as time went on I realised you were just as evil as I was."

Sally took Iain by the arm: "Come away. Just leave her."

Sarah's parting shot was: "I won't bother you any more. I'm going away. Give me a couple of weeks and the caravan will be empty and you will never see me again."

"Thank God for that," said Sally.

****

As might easily be imagined, life for Jack and Sophie was never quite the same again.

Jack had found it easy to forgive Sophie for her antics with Jamie. He never revealed to her his feelings for Catriona so Sophie always believed that her husband had shown saint-like powers of forgiveness.

But the newspaper reports had left them deeply embarrassed. They became obsessively secretive, not wishing their Cornish neighbours to know their backgrounds. They even started to use pseudonyms for their novels and paintings.

However, life was by no means miserable. Their daughters stood by them and each produced a clutch of grandchildren who were a source of great joy for both Jack and Sophie.

Their lives had become diminished, but not tragically so.

Chapter sixteen
Forgiveness

DURING the winter following the events we have described came the decision which folk around Beindow had been waiting for: planning permission for the wind farm was granted.

There was jubilation among the majority of people in the area. They believed that the decision would herald the start of a period of economic wellbeing; they were also excited that the wind farm company had agreed to make an immediate £100,000 grant to the local community – with further annual grants promised for the years to come.

The community council decided to spend the money on upgrading the village hall and staging a number of annual community events.

It was decided that the first of these should be a Summer Arts Festival based around the village hall. There would be traditional highland music, dancing and poetry, but the highlight would be a community play, involving scores of local people of all age groups.

The play, written by a local historian, would follow the history of the area since the time when colossal giants and furious fairies ruled the land, through the clan battles and the Clearances, to the present day.

A committee had been formed to organise the festival, chaired with the greatest possible vigour by the formidable Mrs Myrtle Maclean, with the redoubtable Mrs Fiona MacLeod as her secretary.

One particular committee meeting had been a stormy affair. Mrs Maclean said the community play needed a producer. She declared that she could think of no-one better for this role than a prominent theatre director who happened to live in the area – one Nigel Tavistock.

At first the meeting was in uproar, with several members threatening to resign if the treacherous "anti-wind farmer" was allowed anywhere near the celebration. But Mrs Maclean was adamant that they should put their differences behind them and find the best man for the job.

"This play could put Beindow on the map, which is what we all want," she said. "We might even get on television for some positive reasons for a change – not about us fighting and abusing each other, or murdering each other, or having sex orgies or whatever next."

Fiona MacLeod addressed the meeting in school ma'am style, telling them that the community needed to heal itself and show Christian tolerance to those who had opposed the wind farm. She even suggested holding some events at the Lochside Inn, which had been the headquarters for the hated SPAT.

This idea, to involve the local pub competitors whom she loathed, stretched Mrs Maclean's Christian charity to its limits.

"Those bloody Judds. Are they to reap the benefits from all this?" she declared. But she quickly repented of her rashness and returned to the theme of reconciliation: "Oh, I suppose you're right. In for a penny in for a pound. South Africa's reconciliation process had nothing on us, did it?"

Ronnie McColl, whose nose had already been pushed out of joint when Mrs Maclean was preferred to him as chairman, was silently seething with discontent at the back of the hall. All this talk of reconciliation was too much for him and he pointedly walked out of the meeting to grumble to his chums at the Blackhill.

SPAT members, of course, had been horrified by the result of the wind farm planning application. Individuals were privately licking their wounds.

Nigel and Stella Tavistock were very surprised when Myrtle Maclean appeared at their door, and even more taken aback by her suggestion that Nigel might produce the play. He was so surprised that he said "Yes".

He threw himself into the project with great enthusiasm. To begin with, the locals involved in the play were suspicious of him and laughed to each other about his booming upper class voice.

But, as time went on, they warmed to his essential kindness and friendliness, and began to appreciate that even opponents of wind farms could be decent human beings.

The play was an outstanding success, attracting hundreds of tourists as well as local people. Ronnie McColl went to play golf that day and Hamish McDonald, recently released from prison, stayed in his cottage to drink a bottle of whisky. But most of the Christian people of the area had a thoroughly enjoyable day.

THE END

Printed in Great Britain
by Amazon